NOT
SLEEPING

ALAN WINNIKOFF

CROWSNEST BOOKS

Crowsnest Books

www.crowsnestbooks.com

Distributed by the University of Toronto Press

Edited by Allister Thompson

Proofreader: Britanie Wilson

Cataloguing data available from Library and Archives Canada

ISBN 9780921332749 (paperback)

ISBN 9780921332756 (ebook)

Printed and bound in Canada

NOT SLEEPING

CONTENTS

"*We're born alone, we live alone, we die alone. Only through our love and friendship can we create the illusion for the moment that we're not alone.*"

—Orson Welles

PART ONE

He wakes to Amy's grunts and whines from the bedroom. Josh Sherman, pushing fifty, recently separated, rouses himself from his lumpy couch to find his daughter tearful, pacing in tight circles, stringy, mouse-colored hair swirling. Ethan, cross-legged in Josh's bed, blinks, rubbing sleep from his eyes, and observes his older sister with curious concern. A rank odor thickens the air.

Tonight's waking is undoubtedly the result of the disruption of Amy's carefully managed routine: the strange sleeping arrangements, different eating schedule, the entire circumstance of this weekend outing at Daddy's new apartment. And while her chronic demands and considerable challenges are no longer a part of Josh's day-to-day life, the emotions they trigger — frustration, futility, sadness — are deeply familiar.

In the bathroom, Josh wipes front to back, as all fathers of girls must learn, while simultaneously holding Amy's skinny wrists by her sides. The diarrhea sticking to Josh's fingers and oozing onto his hands will, if not contained, expand its territory, like a marauding army of ants. In no way, thinks Josh, should he be doing this, on his knees, cleaning a nine-year-old girl, even his daughter — especially his daughter. It is wretched, unfathomable, the natural order of things turned on its head.

Ethan leans in the doorway of the bathroom, evoking for Josh an image from an early Bob Dylan album, Spider Man pajamas notwithstanding.

"You're gonna need to give her a shower, Daddy," Ethan says with the singular assertiveness of the all-knowing second grader, round-rimmed glasses glinting in the harsh overhead lighting. His mop of red curls, squished from sleep onto one side, leaves his head appearing asymmetrical. "Mommy always does after she poops like this."

Taking his son's advice, Josh puts Amy under the water, a cloud of steam building around them. As he helps her into clean pajamas, his focus shifts to his phone beckoning from the edge of the sink. From a dark corner of his sleep-deprived brain, the thought begins to take hold: he will let Claudia know what has happened. He knows a text at this hour will most certainly wake her. Claudia is obsessive about keeping her phone by her bed. But would she not want to know? And does he not have a responsibility to keep her informed? Josh scrubs his hands and arms, the stink clinging to his skin. He leads his kids back to the bed, makes sure they are cozy, kisses them both, and returns to the bathroom.

* * *

His disdain for punctuation lends a frantic, stream of consciousness undertone to the message. Claudia reads it, turns the phone away, then reads it again. She will not, she resolves, allow him the satisfaction of a reply. While there is underlying anxiety about her children (no doubt they'll be tired and cranky when he dumps them onto her doorstep tomorrow), she is not his lifeline. He will have to handle this on his own.

Lying in darkness, save for a hint of yellow moonlight along the edges of the curtained windows across the room, Claudia rehashes yet again her struggle to keep their marriage alive. She had refused to give in, even as the full weight of Josh's disconnectedness ground her down. Some part of her had wanted to believe they would find a way. And there were the children, of course.

And so it had been left to Josh to initiate the breakup.

The proposal he'd concocted, in typical Josh fashion, had been less than resolute. He had suggested an interim step, a year off from the marriage, while they both reevaluated. During that time, by default, she would have responsibility for the kids, the house, and everything else they had to this point shared, while he, apparently, would be unfettered. Why, she wonders, hardly for the first time, are men somehow more easily able to get away with this?

And yet, as it has turned out, it is Claudia, not Josh, now enjoying a robust second act. There is something to be said for the shimmery, pit-of-the-stomach tingle of a new romance, particularly when, through her years of marriage, she had dismissed it as something she'd simply never get to experience again. Claudia is beginning to allow herself to envision a life with the silhouetted sleeping man next to her, a man who seems to get her as a person and who, stirringly, if perhaps somewhat prematurely, has already declared his commitment to her.

Claudia waits for sleepiness to return. There is no urgency, no reason they have to be up at any particular time tomorrow. With all the kids out of the house, hers and his, they can stay in bed all morning if they choose to.

She pushes the button on the side of her phone, and her husband's message fades into nothingness.

ONE

The solitary word hovered over their heads, untethered, as though floating inside a cartoon thought bubble. Josh had a notion he could reach up and puncture that bubble with a sharp object. He pictured the letters — *G, M, F, C* — spilling onto the glass surface of the conference room table, shattering into a million pieces. If only he had a sharp object.

After a long moment, Josh heard the clumsily constructed word uttered again.

"Gamification."

There was another pause, then Ryan began to elaborate, gray eyes flitting from person to person. "We're thinking interactive role play with a narrative arc," the younger man explained. "Real-time engagement between users. Social gaming. Totally experiential."

Josh watched James, his boss, hunch forward, elbows coming to rest in front of him. Thick-necked with a wide, flat face, James had a way of using his size to command attention. His mouth hung open before he commenced speaking.

"To be clear," James began, fingering the stained rim of his empty paper coffee cup, "no one is disputing that your digital presence, as it currently stands, needs to be blown up. We're the ones who first told *you* that. But what we all agreed to was an easily navigateable e-commerce destination where customers could buy a pair of shoes and get exactly what they wanted without a lot of fuss or complication. Style, selection, affordability."

James paused to raise his fingers for air quotes. "Replicate the store experience online. Have we forgotten that conversation?"

He nodded in the direction of the man in the knitted golf shirt slouched at the head of the table, phone in hand, belly spreading over his belt, wisps of uncombed silver hair atop his head.

"That's what Bob wanted," James continued with a sigh, tilting his weight farther toward the table's midpoint. His big hands turned, palms up. "We never talked about a gaming app."

All eyes settled on Bob Burns, the Shoe King of New York, a face familiar to millions through years of ubiquitous subway ads and local TV and radio spots, created and produced by the James Gang, the marketing agency James had founded, with Josh as his reliable number two.

More than two decades earlier, Bob had put together a team of investors and transformed what had been a handful of sleepy neighborhood storefronts in Brooklyn and Queens, founded by his immigrant grandfather Morrie Bernstein, into a network of sprawling multilevel superstores. Every new Shoe King opening became an over-the-top media event, with Klieg lights, prizes, circus animals, sports stars, swimsuited blondes, animatronic characters, and games and rides for the kids. Lauded in the business world as a visionary entrepreneur, Bob parlayed his growing public persona into regional celebrity. The Shoe King was soon a sought-after presence at World Series games and Broadway openings. *Saturday Night Live* had even parodied him. Back then, the private Bob had been brash, unpredictable, at times volatile. He routinely fired the James Gang on impulse, only to quickly rehire them. He had been known to throw heavy objects when frustration boiled over. James still took dark pleasure in describing the day he had narrowly ducked a weighty, cut-glass statuette awarded to Bob hours earlier as Man of the Year at an elaborate Long Island Business Leaders luncheon. Recently, however, Bob had mellowed noticeably, and while his longer fuse was welcomed by those who had once been on the receiving end of his infamous tirades, the consuming fire that had driven him to such remarkable, if unlikely heights also seemed to have ebbed some.

Now, since online shopping had drastically reordered the economic landscape for retailers large and small, the Shoe King's stores, having long since colonized all five boroughs as well as Nassau and Suffolk Counties and parts of New Jersey, Westchester, and Connecticut, were no longer generating the foot traffic they once did. Bob's response to this new reality had been slow, glacial, as he had clung to his outdated business model. The Shoe King was in existential crisis, facing an unforgiving new world, in desperate need of radical reinvention.

"We've brought Bob...uh...your dad...into this process every step of the way." James pressed on, gesturing toward the Shoe King again. "No surprises. This isn't something we've just slapped together."

"We're not saying you have," Ryan responded, jaw clenched. "We don't doubt the effort." The way he spat out the word *effort* made it sound dirty, sordid. "The point is, in the digital marketplace you sell through an immersive environment. Consumers online have an infinite number of options. Why would they want to check out our site?" Ryan exhaled. "It worries us big-time that what we've seen so far from you guys feels cookie cutter. Boring."

Josh took note of his boss's grimace — a mere flicker no one else would have likely discerned. It was tough to get under James's skin, and, even when something did, he didn't reveal much. Josh's expressions, on the other hand, were decode-able by anyone who took the trouble to observe him. It was something James would at times chide him for.

James touched the tips of his fleshy fingers together, holding them chest high." You know, Ryan, I totally respect where you're coming from. But we've launched tons of digital platforms and content. I don't think anyone would call us cookie cutter."

"Okay, that's good to hear. I mean, I guess." Ryan lifted a shoulder, unconvinced. "We need to see the goods. Show us what you've got."

James turned his attention back to Bob. "You've been very quiet over there. What are your thoughts?"

The Shoe King stopped scrolling. As he glanced up from his phone, Josh was struck by how tired he looked. His skin was gray, the ash-colored half-moons under his eyes more pronounced than usual.

"Look, I trust you guys. Always have. But we're in a different world these days and," Bob swept a hand across the table, "us old fucks don't always get it."

Josh bristled at being included as a member of Bob's self-identified subgroup. He gazed out at the dreary sky, pressing low and dark against the partially open tenth-floor window, presaging more of the rain that had been falling on and off since early morning.

"Ryan is the master of this domain," said Bob. "That's why I put him — him and Courtney — in charge of digital. They know they have full authority to call the shots on this." The Shoe King chuckled with a snort, which to Josh's ear rang jarring and dissonant, like canned laughter on a sitcom that wasn't funny. "What do I know about this shit?"

On Josh's other side, Ryan's twin sister, Courtney, broke in. "You guys have managed our brand with our dad for a long time. We appreciate everything you've done for the business. For our family. But right now the marketing is stale as shit. The *brand* is stale as shit. And it's pretty obvious," she looked at Ryan, her piercing eyes gray, like her brother's, "we don't have a lot of time to get it right."

Courtney hadn't grown up to be what would be considered conventionally pretty, thought Josh, observing her. But with her jet-black shoulder-length blunt-cut, bangs that fell to her eyes, red lipstick liberally applied and dark crimson fingernails, she was a striking presence. They waited as she paused to shake off her black blazer, revealing toned arms, a tattoo of a tiger stalking along one shoulder.

"Personally, I happen to love shoe shopping," Courtney continued. "But maybe to you guys it's just utilitarian, not sexy. Some people feel that way. Because it's so basic — everyone on the planet needs shoes.

It was our dad who changed the whole dynamic. He turned buying shoes into something fun, experiential. An entertainment destination. It was revolutionary. That same revolution needs to happen again now — but virtually."

"Our digital presence needs to be immersive," Ryan repeated. "Make it social." He paused. "Give users a platform to create avatars. Shoe avatars."

"Shoe avatars?" Josh heard himself blurt.

"Yeah, absolutely." Ryan let his eyes linger on Josh for a long second. "Like one person could be a loafer. Another could be a pump."

"A strappy sandal," Courtney offered.

James nodded, one eyebrow raised. "A strappy…sandal," he repeated with gravitas.

"A Hush Puppy," Bob suddenly threw in, looking up from his phone. "Hey, why not? We've got all of these in our catalog and lots more besides. We've got styles and selections for the whole family."

"The idea is for people to identify with their shoe avatars and become invested in their characters," said Courtney. "Then they're motivated to buy the shoe. They feel ownership. And the app allows them to take their avatars with them wherever they go, while they engage with others in the Shoe King community. Do you see where we're coming from?"

The room fell silent again as they all took a few moments to ponder this. New York City's jangly cacophony drifted up from the street, a downshifting truck, distant sirens, fragments of a disturbed rant.

Josh raised his voice to the speaker phone in front of him. "What about you, Erin? Would love your feedback."

Erin Wasserman, on the other end of the line, led the digital group at LAKreativ, a boutique agency in Los Angeles. The James Gang often partnered with them when they felt they needed a fresh attitude. There were plenty of similar companies in New York, of course, but James was of a mind that New York agencies spent too much time validating one another. In his view, getting out of that bubble was an effective selling point to New York clients. Erin's team, Silver Lake hipsters with a distinctly West Coast sensibility, would focus on the creative while Josh handled the personal side of the client relationships. Over the years, this bicoastal nexus had proven to be a fruitful collaboration.

It was a bit past seven in L.A. Josh envisioned Erin out on her deck, overlooking the beach in Venice, mocha latte in hand, Pacific Ocean stretching out into the distance. She'd once texted him a picture of the view from her bedroom. He recalled a lot of palm trees and a line of blue water along the horizon. In the foreground, a leafy plant on a window ledge pushed out of its brightly colored ceramic vase toward the light.

"Sorry, I had you on mute," they heard Erin say, clearing her throat. "But, yeah, sure." She plunged in, her flat, nasal Western timbre sprinkled with a dash of Valley Girl lilt. "We can take a look at it. Web and mobile gaming. Makes sense. It will delay the build a bit, but we can for sure get into it and come back to you with some ideas. We'll start working on it today."

"Ideas. Game changers. That's what we're looking for," Ryan said to the speaker phone. He dropped his hands lightly onto the table and let them bounce back up, as if trying to prove himself immune to the laws of gravity. "Game changers. It's okay if we have a slight delay. We only have one chance to get this right." He paused, and his tone took a turn. "Look," he said, sounding suddenly uncertain, "I'm not trying to be a dick here. You guys are practically family."

For an instant, Josh had a window into the Ryan he remembered, the insecure twelve-year-old fat kid with the big nose and bad teeth, looking for validation. A long time ago, lifetimes ago, it had been Josh's job to find activities to keep that younger Ryan occupied and amused while, in this same conference room, his father reviewed the agency's latest campaigns.

"Let's be honest here," Ryan continued with renewed confidence, fingers digging into his thick, neatly trimmed stubble. "The future of our business, of the business our dad has built, depends on making this work. Everyone recognizes that the last ten percent of a digital build is the hardest." He eyed his sister, who smiled at him, nodding. Then, almost as an afterthought, Ryan added, "Failure is not an option."

Josh looked at him. Did he really just say that? Jesus. How did this kid get to be such a douche? Or had he always been this way?

Josh recalled when Bob had given the twins his-and-her nose jobs for their sixteenth birthdays. That, combined with a sizeable investment in high-end orthodontia, had accelerated their emergence out of their awkward teenage years. Courtney had gone on to Barnard, then joined up with her father after graduating. Bob had initially put her to work in one of his stores in Queens before calling her back to the Mineola corporate office about a year earlier. Meanwhile, Ryan, NYU MBA in hand, had also recently returned to the fold. Now, with both of them assuming ever more assertive roles in the family business, the ground was shifting.

Erin took charge for the remainder of the hour, hammering out initial thoughts on creative concepts, next steps, and a timeline. Ryan and Courtney, no longer holding court, stared dully at the speaker, heads bobbing now and then. It was difficult to assess how much of what Erin was telling them they were buying. Bob continued to be absorbed by his iPhone, glancing up when something caught his attention.

And then, finally, the meeting reached its end. There was nothing more to say. Josh felt the tension begin to lift from his shoulders. He imagined Erin clicking off her phone and savoring the L.A. sunshine, breathing deeply and filling her lungs with fresh ocean air straight off the Pacific. Meanwhile, Josh was stuck here on gray and rainy 23rd Street with these assholes. It didn't seem fair.

TWO

In his mid-twenties, Josh was living in a studio walk-up in the East Village, selling advertising for a second-tier cable network. Though his job brought minimal satisfaction, he rationalized that it paid well enough for him to enjoy the benefits of life in Manhattan. The city's buzz was intoxicating, and, like the generations of countless migrants that had come before, Josh was of that age when he was easily seduced by New York City's dark, gritty allure. After growing up isolated in New Jersey's suburban wastelands, just walking the streets was a rush. It was like being on a movie set.

Not long after landing in New York, Josh had connected with one of his dorm mates from Rutgers, another recent arrival. In college, Josh and Roger hadn't been close; Josh had never found him particularly easy to talk to. But now, new to the city and living near each other, they'd forged a bond of sorts. Or at least some approximation of one. This friendship of convenience imploded one day after Roger phoned with news of an incipient romance.

"That's great," Josh had said in response. "What's her name?"

"*His* name."

The line crackled. Thinking he had misheard, Josh repeated the question.

"His name," Roger said again, without affect.

Josh was, of course, fine with whomever one chose to be intimate with. But after that, Roger grew distant, as if it were simply assumed Josh would no longer have interest in remaining friends. While troubled by this, Josh found himself unable to muster the energy that would have been required to convince Roger otherwise. Though it was never discussed or acknowledged, they drifted apart not long after.

Still, while he was in the picture, Roger had come with certain advantages. He was building a career in finance and had occasional access to his firm's perqs, most notably, for Josh anyway, corporate seats at Madison Square Garden. It was there, on a bitterly cold February night, as the Knicks stumbled through a listless performance, that a bulky red-faced man with sandy blond hair falling across his forehead dropped into the empty seat Josh had been using to store his overcoat and briefcase. Josh shifted as the new arrival's girth spilled into his personal space. The man appeared a few years older than Josh and was affably garrulous; he seemed to have no hesitation chatting up a total stranger.

"How are they doing?" he asked, lowering himself heavily into his seat. With a glance up at the scoreboard hanging above the court, he answered his own question. "Down by double digits already. Shit. This team can match up with anyone when they decide to play together. It's all about consistency."

Shaking his head, the man turned to his companion on his other side. "I need a beer." His big, deep voice, like a radio announcer's, pierced the buzz of the crowd.

The friend gestured down the aisle at a perspiring vendor, cooler strapped across his belly, chugging up the steps toward them. The new arrival, now fully settled, waved and held up two fingers. "You guys want one?" he asked. Before Josh could respond, the man switched to four fingers. "I'm of the strong opinion that the preferred way to watch these guys is to drink heavily."

Josh chuckled.

"I get to about a half-dozen games or so a year," the man offered,
unprompted. He whirled around and clapped his friend on the shoulder.
"My buddy has season tickets. He hooks me up. You?"

Nodding in the direction of Roger, Josh alluded vaguely to his friend's
Wall Street connections.

"Nice. Always helpful to have friends in high places." The man
handed off two beers, refusing their offer of money. He introduced
himself, leaning across Josh to reach toward Roger first, before drawing
back and shaking Josh's hand.

"Fuckin' Knicks," Josh remembered James saying that night. "I played
a little ball in college. I was a step slow and not a great shooter, but I
was never afraid to put a body on somebody." Then, in what would
become an ongoing refrain on the state of his favorite team, "They
definitely test your loyalty. And yet they have a weird way of getting
under your skin."

Throughout the game, James kept up the chatter, buying beers for
the group as he expounded on a range of topics, from the out-of-con-
trol New York City real estate market to the relative merits of the
women passing by them along the aisle. James disclosed he had
recently left a large ad agency and was in the process of setting up
his own shop. While they didn't discuss Josh's availability specifically,
at the end of the night there was an exchange of business cards,
with James promising to follow up. Josh promptly put it out of his
mind, taking for granted that James's overtures would go nowhere,
writing it off as an isolated moment of alcohol-infused enthusiasm.
It was one of those encounters one has so often in New York, when
business bleeds into, and sometimes overtakes, an otherwise benign
social interaction.

A week or so later, however, James did call and commenced what
would prove to be an extended negotiation. Josh was initially cautious;
the entire proposition, built on the success of James's fledgling business
launch, felt iffy. Still, James was already courting Bob Burns, whose
alter ego, the Shoe King, was by then asserting itself into the public eye.

Josh was also encouraged by an evident personal chemistry with the likeable James, which left him feeling more confident about working together. After the soul-crushing petty politics he'd endured at the cable network, when Josh finally did agree to sign on, he had hopes he'd found a home.

Over the years, their lives had become deeply entwined. Essentially estranged from his older brother Sean, Josh asked James to be the best man at his wedding when he and Claudia became engaged some years later. Josh's relationship with James had grown to be the most enduring of his life. Now, with his marriage in tatters, it appeared that record would remain safely intact.

* * *

Even as a child, Josh had felt distanced from his family. His father, a serial entrepreneur, while never short on ideas, always seemed one unbridgeable step away from cracking the code that could lead to measurable success. This ate at him, leaving him increasingly embittered as the years passed. In high school, Josh's father often seemed indifferent to him, frustrated at Josh's perceived want of initiative. A kid lacking self-confidence, Josh had the misfortune of being raised by a man who seemed to take pleasure in undermining his self-confidence.

Josh and Sean had few common interests. Unlike his older brother, who had played varsity football, Josh was a mediocre athlete, and, though he liked sports, he had little desire to endure the pressure, competition, and potential humiliation that came with being part of a team. If his father had only known the truth; while the football players were smashing pads and grunting and sweating through their long afternoon practices, Josh was in the woods beyond the athletic fields, smoking weed with a handful of other outcasts and misfits.

His father dropped dead of a heart attack during Josh's senior year of college. Josh had tried to mourn, wanted to mourn. Instead, what he felt most, then and now, was relief. Not long ago, Josh realized he'd passed a milestone on his personal timeline and was now older than his father had been when he died. He had taken a bit of satisfaction in that, like he'd finally gotten the better of the old man.

His mother had remained in the house in Plainfield where Josh had spent his childhood. She was still there. But while Josh made a point of dutifully calling every week, they saw each other infrequently. After his father's passing, Josh's mother indulged her inclination as a homebody, rarely venturing far. Early in their marriage, Claudia would make a point of inviting her mother-in-law to their house, but there was always an excuse, and eventually Claudia gave up trying. More recently, Josh had on occasion taken the initiative, packed up the kids, and made his way down to her through the mind-numbing New Jersey traffic. In spite of his ambivalence, he wanted his children to know their grandma. But Amy's constant twirling, spinning, and shrieking, to say nothing of her sudden unpredictable outbursts, made his mom even more tense and anxious than usual. Ethan, emotional sponge that he was, would pick up on his grandmother's unease and begin lobbying to go home not long after their arrival.

* * *

In recent years, James had stepped back some from the day-to-day operations of the James Gang, ceding more responsibility to Josh. James aspired to produce films and spent a good chunk of his time looking for financing, networking with potential funders and mid-level Hollywood strivers. He'd brought in a couple of low-budget independent features so far that Josh had enjoyed and had been generally well received, though James was quick to lament that he himself had yet to make any real money.

The irony was hardly lost on Josh that, while he had spent a career helping to manage a marketing agency, he was, by all objective standards, deficient in the creative acumen one would typically associate with such a job. Josh often felt like a charlatan, destined to be outed at any moment. He wasn't particularly good at original ideas and concepts, he was a terrible artist, and he had no ear for clever copy. What redeemed him was his instinct for making deals. He presented as earnest and transparent, and this approach, uncommon and disarming when employed in the trenches of the Manhattan business world, tended to win over all but the most hard-bitten. And so he became the James Gang's rainmaker; the clients he brought in were largely responsible for keeping the agency afloat. Josh was also the one at the firm who wrangled the staff and the freelancers, making sure deadlines were met and deliverables were, uh, delivered. Those who can, do. Those who can't manage the people who can.

THREE

James and Josh left Bob in the conference room with his phone and walked Ryan and Courtney to the elevator. Shaking Ryan's hand, Josh was unable to make eye contact. The younger man already appeared somewhere far away, his gaze floating. After an awkward hesitation, Josh leaned in to brush Courtney's cheek with his own. As he pressed his hands lightly onto her bare shoulders, she shied a quick second and seemed to flinch, then relented. Josh knew instantly he had misjudged. He should have gone with the safer, more conservative handshake. Observing this, James settled for the one-handed grip while simultaneously casually draping his other arm, bear-like, around both of them. A nice paternal touch, less weird, the perfect instinct.

Back in his office, Josh called Erin. He craved her impressions of the meeting. He needed a reality check.

"They definitely have their point of view, don't they?" she said. In the background there was the hum of her car, the buzz of Southern California traffic at the heart of morning rush hour. "But we can get it done. It's just going to take longer and cost them more money. I've already reached out to my team. We'll meet up in about an hour and start to map it out. I should be able to send you some notes by the end of my day. I'm on my way now." Erin paused, and Josh heard her nasal laugh, a half-snort, over the traffic noise. "Had to cancel my morning yoga class. That's the only thing that sucks for me."

"I'm just finding it ultra-challenging managing those two. The Shoe King 2.0, that is."

"They want a game," Erin replied, "we'll build them a kick ass game. Actually, my guys are pretty excited about it. This is fun for them."

Josh continued to sift through moments from the meeting, trying to decipher the real meaning behind what had been said. This was never easy for him; he leaned on Erin as a sounding board, looking for her to confirm or dispel his impressions.

Then, as the call seemed to be winding down, Erin mentioned she had something more to tell him. "But you need to keep it between us," she insisted, her tone turning intimate, conspiratorial. "Not even James can know."

Josh assured her she had nothing to worry about.

"So, there's this app company in Brooklyn that LAKreativ has been doing some work for?" Josh knew Erin meant it as a statement, but her habit of raising her voice at the end of her sentences made it sound like a question. It was a verbal tic Josh tended to associate with California. "They've thrown out this idea of hiring me to run their marketing. In-house. Still preliminary, but intriguing. Definitely worth investigating."

"In New York?" His pulse quickened. "You mean you'd move here?"

"Yeah, I guess so. If it were to actually happen. Possibly. Maybe. I don't know. Still just in discussions. What do you think? I should go for it, right?"

"That would be amazing." Josh hesitated. "But what about cooking school? What happened to that idea?"

He heard her inhale sharply, a kind of inverted sigh. "Still a possibility too. Definitely in the mix. But I haven't heard from them. I can't sit around and wait. Keeping all options open."

"Well," Josh paused. He wanted to sound warm while maintaining the appropriate degree of professional distance. He wasn't sure how convincingly he could pull that off. "We'd hate to lose you on the Shoe King team, obviously. But if it's what you want, you definitely need to go for it."

"I don't know if it's what I want. That's why I need to go meet with them and check it out. I don't even have any real sense of what they're like or their culture yet. They could turn out to be serial killers for all I know."

"Possible, but doubtful. It's difficult to manage a business when you're hacking people to bits."

"Don't be so sure. Those serial killers get away with some crazy shit. Anyway, I hope I can pick your brain at some point before I actually sit down with them. If that's okay."

"Anything I can do to help."

"Thanks. You're the first person I've told. You know I value your opinion."

It excited Josh to be brought into her confidence. But he thought it best not to dwell on that. Not right then, anyway. "In the meantime," he said, "we should try to work out the timing so you can re-present the new creative, this Shoe King game idea, to Bob and the kids while you're here. Once you have all your ideas locked down, I mean." Then, aiming to recapture the lighter banter of a moment earlier, Josh added, "We're not going to let you escape until you totally blow their minds — Ryan and Courtney, I mean."

"Of course, no worries. Consider their minds blown. I won't let you down. You know that, right?"

* * *

Back in the spring, the James Gang had flown Erin in for their initial Shoe King digital strategy meeting. Josh had promised to take her to dinner, and that evening they had met up at a small bistro on lower Madison. Josh had only recently moved out of his house, and, while he refused to consider this a date, it was impossible to deny its significance. It was the first time he'd been out with a woman since separating from Claudia.

The rain had been coming down all day, one of those raw and chilly early May downpours that make summer seem a long way off. Erin arrived late and damp.

"Not exactly L.A. weather, I guess, huh?" Josh said, watching Erin unpeel soggy layers and carefully lay a colorful woven scarf across the empty seat next to her.

"Part of the appeal," she responded, meeting his eyes with her sharp gaze and warm, toothy smile. A quick detour to the bathroom, and then she was back, picking up the conversation mid-stream. "Unfortunately, my L.A. umbrella proved to be no match for what it was up against out there." Josh followed her glance toward the front windows streaked with fat droplets. She sank into the chair across from him. In the shadowy room, the candlelight flickering between them spotted unevenly across her face. The light illuminated a diamond stud, a tiny pinpoint, embedded on her left nostril. "Had to finally ditch it when I got here. It gave its life to the cause, though. So sad."

While waiting for her to arrive, Josh had been sure to decide what to order in advance. He had a thing about getting to restaurants early. He liked to peruse the menu at a relaxed pace without holding up others at the table. Erin, on the other hand, a self-professed foodie, spent a long time studying her options. Josh leaned back as she read with deep concentration. Physically, Erin was pretty much the opposite of his wife. Several inches taller and wide-hipped, she was broad-shouldered and round where Claudia was angular, padded where Claudia was bony. That morning, she had worn a short dress to the meeting. Josh had taken note of her ample but shapely thighs.

Still processing the seismic upheaval in his domestic life, Josh could feel in himself a yearning to unburden. He craved absolution, or, failing that, at least perhaps empathy. The most logical person to confide in would have been James, of course, but James's short attention span and limited patience for deep confessions and extended narratives eliminated him as a viable option.

Wary of sounding pathetic, needy, self-pitying, Josh had cautioned himself to avoid over-sharing. Yet as they lingered over cocktails, Erin's sympathetic ear proved difficult to resist. By the middle of his second vodka martini, Josh could feel himself cracking.

"When you have a special needs child, there is no break," he said, finally, wading in when the conversation, as it inevitably had to, came around to their personal histories. "You have to be on alert every minute. Which is exhausting, especially when you're already exhausted. We both became convinced we were taking on more of the daily routines and that the burden was unbalanced. And yet it was still perceived as never enough to satisfy the other person. We needed the other person to do more, which was impossible because we were both maxed out." Josh paused to watch a small knot of pedestrians step off the curb across the street and splash across Madison. "I can see that now, of course. But when you're in it, you're only aware of your own needs. You don't recognize how your spouse is also drowning."

"Was there some way to plan it out, figure out a schedule, one person on and one off?" Erin, ever the project manager, asked. "Or something like that?"

"Not really. We just kind of limped along from moment to moment." Josh shrugged and looked away. He struggled to keep emotion out of his voice. "Look, I'm the asshole here, right? I'm the one who abandoned my family, my kids. Even James, when I first told him what I was thinking, was like, 'Dude, just make sure you know what you're getting into before you make a decision you can't undo.' The guilt is horrible. I hurt the people I love. That's something you wind up carrying around with you." Josh inhaled sharply and looked away. "Which is…kind of awful. It never leaves you." He paused again, groping for language. "But at a certain point, it becomes about survival. I couldn't breathe. I couldn't bear to be in that house another minute."

Erin offered an unexpected, hesitant grin. "I must say your impression of James is dead on."

Josh was relieved, grateful to her. He had been feeling his solemn seriousness weighing them down, and for that one moment at least, the heaviness lifted. "I've worked with the guy for a long time," he said with a sheepish smile of his own. Then, lowering his voice an octave to try to approximate James's deep tones, he added, "Sometimes he's kind of a caricature of himself." This elicited another quick laugh from Erin, and Josh felt a shiver of delight run along his spine.

"They say that seventy percent of special needs couples wind up splitting up," Josh told her a few minutes later, still fretting over what Erin might be thinking. Crossing the line from work colleagues to something beyond was a tricky business at best.

"So I guess we're just part of some sort of statistical confirmation. At least we're normal in one way." Josh hesitated again. And again, it was Erin's evident nonjudgmental openness that propelled him forward. Though he hardly knew her, he felt he was on solid ground somehow. He felt safe. "It's not like I don't miss my family. My kids. Claudia, too, if I'm being totally honest. Claudia thinks I gave up, checked out. But that's not what this was about. It's just that, at a certain point, there's no relationship left in the relationship," he said, trying again to articulate something he himself had yet to fully piece together. "The primary thing remaining is resentment and immense fatigue. And a kind of grieving. All of which are not exactly building blocks for a healthy marriage."

Erin looked stricken. "Or anything else. How is your wife managing?"

"Emotionally, it's hard for me to say. She's already started dating someone, from what I can gather, though I don't know what to make of that. A guy from our town that we've known through the local PTA since way before any of this happened. His wife died a while back, so maybe he's had his eye on Claudia for a long time. Who knows?" Josh paused. "Since I'm still paying a lot of the bills," he went on, "she's actually able to afford more childcare help now than when we were together. Kind of ironic, isn't it? In some ways, her life, at least day-to-day, seems better now."

Erin stared down at her plate, thick, wavy off-blond hair falling in front of her face. "I doubt that," she sighed, barely above a mumble. Grimacing, eyes lifting, she pushed the hair off her forehead and studied Josh's face with a hard, piercing look.

"I feel for you. Both of you. I can't say I have any idea how hard it must be to raise a child with a disability." Erin paused before adding, "I'm glad you told me, though."

Their focus shifted with the arrival of the Asian fusion dumplings they had agreed to share.

"Wow, this is really good," Erin said after the first bite, with a small moan of pleasure. "Cilantro and lemongrass. Love it." She chewed slowly, thoughtfully, concentrating on the flavors. Josh took a bite of his own, but he was distracted, still worrying he'd made things weird. But then, the first dumpling sampled, appreciated and dispatched, Erin weighed in again.

"I wasn't sure I wanted to get into this," she said in a measured tone. "But I guess I'll just share with you my breakup tale of woe. It's not anywhere near what you're going through, of course, but since we're doing this, you might as well know my own sorry details."

She told him about Chad, her long-term boyfriend, someone she'd known casually when they'd attended the same high school in Denver. They both wound up settling in L.A., Erin having stayed after graduating from Occidental. They had rediscovered each other through social media connections, had met up, and had sparked. Recently, though, Chad, a musician, had decided to decamp to Portland.

"He went to college up there and loved the area, so it makes a certain kind of sense for him to move back, I guess. I think he finally decided he'd rather be a somewhat bigger fish in a somewhat smaller pond. He felt like he was getting lost in L.A. Which I understand. We all feel that way sometimes. L.A. is that kind of place. I've lived there for twelve years, and I still get like that. But the shitty part for me is that I might have gone with him."

"To Portland?"

"Yeah, maybe. Or elsewhere."

"So what stopped you?"

"What do you mean?"

"Why didn't you go?"

Erin put her napkin to her lips and peered at Josh. "He never asked. It never came up." She leaned back, away from the table, eyes drifting. "He's not the most communicative guy in the world. Funny, he writes moving, sensitive, brilliant songs, but in five years I don't think we ever had a truly honest conversation about our relationship. You keep thinking you can change someone, make him open up, but after living together for all that time, it eventually becomes obvious — or should have anyway — that a person like that isn't going to change." Erin shrugged. "He's not what you'd call emotionally available."

Josh waited silently while she contemplated the next dumpling. "I learned a lot about myself from being with him. Trust me, it wasn't my choice to break up," Erin said, pausing to take a bite. "If it had been up to me, I would have kept it going. That's kind of how I am. I'm weirdly loyal. But now, actually, I can see why it's a good thing that it happened." She shrugged with a frown that tugged at her full lower lip. "Moving on, I guess."

Later, Erin pulled out her iPad and showed Josh pictures of a culinary school in the French countryside. She'd stumbled across it a couple of summers earlier while on a biking trip across the Loire Valley. It had been her obsession ever since. Her dark eyes behind black-framed glasses grew large as she described the pastel-shaded fields and orchards and the foods she'd eaten, all organically grown and locally sourced. She was determined to get back there.

"As soon as I saw it, something just clicked," she said. "It's like I'd been there in a past life or something."

"You need those dreams. But it takes a lot of courage to make them real. I wanted to live in New Zealand after college, but I never did anything about it. Never got there." Josh thought back to the New Zealand idea, now so many years in the past. For so long he had held on to it tightly, like a key to a door only he knew existed. "Still haven't been there."

"What I'm talking about is not a fantasy or a dream or whatever," Erin insisted. "I'm dead serious about this. I don't know. I'm almost thirty. I have to make it happen. I can't wait any longer."

"Otherwise you'll wind up like me," Josh said, forcing a small grin. "Living in the suburbs with two kids and an SUV."

"Don't get me wrong. I'm going to want that too. Eventually." A beat, and she smiled back at him. "Well, maybe I can skip the SUV. But I'm going to want kids someday, the whole thing. I just have other things I need to do first."

Erin was staying with a friend on the Upper East Side, so, when they left the restaurant, Josh assumed they would go their separate ways. But instead of turning toward the subway, she surprised him by declaring she would walk him up Madison and then head farther uptown after dropping him off at Grand Central. The rain, though still falling, had eased considerably. They made their way slowly through Midtown's glistening streets, stepping gingerly over and around puddles, heads close together under Josh's small, saggy umbrella.

Once inside Grand Central, they lingered near the information booth. At this hour, there was only a trickle of people rushing by; the main concourse, cast in golden light, felt cavernous. The few voices to be heard echoed across the expansive room. Though the charming old building was a part of Josh's daily life, like most commuters, he barely noticed it as he raced through twice a day. Erin, however, was captivated. She took pictures with her phone, staring up at the twinkling stars in the painted ceiling. With his train departing in minutes, Josh leaned in to hug her. That hug turned into a kiss, and then another. In the days and weeks that followed, each time Josh would replay the scene on a loop in his mind, he would remind himself that these were far from full-on face-sucking movie kisses. In reality, they were relatively chaste. Still, they were unquestionably full-on open lips, and that wasn't so easily dismissed. As Josh had sensed Erin's warmth radiate toward him, he'd felt his heart quicken, arousal awaken. "Soft caresses all over your body," he'd murmured into Erin's ear as they held onto each other. He thought her knees may have buckled a little at that.

"I should go," she said in a throaty whisper, leaning into him. She glanced at the brass four-faced clock glowing over his shoulder. "And you need to go." A final kiss, gentle, a hint of more, of possibility. Then she broke away with a tender finger wave and was off into the night.

* * *

There was no doubt he'd been smitten. The potential of a new romance, even the most modest flicker of possibility, had always lifted him up, been restorative, an elixir. At this point in his life, the realization came over him, that effect was magnified a hundredfold. He texted her on his way home that night and again over that weekend, trying to get a handle on a moment that felt magical beyond all proportion. Her responses, while open and friendly, were also, he sensed, guarded. His elation began to be supplanted by worry, that she would view him as hopelessly clichéd, the recently separated middle-aged family man looking for romance with a younger woman, not May-December maybe, but certainly May-late October. It was the kind of thing Claudia tended to roll her eyes at when it popped up in romantic comedies. During his darkest moments, he would be consumed by self-loathing, berating himself for losing perspective like a moonstruck teenager. She was young and lovely and desirable and, he fretted, he was none of those things.

Over the summer they would, now and then, text each other friendly, non-work-related notes. And then she sent that picture of the strip of ocean from her bedroom window. For the most part, he eventually calmed down enough for them to resume their professional relationship. Still, he reminded himself, she had been as willing as he. Something had happened.

FOUR

Later in the morning, Josh peeked into the conference room and was surprised to see Bob, still seated in the same chair he'd occupied during their meeting, still engrossed in his phone. Josh waved, but the older man didn't look up. Josh veered toward James's office to report that their most important client had apparently decided to camp out with them for the day.

"Weird. He usually can't wait to bolt out of here and get back to the friendly confines of the Island." James pressed his hands against the armrests on his chair; a moment later he was upright. "What's he doing in there?"

"On his phone. Seems deep in concentration."

James lowered his voice. "I guess we'll have to offer to take him to lunch. I don't really have time for this shit today. Maybe he'll turn us down." James pushed past Josh. "C'mon. Let's go do the deed. See what's up with the great man."

As they edged toward the conference room, James murmured out of the side of his mouth, "We should really be taking the kids to lunch. Or drinks. That seems to be where the power is now."

Josh nodded. "Should I set something up?"

"Yeah, maybe. Yeah. Let's do drinks. Drinks might be better."

"Let me see what I can do."

James stopped short and leaned into Josh, looming over him, coffee breath sour and stale. He spoke so uncharacteristically softly that Josh could hardly hear him. "I have to admit, this client is making me nervous, Josh. And I don't get nervous. That's your territory. You're the one with all the anxiety. I don't like the feeling."

"As long as we keep Bob on our side, I have to believe we'll be okay."

"I hope you're right." James started to move and then abruptly stopped again. "Not sure you are."

In the doorway, they waited for Bob to acknowledge them. But he continued staring at his phone. What could possibly be so mesmerizing? Finally, they entered, James in the lead, Josh trailing close behind.

"Hey, Bob. Wanted to see if you might want to grab a bite to eat. We're buying, so I give you fair warning, we're going cheap."

Chin tucked into his chest, phone in hand, Bob remained unresponsive.

They moved closer. "Is he sleeping?" asked Josh quietly.

James touched the older man's shoulder. "Bob?"

They looked at each other. Josh could feel the hairs rising on his arms.

James shook Bob, gently, then harder. The phone slipped from his hand, clattering against the conference room table as it fell to the floor. The Shoe King slumped to one side.

"Holy fuck," James said, his voice barely above a whisper. He looked up, his face ashen. "This is not sleeping, Josh."

Bob continued to list to his right. Josh instinctively grabbed his arm to keep him from falling over. His skin was clammy and cold, like clay. Josh felt queasy and he pulled away. He thought he might puke. Bob slid farther out of the chair so that his head was now hanging almost to the floor.

"Holy fuck," James said again.

FIVE

Claudia sat alone at a square glass table toward the rear of the airy Upper East Side café, a spray of yellow and white daisies in a blue ceramic vase centered in front of her, menu open but unread. As she glanced at the messages on her phone, she struggled to assess, as one often does upon reconnecting with absent friends, the status of that unassailable chemistry she and Jen had always so reliably shared. Did they still get each other in the same intuitive ways? Or had that magical ability to anticipate the other's thoughts and feelings, so cherished and solid, so woven into their souls, become irrevocably frayed, a casualty of the passing years and their own mutable lives?

Claudia was still troubled by the memory of their last reunion, two years earlier in London. She had stopped for a brief layover on her way back to New York from Zurich. The video production company she worked for had been hired by a Swiss pharmaceutical conglomerate that was in a panic to rush out a new product, having just learned one of their prime competitors was threatening to beat them to market. Within hours of being handed the assignment, Claudia had hired a European crew, pulled together the shoot, and was on a plane. A day later she was returning to New York, having completed her interviews with the company's senior officers.

The nature of the project was not atypical for Claudia, though it wasn't often she was asked to spontaneously hop on a flight to Europe, business class no less. She had worked for the same company since shortly after college; as she'd risen through the ranks, she had fostered a valued reputation as the company's unofficial ombudsman, the trusted troubleshooter on demand. When a project ran up against difficult personalities, impossible deadlines, or some other knotty complication, it was Claudia who was most often called upon to step in and deal with it. She liked the role; it fit her personality. She had authority and control, she didn't have to manage projects from start to finish, and it gave her a degree of flexibility and autonomy.

Upon landing at Heathrow, Claudia had impulsively called Jen, who had sounded delighted by the unexpected news that her friend was in town, if only for a few hours. Jen, who lived in St. John's Wood, suggested they meet up in the bar of a hotel Claudia could reach from the airport relatively easily. But Jen was late, and by the time they found each other, it was nearly time for Claudia to turn around and leave again, irritating them both. Later, after acknowledging their mutual frustration over this brief, unsatisfying reunion, they pledged they would plan something more substantial, perhaps a long weekend away together, perhaps Paris. But life always seemed to interfere, to slip by unnoticed, and now, here it was, another block of time passed.

So, when Jen emailed that she would be on the East Coast to look at colleges with her older daughter Thea, Claudia had made sure to be available. She had arranged to take the afternoon off, hoping they could hang out for the day. She thought they might stroll to a museum together after lunch, as they used to long ago, when their only responsibilities were to their jobs and themselves.

But this was not to be. Just that morning, Jen had phoned to say that schedules had changed and she now would have time for only a quick bite before having to leave to meet Thea in Vermont. The disappointment stung, no question. But Claudia was steadfast in her determination to push aside any hurt feelings. She had been so looking forward to seeing Jen, and she wanted today to be happy. She willed herself to be in the moment, to savor whatever time they had to share.

They had been best friends since the sixth grade, when Jen had transferred into Claudia's school after her family's move from the Midwest. Claudia, a kid who read a lot of books, was inspired by her literary heroes to imagine herself an individualist, an iconoclast who resisted labeling. With Jen, she found the perfect sidekick. Jen truly was an outsider, struggling to adapt to the attitudes, customs, and expectations of well-heeled Westchester County. It was so alien, so different in countless ways, large and small, from the self-contained little Illinois town she'd just left.

Claudia and Jen bonded over their certainty that nobody could possibly understand where they were coming from, that they saw life differently than everyone else. They imagined themselves as complicated misfits, too complex, too intense to be easily categorized. It gave them what their twelve-year-old selves needed; together, they navigated a constricted suburban world that was hopelessly misaligned and clueless. They shared a yen to escape, to break free from the small-mindedness they saw all around them. They would share their daydreams, spinning fanciful tales of journeys to exotic locales they would one day take. The reality, as Claudia would only fully come to understand upon reaching adulthood, was that these carefully cultivated personas were, at minimum, imperfect reflections of who they truly were. Though at that age they would have been horrified at the mere suggestion, the truth was they were both far more conventional than they ever would have accepted. Both did all the typical afterschool activities — Claudia had already discovered her passion for dance — and they had plenty of friends. Far from being outcasts, they negotiated their school's stratified social circles with relative ease. Still, when it came to revealing their truest inner selves, they swore allegiance solely to the other.

They had maintained this impermeable bond throughout their middle grades; it was when they reached high school that their fates began to diverge. Claudia, thin and dark, the prettier one, was attracting steady interest from boys. Jen, plainer and chunky, was self-conscious about her big boobs, flat hair, pigeon-toed gait, and glasses that never seemed to quite fit her face. She couldn't afford the designer outfits and cool accessories the other girls in school seemed to flaunt with calculated ease. When, during their senior year, Jen finally met a guy who showed interest, Claudia was excited for her. It was true that, from the start, Claudia found Neil rather weird and socially awkward. He tended to mutter and had trouble with eye contact. Still, he seemed into Jen, and Jen was won over by the sudden attention. Selfishly, it was also easier in some ways for Claudia because now she no longer had to feel guilty when she sacrificed time with Jen to be with her own boyfriend. Now it was Jen who would suddenly drop out of touch for days at a time.

It wasn't long, however, before it all came apart. One afternoon after school, Jen sought out Claudia and tearfully told her what had happened when she made the decision to sleep with Neil. The whole thing had been tense, clumsy. and painful. At a certain point, Jen had wanted to stop, told him to stop, tried to push him away, but he hadn't listened and continued, forcing himself on her. Now, worse, Neil, who went to a different school, had disappeared, gone silent, totally incommunicado. But an even more devastating blow was to come some weeks later. When Jen missed her period, she took a pregnancy test; in a panic, she told Claudia it had come up positive. Claudia took charge, scraping together the money for the clinic, making the appointment, and escorting Jen at the designated time. Claudia stayed with her that night, holding her, even getting her to laugh when she declared they were through with boys and avowing that from this point on they would exclusively date only women.

After college — Claudia attended Brown while Jen, staying in state, went to SUNY Binghamton — they remained close, moving to the city and sharing an apartment on the East Side, a short distance, as it happened, from the restaurant where Claudia was sitting at that very moment. Once Jen met Rob, Claudia saw less of her. Then, only months after marrying, Jen told Claudia that Rob's career in international banking at JP Morgan was taking off; he'd been promoted and was being transferred overseas. In the years that followed, Claudia was reduced primarily to tracking Jen's adventurous life from afar, connecting with her through the periodic email or phone call and later through her social media posts. It was not unusual for these exchanges to be followed by pangs of envy. Claudia wound up back in Westchester, not far from where she had grown up, her parents having helped her and Josh buy the house in Larchmont. Babies came next, followed by her reluctant entry into the world of special needs parenting. Meanwhile, Jen was raising her two girls and living her life as a cosmopolitan ex-pat, first in Hong Kong, then Dubai, Frankfurt, and now, finally, London. She was experiencing a life Claudia could only imagine.

* * *

Looking up from her phone, Claudia spotted Jen through the oversized windows getting out of a taxi and rushing inside. She appeared as a flash hurrying forward, so elegant in her black cashmere shawl and precisely layered haircut that fell to just above her shoulders, dark blond locks perfectly framing her round face. They threw their arms around each other and squeezed, holding on tightly. As they studied each other from across the table, Claudia observed that Jen still had that bit of fleshiness she had always fretted over. But at this stage in her life, it seemed to work for her. The skin around her eyes and mouth was taut and virtually unlined, and her cheeks retained a soft glow. She looked voluptuous and desirable, with a certain soft poutiness. The thought crossed Claudia's mind briefly that Jen might have had work done. Or that she might be having an affair. But she quickly dismissed both possibilities. Neither would have been Jen's style.

Their initial conversation burst forth in excited exchanges as Jen ran through her crowded itinerary for the next few days. She grew quieter when she asked Claudia about Ethan and Amy, looking concerned and sympathetic as she listened to Claudia describe how the stress of motherhood, already compounded by the care Amy required, had further intensified now that she had been abruptly, unwillingly, transformed into a single parent.

"My heart aches for you, Claudia," Jen said finally. "I'm so sorry you're going through this."

"Don't feel sorry," Claudia replied more curtly than intended, with a wave of her hand. A warning bell went off somewhere deep in her brain. It was hardly unusual for people, upon learning about Amy, to convey their concern through pity. Though this irritated Claudia and she had little patience for it, it was something she had grown accustomed to. But she would have thought Jen would have known better, would have known *her* better.

"We don't feel sorry for ourselves," she said. "Never have given into that. It's a waste of energy. It's not even relevant, really. This is actually one of the few things Josh and I seem — seemed — to agree on. We accept it. It's life — it's what we have to deal with. No different than anyone else with their own shit. You have yours. Everyone does. It sucks. But you deal."

"You're very brave."

"Oh, please," Claudia insisted. She observed two elderly gray-haired women, one wielding a cane, shuffle unsteadily toward the next table. They passed behind her, and Claudia shifted her chair to make room. "The hardest part is having to acknowledge that your child is never going to reach what would have otherwise what should have been her potential. That keeps you up at night." Claudia thought for a moment, considering, before continuing, "That and knowing that at some point we're going to have to figure out her long-term care. She's going to need to live some place, a group home of some sort we can feel confident about."

Claudia looked down at her menu, throat tightening. She didn't want Jen to walk away from today with her primary memory of their conversation being Claudia as a divorced special needs parent. She didn't want Jen to define her that way. There was so much more to talk about, to share, to dig into.

"I always wanted to believe you and Josh were so together on this," Jen said. "What happened? All the sudden he decided he couldn't handle it? I mean, what the hell?"

"Not all of the sudden. Not really. The signs were there for a long time. When he finally decided to leave, he made this big speech about how he had to get out, how his mental health depended on it. As if mine didn't matter...as if my mental health was...you know, extraneous, beside the point. Somehow."

"Pretty shitty."

Claudia tossed her hands, a dismissive gesture. "Well, it's typical Josh. You know, I sometimes think about how middle-aged men are supposed to leave their wives because they are running *to* something — a younger woman or some other midlife crisis male fantasy. Josh did just the reverse: he decided to run away from something. But even when he left, he still made it sound as if he only wanted to take time off temporarily. A year, he said, to...I don't know. Reevaluate, I guess. As if that was ever going to happen. Once he walked out that door, well, you know me well enough...."

"When you emailed me, you said something about him leaving you by text." Jen looked puzzled. "You didn't mean that literally, right?"

"Yeah." Claudia shrugged. "I mean, I knew it was coming and all, but on the day it happened, he messaged me to say he'd found an apartment in Yonkers and had moved his stuff out. By the time I got home that night, he was gone."

"That's so messed up. I don't even know how to respond to that."

"Yeah, well. That's Josh. What can I tell you?"

The waitress — blond, thin, young — deposited two white wines, glistening with condensation, onto their table. They touched glasses.

"To you, my dear," said Jen.

"To us, right?" Claudia said. "And the rest of the world can go fuck itself. Like we used to tell each other."

Jen laughed and lifted her glass. "Something like that. This is what I've been missing. You're still the same bad ass Claudia you always were. I need more of that attitude in my life — for inspiration."

"I'm not sure it's something you really want to aspire to," Claudia said, deflecting with a smile and another half shrug.

They ordered salads, then, with the waitress still lingering nearby, Jen shot Claudia a look from across the table, a look that was reassuringly familiar, though Claudia hadn't seen it for a very long time, of course.

"Share a side of fries?" Jen said.

"Hell, yeah," she replied. "I thought you'd never ask."

After the waitress moved on, Claudia asked Jen about her daughters.

"My kids? My kids are...great. They're really thriving. I can't wait for you to see them." Jen sounded hesitant, careful, almost apologetic. "We're very lucky. Believe me, I don't take it for granted." In a soft voice she added, "I know we're blessed."

"And now Thea is looking at colleges. So crazy how the time goes."

"Tell me about it. But, yeah. It's kind of funny, because my girls have never lived in the States. I mean, they've always gone to American schools, but they've never lived here. So it'll be different for them. They're excited."

"And maybe that means I'll get to see you more often?"

"Actually, that's the other thing. Remember I told you we thought Rob might be relocated back to the U.S.? So it looks like it's going to happen. By the summer probably. You may get more of me than you bargained for."

"I had a feeling from your last email." Claudia touched her friend's arm. "I can't wait. You'll get to meet Marcus."

"Duh. I want to hear all about him."

"Oh, you know, what can I tell you? Just your typical tough Philly street urchin turned urbane, erudite academic."

"Sounds sexy." Jen lifted a sculpted eyebrow. "The intellectual with a hint of menace."

Claudia laughed. "He *is* really smart. But mostly he's just, like, ridiculously normal. It's funny, after all these years with Josh, his diffidence and his whole wishy-washy nature, it's kind of an adjustment to be with someone like Marcus, someone who is actually comfortable in his own skin."

Feeling as though she were dominating the conversation, talking too much about herself, Claudia stopped and stared at her friend.

"But...what?" asked Jen. "You sounded like you were going to say something else."

"No, not really." Claudia paused again for a long moment. "I don't know. Marcus is great and all. But sometimes I think he might be a little *too* centered. I could stand for just a little bit more crazy once in a while. Not Josh's neurotic crazy, you understand. I've had enough of that. Just a little more, I guess, unpredictability. Impulsiveness."

"Unpredictable is kind of overrated, I think. It might sound exciting, edgy, in the abstract — not so much when you're in it. I'll take reliability any day. And for what it's worth, I think it's perfectly natural. You know how it is. You're on the rebound from one relationship, so you seek out the opposite type."

"Ri-ght." Claudia heard herself dragging the word out into several syllables. She wondered again if the communication between them was somehow amiss. What was she not explaining? She took a short breath. "Actually, this isn't a rebound. You get that, right?" She reached out again to put her hand on top of Jen's. "I need to know you understand. I'm not with Marcus because I'm looking for a warm body to sleep with while I figure out my next move. That's not what this is." Leaning forward, forearms on the table, she looked at Jen hard and repeated, "You get that, right?"

Recoiling, Jen seemed shaken. "I'm sorry. I didn't mean it that way. I shouldn't have used the word rebound."

"No, no, it's okay." Claudia felt her shoulders dropping. "I'm sure I'm just thin-skinned about the whole thing. I never wanted to be in this position. Who does? I'm totally feeling my way through it."

"So this is the real deal with Marcus?"

"Actually...more than you might think." She had been looking forward to this part of the conversation, to sharing her secrets with Jen, like they had done so often in the past. "I have to tell you something no one else knows yet. Not my parents, not anyone."

Jen smiled and nodded, fingers locked beneath her chin. A thin silver bracelet slid a few inches down from her wrist. She touched it absently.

"So you know we haven't been seeing each other all that long, right? I mean, it's really only since the first part of this year. So, this might sound a bit...weird. Unexpected. I mean, the divorce isn't even final yet." Claudia watched as Jen continued to nod. "But the thing is, he's already proposed to me. Kinda, sorta."

Jen's mouth dropped open. "You're kidding." Claudia heard a clipped squeal. "That's fantastic."

"I guess so. It's just very, uh, soon. Very fast. A little head spinning."

Jen rested a finger along the side of her chin. "Tell me everything. I need details." Claudia remembered her friend's fondness for romance novels and movies. She wondered if that were still the case. If so, Claudia thought, she might be in for a bit of a letdown.

Claudia said, "The thing is, Marcus has his romantic side. He does a lot of little things that are really adorable. But he's also very practical, rational. He likes to frame our situation as a matter of expediency."

Jen frowned, her lower lip jutting out in exaggerated disappointment. "I'm hoping you'll tell me he took you away to a beautiful place and dropped to one knee."

"I wish I had a better story. It was all about how he and his kids have been spending so much time at my place and how it doesn't make sense to keep two houses, how it's so expensive and how it's not good for anyone, especially for the kids, you know, like that." Claudia took a breath. "Very pragmatic."

"I wasn't even there and I'm crushed," Jen said, chuckling. "So what did you tell him?"

"Well, that's the kinda, sorta part. I accepted. Of course. I just told him I thought we needed more time before we went public and started thinking about a date and making plans and everything." Claudia tensed as she listened to herself describe her life to her best friend. "Marcus is super impatient to move ahead, to get on with it. And I understand that. But his...uh, his urgency, I guess you'd call it? It makes me nervous. On the other hand, you can't control the timing, can you? It's not like I'm going to tell him, sorry, I think you're great but I'm going to pass because enough time hasn't elapsed? Opportunities present themselves, and you either seize them or you don't."

"Single man, widower, raising two kids on his own. I get it. Men don't do so well in those situations."

"Yeah, he's kind of a man on a mission. But I know he loves me. He wouldn't be doing this otherwise, trust me. Nor would I, obviously. I know I'm not just a convenient way for him to find a wife. That would be gross."

"The main thing is that you're really in love with him." Jen tilted her head at her friend.

"Of course I am," Claudia responded.

Jen let the eye contact linger, and Claudia held her gaze. Jen's phrasing, her inflection, put her off. She felt that unease rising in her throat again.

"You know, it's okay if you're still figuring out that part of it," said Jen after a minute. "This is me you're talking to."

"I'm sure of it, Jen," said Claudia and then, to make her point, she repeated, "I'm sure. You don't have to say it like that. Listen, I'm not doubting us as a couple. We just need more time together. Just to be. And on top of all that, I'm still kind of getting my feet on the ground being single again. You know?"

Claudia watched Jen twirl her fork into the shards of lettuce and shredded chicken she'd barely touched. Glancing over at the empty plate of fries, Claudia was mildly alarmed upon realizing it was she who'd eaten most of them.

"How's the sex?" Jen asked, hand half over her mouth.

"Pretty fucking good. Which helps. After not having had much of it for, uh, well...a while, that's one thing I'm not complaining about.

He's, uh, let's just say he's more present than Josh. Proof that you can teach an old dog a few new tricks. Though I may have shown him a thing or two as well. It's just weird fucking someone new after all these years. It takes some adjusting."

Claudia became aware of the two ladies at the next table, eavesdropping. The one with the cane caught Claudia's eye, the old woman leaning in her direction. Momentarily unsettled, Claudia had a sudden glimpse of herself thirty or so years in the future. She forced a smile, then, with a slight shudder, looked away and returned her focus to Jen.

"Glad to hear someone is getting it," Jen said, lowering her voice, with a glance over at the ladies. "That makes one of us."

"You and Rob are...?"

"No, no, we're fine. It's more that we just never see each other. He's either traveling or working crazy hours. And I'm so wrapped up with the girls right now."

"Well, that part will change soon, right?"

"Yeah, that's one reason I'm glad we're moving back here. I'm ready to come home. I think Rob is too." Jen smiled at Claudia and exhaled. "It'll be good for us. It's time."

When they left the restaurant, they stood on the sidewalk and held each other again. The autumn breeze gusted and ebbed, scraps of decaying newspapers and plastic bags swirling at their feet, wrapping around their ankles. Jen took a few steps toward a black town car idling by the curb, the driver lingering a few feet away. One hand resting on top of the open rear door, she promised to be in touch as soon as she returned to London. Claudia watched as her friend slid into the back seat, ran a hand through her hair, leaned forward, and said something to the driver. Then they were off, headed uptown, melting into the dense Third Avenue traffic.

Claudia turned and unhurriedly began making her way in the other direction. She thought she might do a little shopping, maybe wander through a few stores as she meandered toward Grand Central. It was rare for her to have unstructured free time like this. She was torn over how to use it. On the one hand, she felt the need to do something productive. On the other, she had an equally strong desire to simply fritter away her hour or two in the least constructive way possible.

She pictured Jen up in Vermont with Thea. She tried to imagine that feeling, mother and daughter together, the latter on the cusp of adulthood, ready to embark upon her life as an independent young woman. Claudia had a daughter too, but they would never be visiting colleges. Amy would not be going to college, nor would she be dating or getting married or having babies of her own. Instead, one day, perhaps sooner than Claudia wished to acknowledge, she and presumably Josh would be going to visit those residential care facilities, searching for the place where Amy could thrive to the best of her ability. Though no longer a couple, she and Josh were still Amy's parents, and they were going to need to decide together on this, on finding a place where Amy would be safe and happy. They would do it with no way of knowing for sure if they were making the best choice. There were no guarantees. And then Amy would live somewhere else, with other people to look after her, far into the future, even after Claudia and Josh were no longer around. This was to be their daughter's fate; it was the best they could do for her, the best they could hope for her.

SIX

The Shoe King's sudden and untimely demise had not gone unnoticed in the wider world. Even *The Times* had regarded the news noteworthy enough to devote an entire column to it in its Metro section:

'The Shoe King' Passes
And With Him, A New York Era Fades

In accordance with Jewish tradition, the funeral took place quickly, just two days after Bob's expiration. As James and Josh entered the Long Island synagogue near Bob's home, they'd had to shuffle past a gaggle of photographers and local TV crews. Since it had been they who discovered Bob, the pair were of particular interest to the media. But James had made clear to Josh they were not to speak to anyone.

"If we start giving quotes to the press," he warned, "there's only one way it can go. Badly."

Josh stayed close to his boss, falling in step with his heavy gait. He was relieved when they made it inside without being approached by any of the lurking cameras.

The two men sat down near the back of the crowded chapel; soon they heard an organ playing and someone chanting in Hebrew. The yarmulke on Josh's head felt awkward and unnatural. James, too, looked like a gentile fish out of water. The James Gang had been given responsibility for the design, printing, and delivery of the programs, a copy of which Josh now held loosely in his hands. It had been an anxious couple of days getting them done; Josh was relieved to see how well they had turned out, Bob's craggy face beaming up at him.

James elbowed Josh and motioned with his chin toward a thin dark-haired woman wrapped in an oversized shawl, perhaps mid-thirties, seated by herself across the aisle.

"That's the girlfriend," James said in a hushed tone. "Bob's latest paramour."

"No shit," Josh murmured. "Does Marissa know about her?"

"Not sure. But you would think so, right? With Bob's track record, you've gotta figure at some point it becomes fairly evident."

Josh considered this. "How do you know who she is? You've met her?"

"Met her? Hell, yeah, I've met her. Been out with them, had dinner with them. Her and Bob." James paused. "She's a hoot, actually."

Josh looked at his boss again. There were so many secrets out there he simply had no idea about. He sometimes felt as though his entire life was spent out of the loop. Or at least the loop that mattered in any meaningful way.

James looked over at her again, caught her eye, and nodded grimly. She looked back with pursed lips. Then he turned back to Josh and whispered, "Now that you're single, maybe you want to give that a shot. I've heard she just recently became available."

"You are a sick fuck," Josh whispered back.

Although Bob had donated heavily to this synagogue, and he had insisted on elaborate, dual Bar/Bat Mitzvahs for his children, he had been far from devout and had professed little more than a passing interest in tradition or ritual. Josh had been part of more than one Yom Kippur day business lunch that Bob had dropped in on after spending his morning fasting and atoning for his sins.

Josh was in no position to judge a person's religious leanings and had no interest in doing so. Somewhere way back, at least part of his family had been Episcopalian. But his parents were committed nonbelievers, and, growing up, he had barely set foot in a church. When he met Claudia, she had expressed disdain for what she pointedly referred to as "organized religion." While she affirmed that the search for personal spirituality was a quest to be taken seriously and with gravitas, she believed that it was up to each individual to discover his or her own unique pathway to uplifting, meaningful existential enlightenment and a higher consciousness. The thought had occasionally occurred to Josh, particularly when in settings such as this; if he had married a woman for whom traditional religion mattered, he might have had a very different life.

"When a member of our community passes, how shall we remember him and honor that memory?" the rabbi began. He was younger than Josh had anticipated, with a close-cut dark beard and an earnest expression. His lilting cadence was mesmerizing; Josh found himself at points paying more attention to the man's rhythmic speech pattern than his words. "Bob Burns was a successful entrepreneur, a provider, a builder, a community leader, and a giving soul. He was a family man first and foremost. He was a loving husband to his wife Marissa, and he adored his twin children, Ryan and Courtney. And that adoration was returned, to the point where the three of them ended up working together. It was one of Bob's greatest thrills and satisfactions to be able to bring his children into the family business."

When it came time for the family to speak, the twins slowly approached the steps to the podium. Their mother remained seated in the first row, huddled into herself, sobbing quietly, a black veil covering her face.

Both Ryan and Courtney had been drawn to the spotlight from an early age. Courtney had pursued theatre — Josh remembered being forced to go with James to see her as Laura in her high school production of *The Glass Menagerie*. Ryan had fronted a metal band since middle school and still played with those same guys on occasion, when the opportunity presented itself.

So, in spite of this most somber of settings, the two of them, falling back on those instincts as performers, seemed to relish their moment before this packed chapel, their captive audience rapt. Shoulder to shoulder, they were in command of the room, taking turns sharing stories about their father, at times finishing the other's sentences.

"Bob Burns embraced the best of Jewish values," began Ryan, his voice rich with emotion, eyes drifting across the attentive faces. "He believed in the concept of Tikkun Olam — 'repair the world'— the idea that we are responsible for the welfare of society at large. This was something our father could totally get behind. And, like most things in his life, it wasn't just lip service. He walked the walk. It was in his DNA to give back. He tried to do what he could, through his generosity of spirit, to make the world a better place. When we were growing up, every year at Thanksgiving our dad took us to a soup kitchen, where we handed out meals to the less fortunate. Believe me, as kids, my sister and I didn't always want to go." Here, Ryan glanced over at Courtney, who shot him that same tender smile Josh had noticed the other day during the meeting. "But he insisted."

"And we're so fortunate he did," Courtney added, picking up the thread. "Because it was moments like those that taught us about character and what it means to be a good person."

"This is the Bob Burns he kept private," Ryan continued. "This was the man no one knew about."

"Actually," whispered James, looking down at the floor, "everyone knew. We made sure the PR firm got the local news down there to cover Bob doling out those plates of turkey. Which they did, by God. We made sure of it."

Josh nodded as James continued to mutter random commentary. Josh knew it all too well. The real truth was that James handed off the annual Thanksgiving Day assignment to Josh, and Josh was the one who had to make sure the PR firm didn't fuck it up. He had spent many a

Thanksgiving morning on the phone in his home office coordinating and confirming. It drove Claudia nuts; she had been adamant that that time should be off limits and reserved for family.

"Seeing so many of you here reminds us just how much our dad was loved." Courtney's voice wobbled, and she took a step back, away from the podium. Ryan rested a hand gently on her forearm; she gathered herself and started again. "Our father, who never even finished college, was the epitome of the American dream. He was a joyful man, and that joy is something we will cherish and carry with us throughout the rest of our lives. He truly lived the adage, *If you love what you do, you'll never work a day in your life.*"

Oh, how Josh hated that expression. Ninety-nine percent of the assholes out in the real world were not doing what they loved, or even liked. Most people tolerated their jobs. They were doing it for a paycheck, and that was just how it was and how it was always going to be. That stupid expression just gave most people yet one more reason to feel bad about themselves.

* * *

After they'd driven out to the cemetery, after the coffin had been lowered into the ground, after the final prayers had been said, and after everyone had had their turns tossing a handful of dirt on top of the Shoe King, Ryan approached James and Josh, while Courtney, dark dress clinging provocatively to her shapely figure, lingered nearby. The October air was brisk, with a steady breeze. Cotton candy clouds, some dark and threatening, scudded across the sky. With a tilt of his head, somber black tie flapping against a crisp white shirt, Ryan ushered them toward a stone crypt, up a hill a short distance away. The small low door, half open, creaked softly on its hinges with each gust of wind. Ryan indicated they should go in.

"Here?" James asked dubiously.

"We just need someplace private for a few minutes," responded Ryan. "We'll never be able to talk out here. Too many hands to shake." He looked back toward the dark-suited mourners milling near the gravesite. A cluster of older men standing by themselves, some bald, some with slicked back graying hair, peered up in their direction. "We just need a few minutes," Ryan repeated with a quick glance over his shoulder.

James and Josh exchanged looks, then stooped and stepped through the arched entrance into the cramped space.

"Have a seat," Ryan said, pointing toward a small granite bench against the back wall.

James lifted a handful of dried flowers off the bench and looked at Josh again curiously before gently placing the withered bouquet onto the floor. James and Josh squeezed together, their eyes adjusting to the dusky light. Ryan, facing them, leaned against the opposite wall, twisting his neck and shoulders to accommodate the tight quarters.

"Let's get right to it," Ryan said. "We haven't come to a final decision yet, but we want to be fair and tell you we're seriously thinking of making an agency change. We're looking at the big picture, and, unfortunately, it's hard to conclude in any other way but that you guys don't get what we want. The chemistry just isn't there."

James inhaled deeply. "Can we talk about this in the office or over lunch?" His eyes flashed sideways, then returned to Ryan. "I'm not entirely comfortable having this conversation here."

"No. We need to do it now, while we're all together," countered Ryan. "There's an urgency. We need you to know how we're feeling. We need you to hear us."

"Out of respect for your father. Let's do this later. Unfortunately, I have to fly to Toronto tonight, but I'm totally available to you the first of next week. This is not the time. Or the place."

"My dad was a businessman and a straight shooter," Ryan pressed on. "He would have wanted us to have this out as soon as possible."

Standing in the doorway, arms folded, framed by a wedge of greenery, Courtney listened to her brother, expressionless. The grassy expanse behind her, lit up by the late afternoon sunlight that had suddenly reappeared, stretched off into the distance, checkerboarded by a sea of gravestones.

"We want to do the right thing," Courtney said. "That's important to us. We've decided we're going to give you sixty days. The reality is, we can't afford even that kind of time. But it's for our dad." With a weak smile, she continued, "I know he liked you, James. Besides, we really do want to give you guys every chance to pull it together. We're not here to screw you over. But by the first of January, we're moving on, one way or another. This digital strategy has been a shit show for too long. We've got to get it straightened out and launched and get this business back to where it needs to be."

"This isn't easy for us," Ryan added. "You guys have been with our family for a long time. We understand the personal side to all of this. We're hardly blind to it."

"It's not personal," Courtney interjected, contradicting her brother. "It's just business. We can't be responsible for letting everything Dad built fall apart. There's a humongous amount of pressure on us. I'm sure you can see where we're coming from."

In the distance, they heard cars starting up, engines turning over and idling.

"We need to get back to our mom," said Ryan with a backward glance toward the swath of daylight through the doorway. "She's waiting in the limo. To be honest, it would be awesome if you guys came up with something truly fucking amazing. We'd love it if that could happen."

SEVEN

Claudia was pregnant with Ethan when they learned of Amy's diagnosis. They'd known for some time that their daughter had developmental delays; Amy had been working with therapists since she was just over a year old. But Josh and Claudia had convinced themselves that whatever the problem was, it was correctable, that she would eventually catch up. They hadn't been prepared for the severity of what they were facing. Once the situation was made clear to them, they felt foolish and sheepish, as it dawned on them they had been the last to know, blind to what had been obvious to the professionals. The statistics showed that autistic children were primarily boys. Amy was an exception.

Though by and large sweet-tempered, Amy was prone to explosive tantrums. Essentially nonverbal, she became frustrated when she couldn't communicate or didn't understand how to process basic sensations such as hunger or cold. She could be inconsolable at those times, and her wailing, unstaunchable howls of misery and torment ate into their nerves.

While other parents celebrated their children's milestones and looked forward to what lay ahead, Josh and Claudia felt like they were running in place. It was like raising a toddler in perpetuity, a dark version of *Groundhog Day* you could never escape.

Pulled into the world of special needs families, they involuntarily bore witness to other parents' sad stories, each its own custom-made nightmare, many far worse than their own. Some of the kids in Amy's therapy groups could be violent. Some wore crash helmets to guard against serious injury in case they bashed their heads into walls. There was the elderly couple with their thirty-something daughter, glassy-eyed, slack-jawed, and wheelchair-bound. As they grew older, the parents were losing their ability to manage the wheelchair, to say nothing of the countless other day-to-day tasks their daughter's care required. But they refused to entertain the idea of moving her out of the only home she'd known, so instead they fought desperately against the inevitable pull of aging, renewing the struggle each day.

Josh began to hear that statistic, the seventy percent break-up rate for special needs couples. It seemed to be accepted within that world as common knowledge, as gospel. But there was no solid research for it that Josh could find, and he began to wonder if that number were not a bit of an urban legend. Finally, he decided it was irrelevant because, ultimately, the particular strain Josh and Claudia were under was unique to their unique situation. The battle to keep their marriage alive was theirs and theirs alone.

Amy was unable to independently dress, bathe, or feed herself. She also had never been successfully toilet-trained, in spite of their unceasing efforts. This alone added tremendous stress to their daily lives. Sometimes, during those moments when they felt they needed nothing more than a few minutes alone with their own thoughts, Josh and Claudia would lurk in opposite corners of the house, pretending not to notice the smell, until one of them finally relented and cleaned her up. Josh began to think of this, with grim humor, as a game of diaper chicken. Who would be the first to crack?

The reality of their lives made it impossible for them to function as a typical couple — or a typical family — and this want of normalcy eventually piled so much pressure onto their fragile partnership that it splintered.

* * *

In hindsight, Claudia believed, she could track how their marriage had deteriorated in stages. First, they gave up travelling. Then they lost friends. Then they stopped having sex. While other families did take vacations with their special needs kids, even flying with them, Josh and Claudia were terrified of the idea of Amy on a plane, in a confined, crowded space for hours with a bunch of irritable strangers with little tolerance for their situation. They weren't even comfortable contemplating long driving trips, not at all confident Amy could manage a night in a hotel room, away from her familiar surroundings. They had less control over their shrinking social circle. Some of those they had felt closest to appeared flummoxed by Amy and at times genuinely fearful. More than once, Claudia had caught one of the moms she thought she knew well physically restraining her child when Amy was nearby, as if autism were contagious, something you could catch from a sneeze or dirty hands. Predictably, Josh and Claudia's new group of friends were families that more closely mirrored their own. It took a lot to freak out special needs parents. If Amy decided to take off her clothes and dance on the dining room table while everyone else was enjoying a Sunday brunch, they would simply remove her, get her dressed, and go back to eating their bagels and cream cheese. But it was the hit their sex life took that was most painful. Intimacy became overwhelmingly difficult to initiate. Extreme fatigue and chronic worry, combined with a simmering but unabated enmity between them, made Josh and Claudia forget the qualities that had once, long ago, drawn them together and that they had actually once liked about each other.

* * *

Claudia confessed to Josh there were times she would become so overwhelmed that, while driving, she'd have to pull over to the side of the road, weepy and incapacitated. Josh didn't know how to respond to that, how to comfort her, so he said little, which then, in turn, further alienated Claudia. It wasn't that he lacked empathy. If anything, he experienced her pain too acutely. But he also felt paralyzed. It terrified him that the woman he had married, so solid, so unshakable, was having so much trouble coping. A foundation he had come to rely on had been rocked.

Then there were the episodes Josh kept locked away, hidden from everyone. One evening, when Claudia was working late, Josh came home to relieve their nanny Anna after a long and difficult day, in which he had taken abuse from one complaining client after another. He brought Amy upstairs, and she began bouncing on her bed, violently though happily. Spent and strung out, Josh only wanted to get through the bedtime routine quickly. He needed to eat something and watch mindless TV for an hour. He leaned in to grab his daughter and calm her. Just as he bent over, she flew up again, slamming hard into his left eye with the top of her head. Josh stumbled backward, blinded by searing pain, literally seeing stars, while Amy continued to laugh and bounce.

Frustration surged out of him. He snapped. It was primal. "Goddamn it, fuck, fuck, fuck you," he screamed. He couldn't have said for sure if he were screaming at his daughter or at the cosmos in general, but believing Amy was unaware and unable to comprehend, oblivious to the scene in front of her, seemed to give him license to rage.

After some minutes, he regained a measure of composure, willing himself to pull it together, well aware he had no alternative. He held Amy tightly, waiting until he felt her soothe, felt the tension in her body slacken. He kissed her goodnight, pulled the curtains shut, and closed her door with a muted click. Head throbbing, he went downstairs to find ice for the sizeable, tender bump that had emerged above his eyebrow. He dropped a second handful of ice into a tall glass, filled the glass with vodka, and sat on the couch in the living room twilight, excoriating himself for being such a shitty parent, for unburdening so unfairly, so inappropriately, so cruelly on his vulnerable child.

"That can't happen," he muttered miserably, repeating it like a mantra. But of course, it had.

It felt like a long time later when he moved quietly back up the stairs, to Amy's room for another check-in. To his surprise, she was still awake, on her back on the bed, atop her Dora the Explorer comforter, making muffled gurgling sounds, talking to herself in a private language only she could comprehend. In the dim light, Josh could see her shadowy figure lifting up as she heard him enter. He stepped gingerly across the carpeted floor, feeling her eyes on him.

"Daddy, daddy, daddy," he heard her mumble, garbled but clear enough for him to understand.

You never knew whether Amy was actually attempting to use language to communicate or if her words were merely echolalia, meaningless babble, a function of some sort of endless tape loop running in her head. Hearing her voice now, Josh wanted to believe, was compelled to believe, that she was making a connection, purposeful and appropriate, even if it was just this one isolated instance. Something stirred inside him, undefined, inchoate. He approached the narrow bed and squeezed in alongside her. Amy raised a hand and touched his face, pinching and pushing gently, feeling her way with her fingers, along his chin, his mouth, his nose, as a sightless person might.

He heard the soft, thick murmuring again, "Daddy, daddy, daddy."

Josh brushed a strand of dark hair away from her face, kissed the soft skin of her cheek, and rested a hand on her belly, absorbed in the sensation, the gentle rise and fall against his palm.

After a few minutes, he could hear her breathing growing rhythmic, steady, her little snores the only sounds in the room. He knew all too well that in the morning, when Amy woke, she would be spinning and shrieking and rocking; the struggle would be renewed. But for now, there was this lull, a respite. He stayed on the bed with her, motionless, as the deeper darkness settled over them. In time, the snores faded into quiet breaths, tiny gasps, barely audible. He felt his eyes begin to flutter, dimly aware of his own breathing turning shallow and measured. He let it happen, offered no resistance, allowing the need for sleep to gradually, but immutably, overtake him.

EIGHT

Josh drove along the familiar streets, through the last of the dusky twilight, headlights illuminating scattered leaves drifting across browning lawns. He pulled up in front of the house in Larchmont, the house that had been his for over a decade and from which he was now effectively exiled. Claudia was perched on the front porch with the asshole, Marcus, a large gray wool blanket hanging loosely across their shoulders. The big front windows on either side of them glowed yellow behind white curtains.

As he cut the engine, Josh watched Claudia rise and make her way down the brick steps in his direction. The piney scent of someone's fireplace drifted through the chilly autumn air.

"You're letting your hair grow," he said as she came near, stopping under the arc of the curbside streetlight. "And the color too?"

Claudia reflexively fingered the strands that reached nearly to her shoulders. "Yeah. The color isn't too radical, just a shade or two darker." She glanced toward Marcus. "I decided it was time to try something different."

Josh eyed her. He'd always preferred her hair short. It fit her better.

"What happened to you?" Claudia asked. "You're like an hour late."

"I told you. It was Bob's funeral today. I did the best I could."

"Yeah. I'm aware," she said. "I knew about the funeral. But you couldn't call? Or text?"

"I thought I could make it on time. I also had to drop off James at the airport. He's got some meetings with a bunch of Canadian millionaires who might want to finance his next movie."

Claudia smirked. "Of course you did. God forbid James should consider a car service. Did you carry his bags as well?"

"We were coming from Long Island, Claudia. It made sense for me to take him. LaGuardia was practically on the way."

"LaGuardia isn't practically on the way to anywhere, Josh," she replied with the same smirk.

"And then the traffic on the Hutch just killed me. I didn't think it would be advisable to be texting in that mess. If it wasn't for that, I almost would have made it."

Josh looked past her. Marcus was still on the steps, the blanket now bunched at his feet, trying to pretend he wasn't listening, eyes locked on something off in the distance.

"Well, Amy got tired really early tonight. Anna gave her dinner and put her to bed. You can take Ethan if you want. He's been pretty patient, all in all. He was determined to wait. I think he was worried you forgot."

"Why would I forget?" Josh responded. Claudia's aggressive tone was grating. It had been a long, difficult day, and the last thing he needed right now was attitude from her. "I did the best I could. If it makes you feel any better, I've got to drive back out there tomorrow for the shivah. Lucky me."

They moved slowly up the walk, Claudia a few paces ahead. Josh couldn't help but notice how good she looked in her jeans. Even after two kids and all these years, she had done an admirable job preserving that lithe dancer's body she'd so carefully maintained throughout her youth. Though it may now have seemed unimaginable, Josh remembered well how there had been a time not all that long ago when he couldn't get enough of that shapely little ass.

Josh extended his hand to Marcus, the man now fucking his wife. Marcus's return grip was firm and solid; he nodded with a thin smile and unblinking eye contact. Josh had met Marcus a few times over the years, going back to well before any of this had started. He was slim and dark, with small square glasses, his hair cropped short and receding at the temples. A silver-dollar-sized patch of scalp was visible where the top of his head began to slope down toward his neck. Josh took some satisfaction in his height advantage, two, maybe three inches.

"We should have rescheduled," Claudia said, turning back toward Josh, hands on hips.

"I didn't want to. We've had these plans, and I didn't want to disappoint Ethan." There was a silence and Josh looked at her. "I'm really sorry, Claudia. I hadn't accounted for my client of twenty some-odd years dropping dead in my conference room. It kind of threw off my schedule."

The front door swung open, and Ethan bolted down the steps toward them. "Dad-dy!" he sang out. The boy buried his face in Josh's belly. "I thought maybe you weren't coming."

"Hey. Would I do that to you?"

"We're still going, right?" Ethan asked. He shot his mother a quick look.

"Of course we are. Right now." Josh leaned down, his nose in Ethan's freshly shampooed curls. He was swept back to those many evenings of leaning over the tub, inhaling soapy steam, scrubbing the small perfect heads of his children.

"I'm starving. I want a grilled cheese and French fries."

"I will say with some confidence that we can make that happen."

"Starving means very, very hungry," Ethan explained to his father as they crossed the sidewalk. "Like super hungry."

"Try to get him home at a reasonable hour," Claudia called from the steps. "He has a full day tomorrow."

* * *

Arms folded, Claudia watched as Josh opened the back seat for Ethan and leaned in to help with the seatbelt. She waited for them to disappear around the corner then turned back toward the house. She became aware of Marcus's hand resting on her shoulder.

As Josh had emerged from his car, the gray, dented Camry she knew so well, Claudia had been briefly startled to see him in his black suit, white shirt, and dark tie. It was not his usual look. Josh was still an attractive man. He had always made a point to invest in good haircuts and nice clothes, even when money was tight. His chameleon eyes, sometimes blue, sometimes green, had always been his best feature. But tonight he appeared tired, drawn. His russet-colored hair seemed to have gone grayer, even since she'd last seen him. She wondered if he was getting any exercise. She was relieved that the minutiae of his daily life was no longer something she had to worry about or be invested in. Still, it was a funny thing about a marriage ending; you wanted to believe you no longer cared, that the love had dissipated into nothingness, that you were making a clean break. But the reality was, it wasn't clean — it was messy. Pieces of your ex clung to you. It was a lot more complicated than you wished it to be.

"He's so clueless sometimes," she sighed to Marcus in the hallway as she pressed the front door shut. "He should have rescheduled."

NINE

They met in an elevator. Claudia, then an assistant at the same video production company she still worked for, was heading out for a midafternoon coffee run. Rushing back to his office after a client meeting, Josh was thinking about the next thing on his to-do list. He was drawn to her compact body, olive skin, and bob haircut. She side-eyed him as she watched the numbers drop, taking note of his vintage sharkskin jacket with the thin lapels and how its drape fell so nicely across his shoulders.

They shared a capacity to be convincingly alluring when properly motivated; once they realized they were in similar creative fields, the conversation flowed easily. The trip to the lobby was all the time needed for them to become fully engaged in flirtatious small talk. Still, it might have ended on the sidewalk in front of the building had they not happened to be walking in the same direction. In an uncharacteristically bold move, before turning to get on the subway, Josh asked her out for a drink. She gave him her number.

Josh was destined to fall quickly. Claudia's straightforward, firmly grounded, unclouded approach to the world was seductive. There was little of the incessant guessing, indirectness, and ambiguous subtext that had so often left him at a loss with other women he'd dated. It was this, as much as anything else, that he found sexy.

Claudia was more reticent. She had recently broken up with a man who, after pursuing her with single-minded tenacity, had turned darkly passive-aggressive. He had a nasty habit of following up his indirect but unmistakably belligerent comments with open-mouthed surprise and a steadfast denial of hostile intent. Claudia was left off-balance by this, doubting her instincts and, at moments, questioning her sanity. She had emerged from the turmoil of that dispiriting experience with a new wariness and a tougher skin.

So when she met Josh, she was not at all convinced she was ready to start anything new. Yet she found Josh's quirky guilelessness refreshingly disarming. His evident desire to please, to put her happiness first, pulled her toward him. Over time, she began to believe she could trust him. She came to believe he had a good heart. Years later, as she attempted to trace where things between them had begun to turn, she realized how easy it could be to confuse Josh's peculiar brand of charming diffidence with something deeper, something more closely akin to genuine, authentic kindness.

TEN

With Ethan out to dinner with his father and Amy already in bed, the house felt very still. The only sounds were from down the hall, where Will and Daniel, Marcus's two boys, were scrolling through channels on the television. Settling next to Marcus on the cream-colored couch in her living room, Claudia picked up her phone, checking emails and her Instagram feed. Glancing at the time, she did a quick calculation in her head, trying to estimate when Josh would return.

"Did Josh ever hire an attorney?" Marcus asked, breaking the silence, nodding toward the official-looking manila envelope on the desk in the corner.

"Don't hold your breath. He's still convinced he doesn't need one." Claudia peered at him, returning his skeptical gaze. "What am I supposed to do? All the paperwork has been sent. The divorce is going to happen one way or another. My lawyer says we can file a default if Josh doesn't respond. Hopefully it won't come to that. All he has to do is sign the damn thing."

Distracted by Will and Daniel's muffled voices, Claudia considered the seismic events that were continuing to roil her life. For weeks, Marcus and his boys had been slowly moving in. They were now spending nearly as much time at Claudia's house as their own. Though she'd been anxious about Ethan's ability to handle another upheaval, to her surprise he had so far seemed generally okay with these new people living under the same roof, so long as everyone respected his stuff and asked before playing with his toys. It helped that Will and Daniel, two and four years older than Ethan, had made an effort to include him in their activities. And the two older boys didn't appear freaked out by Amy. They seemed to accept her as just another member of the family. Another relief. For Claudia, trying to predict — or even make sense of — the behaviors of preteen boys, the good and the bad, was hopeless. For the moment, she found herself mostly just trying to observe and be present.

"Maybe if you explain to him more directly about...about us," said Marcus. "Try to make him understand how we're committed to each other. That might impel him to move ahead."

"I'm not sure Josh is the impel-able type," she said. "And I'm not ready to get into that kind of detail with him at this point. One thing at a time. We're not up to that yet."

Marcus shot her a look of frustration. "He's going to need to know about us eventually. You can't get married while you're still married."

"Yes," said Claudia. "I am aware that the legal system tends to frown on polygamy. Unless you're prepared to move to certain parts of Utah."

Marcus laughed, but it rang hollow, his dark brows pulling together above liquid blue eyes. "What about the custody? Nothing new there either?"

"Nothing's changed, Marcus." Claudia stiffened, she didn't like him pressing her like this. "I'm on it. It's not like I'm keeping anything from you. And I'm more convinced now than ever that it would be terrible having my kids move back and forth. They do so much better when they're rooted. Amy, obviously, but Ethan too. So that's the deal. I get full custody and he pays child support. Which," she added, with an exaggerated eye roll and a shake of her head, "he says he understands."

"Hard to believe he actually said he doesn't want his kids," Marcus said, chin resting against a folded fist. "That's kind of messed up. Sorry, it just is."

"He would never put it like that. And it's not that he doesn't want them. He just doesn't want the responsibility for them. Classic Josh. If you knew him better, you would understand it. None of this surprises me, to be honest."

Marcus rose and headed toward the kitchen. Claudia could hear the refrigerator open, glasses clinking, wine being poured. When he returned, he passed a glass to her. She stared at it in her hand, then picked up a coaster from the coffee table, set it down, and slid it a few inches away.

"You know, I know my marriage is over. I want it to be over. But it's just so difficult to get to the..." she hesitated, "...the next stage. The finality of it is...." She couldn't find the words she wanted and trailed off. "The reality is, I've turned the page. But it's also true that I'd just like to know he's moving on with his life too. Why that should matter to me at this point...I don't know. I couldn't really give you a logical explanation."

"He's not your responsibility." Marcus said. "Don't let him manipulate you." Seeing Claudia grimace at this, he took her hand, and his tone softened. "I mean, I get it. It's not an easy thing. For anyone."

"No. It's not." Then, with a sudden burst, "But he's the one who fucking walked out on me. Right? Right? He's the one who made the big speech about his mental health." Claudia cringed at the shrill notes coming out of her. She didn't want Marcus witnessing her angst and uncertainty. It was too raw, too naked. Too soon. And yet her need to vent was overwhelming. She forced a smile.

"I understand," Marcus said in a calming voice, the way one might speak to a child.

"As you may be aware," she said, lowering her voice, "I didn't ask for this. So it shouldn't matter to me what he thinks or wants or does at this point. It shouldn't, right? But it does. It does. Weirdly." She touched the back of her neck and thought, randomly, she needed to get her newer, longer hair trimmed. It was losing its shape. "Maybe I'm just more of a mush than I realized." She paused, then added with a twisted smile, "God, that's a disturbing thought."

"That's one of the things I love about you," Marcus said smiling at her. "You're not as tough as you think you are."

Claudia knew Marcus meant well. She knew he thought he was helping. But saying this to her was not a compliment. Amazing how men, even sensitive, caring men, could at times say the most fucked up, inappropriate shit and be completely oblivious to its impact. Still, she let it go. There were certain things, at certain moments, that were not worth getting worked up over. If she'd learned nothing else from her marriage, that was one lesson that had stuck.

She touched his stubbly face and looked into those blue eyes. Claudia knew she would never be able to fully comprehend the unimaginable hell Marcus and his boys had had to endure. Some years earlier, Marcus's wife, Debbie, whom Claudia had known casually from the train as a fellow commuter, had been diagnosed with breast cancer. After enduring surgery, chemo, and radiation, one day Claudia saw her reappear at her usual spot on the station platform, as if her extended absence had been nothing more than a minor hiatus. Seemingly recovered, high-energy, and perky as ever, she appeared to effortlessly resume her active life as wife, mother, small business owner, and weekend long-distance runner. When the cancer returned, two years ago, Marcus told Claudia, his voice shaking, during one of their first nights together, it progressed so shockingly swiftly and horribly that Debbie was gone before he'd had the chance even to fully come to terms with the gravity of the situation. Trying to care for his children while finding time to mourn was overwhelming. Day by day — sometimes minute by minute — became his survival strategy.

Will and Daniel naturally ached terribly for their mother. Marcus had put them in therapy for a while, but they hadn't liked it, so he agreed to let them stop going. Yet you wouldn't necessarily know at first glance that they'd suffered such a horrifically painful loss. For the most part, they went along with their daily lives like any other boys. But then there were those moments when one of them would spontaneously become weepy, often with no obvious trigger. The brothers seemed to have evolved a kind of symbiosis that held each other up — when one was upset, the other was there to comfort him. Claudia was moved to see how they leaned on each other, and she felt deeply for them. She yearned to hug and kiss them, to take their pain away. But though they accepted her casual warmth and care, she sensed they weren't ready for her to assume a more central role in their lives. So she held herself back, keeping some distance, waiting for what was at best destined to be a complicated relationship to develop organically.

Meanwhile, there were the pragmatics of blending two families and two households. Getting four kids ready for school in the morning added another level of chaos to a hectic routine. Marcus, who taught literature at Iona, had a little extra time, so on the days when they were all together, he had volunteered to be the one to get everyone up and going, prior to Anna's arrival. Claudia had managed to get past her initial reservations and make the leap of faith; she was adjusting to the sensation of walking out the door with the start-of-day craziness still swirling around her. It was, admittedly, a refreshing change to be able to get to work on time. No more running into the office breathless, already behind schedule. At first, Ethan had clung to her as she prepared to leave, but lately he seemed to be adjusting to this shift in routine as well.

And so it was, so far at least, that everyone, by all outward appearances, was adapting surprisingly smoothly. Still, Claudia continued to chafe at Marcus's unshakable, relentless conviction that hurtling ahead at maximum speed was the best way for him to heal. It was not in her nature to be a passive passenger like this, to be pulled along while he dictated the pace of the relationship.

From the beginning, Marcus had been the initiator. It was he who had spontaneously asked Claudia to coffee when they had bumped into each other in the village on a Saturday morning when they both happened to have childcare, who had listened mindfully as she told him of Josh's decision to leave her, who had surprised her with tender kisses on the sidewalk afterward, and who had led her to his bed as they began to see more of each other in the weeks that followed. Not that, to be fair, Claudia had offered up much resistance to any of it. She had been craving adult companionship, and none of this would have happened if she hadn't been a willing partner.

Claudia looked over at the man sitting next to her, the man she was sleeping with, the man who was now more or less living under her roof and who it was looking likely she was going to marry, perhaps sooner than she could have imagined even a few months ago. A not unpleasant rush of nervous energy surged through her.

Marcus had flaws, of course. Who didn't? But he was a good man, a man of strength, of character, with good values. The way he was around Amy, for instance, touched Claudia deeply. Whereas many people, including Claudia's own mother, would speak to Amy in that artificial, high pitched, sing-songy, too loud voice, as if she were deaf, Marcus addressed her with the same easy, unaffected tone he would use on anyone else.

Marcus had seemed genuinely puzzled when Claudia commented on this. "She's a sentient being," he contended. "Just because she perceives the world differently than you or me doesn't make her any less present."

Claudia leaned into Marcus and heard herself sigh as he wrapped an arm around her. She thought about the first time he'd told her he loved her. He'd blurted it out one night while climaxing inside her, something else, in Claudia's experience, men had a weird habit of doing. Later, while admittedly sheepish about the circumstances in which he'd vocalized it, he didn't back down; on the contrary, he reaffirmed his feelings were real. "I want to be with you," he had said with conviction. "That's not going to change. I'm certain of it."

Claudia didn't doubt she wanted to be married again. She didn't intend to go through the rest of her life alone. If he were truly the one, if the chemistry were right, if this second act were meant to be, then in the long run, none of her concerns should matter. The pacing of things would even out over time. She would eventually catch up. And as far as the rest of it, they'd figure it out. That was what you did in relationships.

If both parties were truly willing to do the work, they could always find a path forward. She'd managed to stay married to Josh for ten years, for God's sake. She could figure *this* out. A divorced woman with two children, one with special needs, does not simply let this go. A good man. A *good* man. A good man is hard to find. Stop looking for flaws. Appreciate it for what it is, not what you wish it to be.

ELEVEN

On the Monday after the funeral, Josh made sure to arrive to work early. He wanted a few quiet minutes before the day started heating up. Keys in hand, he turned the locks, then realized they'd already been undone. He was startled to see James at his desk, oversized paper coffee cup close at hand, punching away at his keyboard.

"What are you doing here?" Josh asked, raising his voice to announce his presence as he drew closer. "This must be some sort of record. You're supposed to still be sleeping."

James stopped typing and peered around his screen. "Hey, I work for a living," he boomed. "Where the hell have you been?"

Josh entered James's office, took off his coat, and sank into the black leather couch against the far wall. "How was Toronto?"

"Yeah, it went pretty well, I'd say. A bunch of oil dudes who've spent too many years in some frozen shithole somewhere out on the prairie, looking for something fun to do with a little of the massive amounts of cash they've made fucking up the planet. They could do a whole lot worse than throw some of their dirty money my way."

"I hope you said it just like that. I'm sure they appreciated the candor."

"I think they got the idea once I explained how the whole executive producer thing works. People love seeing their names on the big screen." James continued to type for a minute, then slid his chair out from behind his desk so he could look directly at Josh. "So, uh, Courtney called me while I was up there," he said in what, for James, passed as his inside voice. "Turns out, we have...we have a bit of a situation."

"Well, yeah okay," came Josh's languid, careful reply. "That much we knew. I can only imagine what those two are cooking up. We're going to really miss Bob."

"Too true. But you don't even know the half of it." James stared at his fingers drumming on the side of his desk, hair falling across his forehead. "Courtney...well, she was pretty...enlightening. Apparently, Bob has been borrowing money to keep the business going. Like, substantial amounts. They owe a lot to a lot of people. And I'm not even talking about vendors like us. In the scheme of things, we are among the smaller of the small potatoes."

"You mean bank loans? Lines of credit?"

"I wish it was that straightforward." James sighed and leaned forward. "I've never told you this, Josh, but when Bob first decided to expand, before you and I even started working together, he was practically broke — he had no credit, and he couldn't get a bank to give him a loan. So it was his Long Island homeboys, the guys he grew up with, who became his backers. Even back then, they were doing well with their own businesses — construction, parking lots, trash hauling, that sort of thing. They had the capital. They got equity. The money they've invested into the Shoe King — it's brought them a very nice return over the years."

Josh stared at James for a long moment. More secrets he wasn't privy to. "How is it I've never heard this story before?"

With a hand to his mouth, James belched softly, grimacing. "Frankly, Josh, it wasn't something you needed to know about, and I didn't see the point of getting you involved. Trust me, you're better off knowing as little as possible about the shady side of Bob's operations. You look under rocks, you find things you may not like."

"Well," Josh said, a little defensive, "it's not like I wasn't aware he had investors. I just always assumed they were the more, uh, conventional kind. More like Wall Street guys in suits."

"Yeah, well, I don't think these guys own many suits. The point is, that cash is now flowing in the wrong direction. A few months ago, Bob's buddies agreed to float him what he needed to keep things going. He convinced them that once the digital strategy kicked in, it would start filling in the revenue gaps. And now Bob is gone." James paused to pull something off the front of his tongue, rolling whatever it was between a thumb and forefinger, inspecting it. "Bob's posse has always made me nervous. You don't want to piss those guys off." His focus returned to his screen. Leaning over, he took a minute to read something before resuming the conversation.

"Everyone is owed, and everyone is looking to collect," James went on. "And we're just one more of the assholes with our hands out." He fell silent, then looked at Josh again. "Thus, our dilemma. On the one hand, we can't keep doing work on the Shoe King account if they don't start paying up. But of course, at the same time, without them, we'd be hurting. Big-time."

Josh nodded, still thinking about Courtney. "It's weird that she was so open with you."

"She wasn't supposed to be," James replied. "She made it clear Ryan doesn't want her talking to me about it."

"But she did anyway."

"Strictly unofficially." James rubbed his chin and stared at a spot near the ceiling. "I guess Ryan figures if we don't know the dirty secrets behind the dirty secrets, he can keep us working a while longer while conveniently ignoring our invoices. The little shit."

Josh thought it a positive sign that Courtney saw James as someone she could confide in, someone she trusted. But James had a different take.

"It's not about trust, Josh," he said. "It's fear. They're both terrified. In spite of all of the attitude and bravado. They're kids, children really, they don't have a fucking clue, and Daddy's no longer around. Even if, let's say, the business was humming along perfectly, which it's not, and they were making money hand over fist, which they're not, I'd still lay odds that there'd be a better than even chance they'd fuck it up somewhere down the line. I don't know...it's hard to see how they're going to pull out of this."

"So how bad *are* the finances?" Josh asked in a slow monotone.

"I'm not sure. I'm not sure anyone knows yet. The accountants are going through everything, but it might take a while. That's another thing Courtney let slip out. Bob had books...and then he had...other books. If you get my drift."

"I spoke with Bob about our money. I told you about that at the time." Josh paused, his eyes landing on a framed photo on the wall above James's head. It was James and Bob at the Shoe King Hartford opening. They were in the parking lot, a giant banner with the company logo behind them, arms around each other, laughing into the camera. James held a *Shoe King Grand Opening* balloon in his free hand, but the balloon was out of the frame, so all you could see was the string pulling upward into a cloudless sky. "Bob swore we'd be taken care of by the end of the year — that they'd get us caught up."

"Yeah, well, I don't think Bob is in much of a position to be following through on his promises right now," James said. "Financially or otherwise."

They heard the click of the front door and footsteps echoing across the wood floor. James's assistant Ashley poked her head in and issued a cheerful greeting. Craning his neck to look back over his shoulder, Josh caught a glimpse of purple tips and silver bangles.

Lingering in the doorway, Ashley asked about the funeral, then James told her about his Canada meetings — a slightly more sanitized version of what he'd related to Josh a few minutes earlier. Satisfied with this quick download, Ashley pulled James's door shut; they could hear her chunky heels as she retreated to her desk on other side of the open floor.

James leaned closer, and his voice dropped a shade more. "Look, Josh. I don't honestly know what's going to happen here. Even if they do decide to keep us on after our bullshit" — shaking his head, James stopped to make air quotes — "sixty-day probation, where is the money going to come from?"

"So what are you saying? That we should fire them before they can fire us?"

"Not exactly. Since we're not supposed to know any of this whole backstory anyway, I say for the moment we just keep moving ahead as if everything is status quo. We have leverage, obviously, because they need us to finish the app. So we bring in Erin as planned, LAKreativ kicks ass on the new gaming demo, and then we see where we're at." James shrugged, swigging his coffee. "I want to let it play out. Once they realize our app is amazing and they can't live without us, we put the screws to them. They'll have to come up with the money, pay what they already owe, and then pay us up-front before we do the rest of work. The point is, once we get our money and deliver the final app, I really don't give much of a shit what they do."

James stopped, fell back in his chair, and sighed. Peering over at Josh, his eyes widened and he let his head drop to one side. "Sorry if this sounds harsh, my friend, but we're in survival mode here. Fuck 'em. It's not like Ryan and Courtney are going to worry about what happens to us. There's no loyalty. My only concern is to get what's coming to us before their fucking ship goes down. Which, I predict with some confidence, it will."

"You can be a cold bastard," Josh said. "What about your history with Bob?" he asked, stealing another glance at the photo on the wall. "Does that not count for anything?"

"What did I just say? Bob's not here. So, uh, that would be no." James stopped, then repeated, "The answer to that is no."

James's tone was clear. He was not to be pushed on this. "Okay," said Josh. "I'll play it however you want. Of course."

"Dog eat dog, baby. It's a cruel world out there. How many times have I told you? You're too fucking nice."

"I'm not that nice."

James eyed him with a flat, level stare, lips slightly upturned, half bemusement, half scowl, that Josh instantly recognized and unequivocally despised. That look was James at his most patronizing, reserved for those moments when he seemed inclined to view Josh as the slightly daft little brother who missed signals and couldn't quite keep up.

"So we keep this whole money thing between us, then?" Josh asked, forcing himself to shake off the look and stay focused. "You don't even want Erin to know?"

"Not for now, no. There's no reason to freak out the L.A. guys. Whatever happens, I'll make sure they get what's coming to them. But I have to be honest with you, Josh." James sat up straighter. "You and I have been together a long time. I don't want to see you get fucked either. But if this gets to the point where I can't pay you...."

"Yeah. Yeah." Josh exhaled with a prolonged sigh. "I get it."

"Listen to what I'm telling you. I'll take care of you as long as I can. But if, or I should probably say when, the Shoe King crashes and burns — whether it's a month or a year from now — I can't make any guarantees."

James stopped talking and returned to his screen. Taking what he thought to be his cue, Josh pushed up from the couch and prepared to exit. But James wasn't finished yet. Josh stood awkwardly, waiting.

"This actually may be the universe trying to tell us both something," James went on, almost as if he were speaking to himself. "The truth is, I've been questioning how much longer I want to keep doing this. The film thing...it's going okay right now. Maybe more than okay. We've had a nice run here but, I don't know...maybe it's time to consider a complete life overhaul. I need to think about what I want to do with the rest of my life."

Josh was stunned. His boss seemed to be connecting an awful lot of dots that, to Josh's thinking, were not necessarily readily connectable. Losing the Shoe King would be very bad, undoubtedly, but by no means did it have to be fatal. "You're serious? You're actually thinking about the movie thing full-time?"

"Maybe. Yeah. Maybe. I have other ideas too. Anyway, we can talk about me some other time. Right now, as your boss and as your friend, I'm telling you straight-out, you need to listen to your own universe.

You need to start thinking about your own next act. I'm giving you this as an assignment, and it's not optional. You need a Josh Sherman Plan B. Take this as seriously as you would a client project. Pay close attention to what your universe is telling you. It's the best advice I can give you. And it's the best thing you can do for yourself right now."

* * *

As a general rule, Josh had never had much faith in his personal universe. He had always believed that fate or providence or whatever it was that was out there pulling the strings, unseen and unknowable, was profoundly indifferent to him.

He remembered a day not long before when, rushing to a meeting, he had approached the subway entrance and found himself behind a thin woman with a flowing lavender scarf struggling with several good-sized shopping bags and a stroller. She made it through and pushed ahead to get on a train that was just pulling in. As Josh followed, he saw her wallet tumble onto the platform. He called out, but she was already boarding as the doors closed. Coming through the turnstile and scooping up the wallet, he could see her, a flash of lavender through the smeared, scratched window; she was bent over, attending to her child. Then the train was gone, its lights disappearing into the dark tunnel. No more than a minute later, an express rolled in on the opposite track. The situation demanded a quick decision. On impulse, Josh decided to board, on the off possibility that if this downtown express arrived at its next station before her local, and she was still on it, he just might catch her. It was worth the try.

The wallet was faux leather, pink and oblong. On the ride down, Josh clutched it tightly to his chest until, realizing how ridiculous he must look, he awkwardly stuffed it into a jacket pocket. He arrived at the next stop, exited and waited, wired and anticipatory. The local train pulled in a few minutes later, and sure enough, there she was — woman, scarf, stroller, child. As the doors opened, Josh bounded into her car, triumphant, unable to suppress a broad grin. He gently tapped her on the shoulder, and, wordlessly, like a scene from an old silent movie, handed her the wallet. Confused and guarded at first, the woman assessed the situation, recovered her composure, and quickly thanked him. But from Josh's perspective, she was inappropriately low-key; the exchange between them was clipped and terse. The woman tucked the wallet into her handbag, leaned down to pass her child a cookie, and proceeded to ignore Josh from that point on. Pressed close to her in the crowded car, waiting to disembark at the next stop, he felt awkward, resentment growing. It wasn't as if he'd merely held the door for her. He had gone to extraordinary, even heroic lengths. His act of selflessness merited a deeper level of appreciation. The experience, rather than exhilarating and affirming, had turned darkly dispiriting.

Clearly, one did not do the right thing with the expectation that one would be rewarded. You did the right thing because it was the right thing to do. And after his initial disappointment, he was eventually able to come to terms with the woman's underwhelming, blasé demeanor. This was New York, after all, and you should know better than to expect much from people. He'd felt good about what he'd done regardless, and he reminded himself that he would do it again, even if he had known ahead of time that it would lead to the this less than satisfactory response.

No, the woman, though unquestionably annoying, was not what most got under his skin. It was the universe itself that had really pissed him off. It felt perfectly plausible to Josh to expect the fates to acknowledge his kindness and reward him by making his anxious, quotidian life marginally easier, at least for a second or two. Like a ten-year-old, he wanted the universe to muss his hair and tell him what a good job he'd done. Maybe an unexpected check would arrive to help him pay some of the mound of bills collecting dust on his coffee table. But in the days and weeks following the dramatic wallet rescue, his life didn't change at all. There was no reward, only silence. It was as if the entire episode had never occurred. And it had always been that way for Josh.

Further proof that fate, while not necessarily mean-spirited perhaps, was chronically disengaged.

Yet thinking about it now, it did seem possible that James's admonition regarding Josh's universe was fortuitously timed. Something had happened over this past summer, thousands of miles away, in a crowded bar in the desert, something James knew nothing about. Events on that day had at the time appeared random, unlinked. But what if they weren't? What if this normally dispassionate universe had at long last decided to take an interest in providing Josh a hand?

This was the basis for Josh's nascent Plan B. It hadn't really come together yet; he wasn't even sure where it was leading. To be honest, Josh wasn't even sure he wanted fate sticking its nose into his business. He didn't trust that it was operating on the level. But on the other hand, if the universe did finally decide at the eleventh hour not to fuck him over and actually was sincere about trying to help, Josh's Plan B might just be the chance for reinvention he had been looking for.

TWELVE

Cocktail in hand, seated in a high-backed chair in the corner of a dimly lit lounge on the edge of a casino floor that, in its ubiquity, was indistinguishable from the countless others spread across every corner of this town, Josh could feel the stress and adrenaline finally melting away at the end of the long and exhausting week. As the alcohol began to numb the anxiety receptors that normally vied for dominance in his brain, the sensory overload — flashing lights, jangling machines, occasional shouts of players hitting their numbers — was oddly soothing.

Until a few minutes earlier, Josh would have expected by now to be on his way to that Italian restaurant in Summerlin he'd had his eye on since finding it online weeks ago. Instead, he was having a drink in a casino bar, teeming with a mashup of convention goers, vacationers, partying millennials, and committed gamblers. The place buzzed with a thousand different agendas. Across from him was fellow conventioneer and quasi-friend Don Bieler, also checking out the scene.

Every year at the height of summer, Josh went out to Las Vegas to attend this gathering of digital content developers. Occasionally he would have a client to keep an eye on, but mostly he went because it was a good place to troll for business. He always came back with one or two new projects, and James, who couldn't stand Vegas, was happy to foot the bill as long as he didn't have to deal with it.

Josh looked forward to going, even though he no longer had the disposable income for gambling he'd once enjoyed, and even though the intense July heat meant each time you dared set foot outdoors, it was as if you'd stepped through the gates of hell. The trip was a break from his normal routine, and for that alone, Josh was grateful. Admittedly, Vegas was a weird place to go for work. In spite of its rebranding as a premiere convention town, at its heart, at least to Josh, the place wasn't really designed for that. In the morning he would get up early, work out in the hotel gym, slam down a coffee and a quick breakfast, put on his badge, and head out in black blazer, blue dress shirt, and gray slacks, laptop bag in hand. As he cut through the casino, passing the vacationers in Bermuda shorts, already set up with cocktails, throwing out chips and whooping over their wins, large and small, Josh had to have tunnel vision and not allow himself to be distracted lest the feeling of missing out on someone else's good time become too overwhelming.

And while an expenses-paid trip to Vegas was appealing, it was an appeal with a short shelf life. After several noisy, crowded days breathing the artificial air in that hermetically sealed environment, he was done. Over the years, he had developed a tradition of rewarding himself by going out alone on this last night. He would research a well-reviewed neighborhood restaurant that was far enough away from the Strip that he could be assured he wouldn't run into anyone he knew. After dinner and a couple of drinks, he might do a little cut-rate gambling at some off-the-beaten-path spot frequented by locals, then head back to the hotel, call it a night, and get ready to catch his early flight home the next morning. That solitary final evening's escape was his way to decompress, and he looked forward to it.

Josh also tried to avoid being one of those last stragglers, the handful of dead-enders still hanging around as the convention closed. For three days, the place would be a hub of energy and activity, a self-contained, hyperactive little mini city. Then, in the blink of an eye, the show would end, and in a heartbeat, the place would come tumbling down. It saddened him to be a witness to that; the finality of it depressed him somehow. So he would be sure to escape before the conference approached its last hour.

This past year, as he left the building toward late afternoon and went out into the blinding sunlight, he reached for his phone to check the address of the restaurant. He patted his jacket pocket, then his other pockets, then stopped walking. He opened his bag and rummaged through it. The phone was nowhere to be found. How was this possible? He was so obsessive about making sure he had everything. Wallet, keys, money, he had a specific place for each item and the order of things never varied. But somehow, today, he'd managed to lose the phone. It must have been at his final appointment, the one with Gary DeVito, a new contact he had just met with for the first time. Gary, an app developer from Seattle, evidently had also been anxious to wrap up, as he had rather abruptly hustled Josh through the meeting, even though, from Josh's perspective, there was still more to cover. Josh had had to quickly gather his papers and awkwardly scamper away. It wasn't until he was down the hall and found a quiet corner that he'd been able to stop and properly put everything back into order. That must have been how the phone had been left behind. At least he hoped that was what had happened.

Josh turned and commenced the brisk walk back toward the convention floor. He'd been outdoors for less than five minutes but was already perspiring. Moderately frantic, the sweat began to run more freely down his face. He could feel his shirt sticking under his jacket.

The convention hall had just closed when he reached the entrance. Lights were dimming; whole sections were already in the process of deconstruction. He could see booths being dismantled, materials being packed away. The security guard stopped Josh with a raised hand. You needed, explained the uniformed man, to be an exhibitor if you wanted to enter during off hours. Stress level rising, Josh pleaded his case. But the guard was steadfast, and Josh remained stuck on the outside looking in. Just as he was about to give up, the guard, perhaps feeling pity on this sweaty, anxiety-ridden guy pacing in front of him, abruptly relented and motioned with a slight tilt of his head and a single beckoning finger for him to go through. Josh didn't question the change of heart; he muttered a quick thanks and barreled forward.

Gary, naturally, was in the farthest corner from Josh's entry point. By now nearly sprinting, Josh finally spotted the desired destination ahead of him at the end of a long aisle. The colorful flashing neon sign with Gary's company name — *Northern Lights Media* — had served as a beacon all week, hanging from the rafters high above. But now the sign, removed from its lofty perch, was just a bunch of drab colored tubes laying on the floor, propped up against a prefab wall that was itself soon to be disassembled. Gary was there in the midst of all this, standing surrounded by wooden packing crates, large bellied men in T-shirts and tool belts buzzing back and forth.

Shaved round head atop broad, squared shoulders, Gary was deep in conversation with another man Josh didn't know. As Josh drew closer, he could see Gary vigorously stabbing a finger toward the man with some frequency.

Josh spotted his phone on one of the white round meeting tables, right where he'd left it. Hoping to be inconspicuous, he made a beeline in that direction.

Gary stopped in mid-finger point and turned, registering Josh's presence. His heavy brows lifted.

"Forgot this," Josh said, trying to sound nonchalant, like it was no big deal, like leaving his phone had all been part of the master plan somehow.

"Yeah, we were wondering who that belonged to," said Gary, watching him. "Another ten minutes, we were going to have someone drop it at the lost and found."

"Or sell it on eBay and use the money for betting the tables," the other man chimed in, unhelpfully, with a chuckle.

"Have a good trip back, Josh. Send me an email." Gary turned back to the man. The finger resumed its steady, rhythmic stabbing motion.

Josh prepared to exit the convention floor for a second time. He was preoccupied, exhausted, trying to regain his equilibrium, only half aware of the union guys darting about with well-practiced purposefulness. As he strode past the security guard from earlier, he heard his name shouted over the drone of a nearby forklift, once, then again. Rushing toward him, one arm extended straight out in handshake mode and the other raised high, preparing to clap him on the shoulder, a familiar figure greeted him heartily.

"Hey, buddy," said Don Bieler with a big grin. "I was wonderin' if I might run into you after all. You're like me. One of the diehards workin' till the bitter end. Sorry we couldn't meet up earlier. When you emailed me I just couldn't find an open half-hour in my schedule. Fuckin' crazed. So glad this fuckin' circus is over. But hey, we're here now. It must be meant to be, right? What's shakin'?"

Don was stocky, with a fire hydrant body, a brush cut, and a fondness for polo shirts and khakis. Not the kind of guy you'd think would be a natural fit in his adopted hometown of Los Angeles, but somehow he made it work. Maybe it was his Oklahoma roots that Angelenos found disarmingly authentic in a town not exactly known for its authenticity.

"It's been a long week," Josh said. Mentally, he had already been in the process of shutting down. Now he had to force himself to rev up back to convention level schmoozy-ness. "You know? Ready to get out of Dodge."

"I hear that. I'm pretty toasty myself."

Josh was a dogged networker — he had an extensive pool of contacts, and he was good about keeping in touch. Don was one of those people. They usually saw each other at conferences such as this or would occasionally meet for dinner on one of Don's trips to New York. More than colleagues, less than friends, it was the Dons of the world who made up the vast majority of Josh's social circle.

Don's company had been among the first to recognize the potential in working with YouTube personalities, "influencers" as they were known in the business. He represented a number of them, making sponsorship and licensing deals and getting these YouTubers, many of whom were just kids, paid outrageous amounts of money for their endorsements. Don and Josh had periodically explored ways in which they might team up and join forces, but they'd never found the right project.

Part of what held Josh back was James, who, while never one to discourage Josh from pursuing any business opportunity that might bring in revenue, was wary of Don. He thought him to be generally full of shit and didn't completely trust him. Years ago, there had been some sort of deal between them that had gone sour. Josh was only vaguely aware of the details, but he knew that it involved someone not paying someone something they were thought they were supposed to have been paid. The bad blood had never totally been forgotten. Still, at this point it seemed to be James's issue more than Don's, since the latter continued to work through Josh to try and find a way their two companies could collaborate. Josh made sure James knew about his continued interactions with Don, and James had grudgingly agreed they should keep the lines of communication open. Just so long as he didn't have to deal with Don directly.

Josh actually found Don likeable, in spite of his boss's reservations. Or perhaps, more precisely, Don seemed to like Josh for whatever reason, and that, in turn, made him more likeable in Josh's eyes. So, when Don told Josh he was headed to the lounge inside the casino and asked him along, Josh was inclined to put his solo Summerlin dinner plans on hold.

"I've never had any serious objections, moral or otherwise, to drinking alone," Don said as they ambled together in the direction of the green velvet tables a short distance away. "But it's always more pleasurable to have a compadre. Besides," he added, eyeing the beads of sweat only now beginning to dry on Josh's flushed face. "You look like you could use a pop or two."

"Been doing a lot of running around," Josh explained without much conviction. "Where's your usual posse?" he asked. "You always seem to have a crowd around you."

"Yeah, the scumbag pricks deserted me. They wanted to get away from the old man for a while, I suppose. I'll track them down for dinner, most likely. Someone has to pick up the check, after all."

Josh was skeptical they'd find seating in the packed lounge. But Don seemed to have a nose for this sort of thing and quickly zeroed in on a back corner, where two blonde twenty-somethings in tight short skirts were just getting up.

"Hey, lovely ladies," Don said, letting his Oklahoma drawl thicken to the point of parody. "Don't y'all leave on our account. We were just comin' over to join y'all."

The women exchanged looks and giggled as they backed away. "It's all yours," one of them said.

"Can't convince y'all to stick around and let us buy you a cocktail?"

"Not this time. But thanks for the offer."

"Do you know them?" Josh asked, watching their shapely backsides recede into the crowd.

"Fuck no," Don said, shaking his head. "But you never know when you might get lucky. It's Vegas, after all. Don't you think you and I would be having a lot more fun right now if those two had taken us up on my very kind offer?"

Josh laughed. "Maybe. Or more likely they'd just be looking for free drinks."

"Which I would happily oblige. Nothin' wrong with buying a pretty girl a drink in exchange for the pleasure of her company."

The waitress, platinum hair, heavy mascara, low-cut top, somewhat past her prime, scooped up the two lipstick-smudged glasses left behind while dropping fresh cocktail napkins onto their table. "Hey darlin'," said Don, eyes at chest level. He broke away and shot a side-eyed glance over at Josh. "What're you havin'? This is on me."

They ordered and the waitress departed. As Don surveyed the room, he asked Josh about his week. "You need to go back to New York and impress that slave driver boss of yours," Don said. "Tell 'im you killed it in Vegas. How is ol' Mr. James Gang, anyway?"

Josh laughed a second time. "James is okay. You know about his movie career, right?"

"You may have mentioned it once or twice. So that's progressin' according to plan?"

Josh said it seemed to be.

"You make sure and convey my warmest personal regards to my good friend James."

There was something uncomfortable about Don talking about James, knowing how the two of them felt about each other. Josh wondered about a subtext he wasn't quite picking up on. Was this Don's brand of sarcasm, so thoroughly cloaked in good ol' boy bonhomie that the standard L.A. passive aggressive nuance was effectively rendered untraceable? Or was there actually a genuine desire to use Josh as a liaison for bridge-building, a step toward repairing a long-frayed relationship?

"How's your business?" Josh asked, refocusing the conversation. The waitress returned, and they fell silent while she put the drinks in front of them. Don winked at her and handed over his credit card.

"Goin' great, actually. We've been expanding, hiring. The best thing I ever did was change our business model to focus on the YouTubers. It's a fucking goldmine, to be totally honest with you. You know how you only have to be smart once in your life? This may have been my once." Don took a long pull from his drink and let his gaze wander again. His eyes settled on a group of women, spangled and sleeveless, leaning against the bar.

"We should talk sometime about you using my clients in your projects," Don said. "It could help you reach an entirely different audience. I can show you the analytics. It'll blow your mind."

Josh considered the idea, the Shoe King being promoted by some YouTube kid with millions of followers. Bob wouldn't get it and likely wouldn't think it a fit for the brand. But Josh could see where Ryan and Courtney might love the idea. He thought he'd run it by Erin first.

"Family all good?" Don was saying now. "What's going on with your kid, the one with the, uh, the disability?"

"Autism. Yeah. My daughter."

"Right. How's she doing?"

"You know, it's challenging. But we deal with it. Like anything else. We try not to make it about us, you know? Like *why me*? That doesn't get you anywhere."

"I can appreciate that. Still, it's gotta be a rough kinda deal."

"Everybody has their things they're dealing with. There's some godawful shit out there. Nobody gets out of this life without some damage, as they say."

"Do they say that? Yeah, I suppose they do." Don sighed, answering his own question. "Still, some have more than others. Shit, man, I'm sorry you're going through it. That's also got to put a hell of a strain on a marriage."

"Yeah. It does. It does." Josh eyed the distance from his hand to the table, then set his drink down gingerly on the napkin in front of him. He considered for a long beat before speaking again. "Actually, my wife and I are in the middle of separating." He thought momentarily about mentioning the seventy-percent thing. But he held back. It was too much detail, would require too much explanation, for this conversation.

"Oh, shit," said Don. Josh was surprised at how upset he seemed by this news. "That sucks. I've been through it. Know all about divorce. It takes a huge whack out of you, that's for sure. Emotionally. Financially. You name it."

"Well, we're still just separated. Nothing's final yet." Josh wondered why he felt it necessary to add that. "But I didn't know you got divorced. When did that happen?"

"Oh, no, not now. I'm talking about my first marriage. Years ago. I don't usually bring it up too often. I have grown kids with my first wife. Grandkids too now, from what I've been told. I don't see 'em, though."

"I thought your kids were teenagers."

"Those are from my second marriage. Yeah. Just about teenage now. Good luck to me with that." Don smirked. "My older one, my little girl, is thirteen. She's a hot little number. First motherfucking pimply-faced twerp that puts a hand down her shirt is going to be missing some teeth, I can assure you."

Don had ordered more drinks, and the conversation halted again as the waitress arrived. Josh was definitely feeling buzzed. It seemed less and less likely he was going to make it to Summerlin. Room service and a ballgame on TV seemed more likely at this point.

"I've been married this time around goin' on twenty years. I was too young the first time. Wasn't ready," Don said, pouring the ice from his current drink into the new one, then handing the finished glass to the waitress. "Thank you, beautiful," he said as she smiled at him and stepped away. "It was my own fault. I fucked it up. I messed around on her way too much. When I got remarried, I knew I'd have to stick to the straight and narrow. Which I have. For the most part." Don winked at Josh. "Maybe the occasional slip-up, but nothing really worth mentioning. Besides, I'm getting older now. Moving slower. I don't have the energy I once did."

"I don't know. You seem like your motor is still running pretty well. Must be your clean living."

Don cackled. "Nah. Tell ya the truth, I'm wearin' down. Part of me thinks I should just focus on making as much money as I can over the next few years and then get out of this fucked-up business. Go back home to Oklahoma and buy a little ranch. Spend my days sittin' on the porch, drink in hand. Maybe get a dog and do a little huntin'."

"I didn't know you were a hunter."

"I'm not. Actually, I hate guns. I just like the idea of it. It's a nice visual. Goes with the narrative." Don was glassy-eyed, unfocused, perhaps picturing the scene he had just described. "I do like dogs, though," he added with unexpected gravitas.

"I thought everyone in Oklahoma owned a gun."

"Fuck, man," Don said with an abbreviated snort. "You must think I'm one hell of a redneck. Hate to disappoint you, but I grew up in the suburbs, just like you in your little candy-ass New Jersey town." Don was getting wound up, becoming louder and laughing at his own performance. "Here's a little something else that might surprise you, my friend. I went to a liberal arts college in Iowa. Yeah, that's right. Don't look so surprised. Hell, I was a creative writing major."

"Seriously?"

"Scout's honor," he said, flashing two fingers. Don leaned back and laughed again. His belly shook. He seemed to be enjoying himself immensely. "You can see where that got me."

"I don't think I'll ever retire," Josh said, happy to play the straight man. "No matter how appealing the whole ranch, dog, gun, porch thing might be. I need to make money for as long as I can."

"Yeah, well, hate to tell you this, but now with your divorce, I'm sorry to say, that's only going to get worse. The child support alone will kick your ass." Don saw Josh's face tighten, and he shrugged. His voice dropped. "Sorry, man. Don't mean to bring you down. On the other hand, think of it this way. You're a free man. I remember what that felt like. Of course, I was a lot younger than you are now. Still that's how you have to approach it. You don't get many opportunities in life to press reset. You have a chance to declare a do-over and fix the things that got fucked up the first time around."

"Or, on the other hand, it sets you up perfectly to find entirely new ways to fuck those things up."

"Well, that's another way of looking at it, I guess."

"Look, I'm not that free. I've still got my kids, my job, the house that my wife is now living in with her asshole boyfriend, the usual adult shit. I can't just go off and wander the world."

"Yeah, obviously," said Don, swatting impatiently at the air. "You still need to make a living. But there are things you can change. If you want to. I mean, I know you're loyal to James, but if you were so inclined, you could really start fresh. Look, I'm not here to tell you what to do. We don't even know each other that well. A man only knows his own story. I moved to L.A. It changed my life. I'm not saying L.A. is perfect. There are a lot of things I can't stand about the place. But one thing I can say based on experience: it's a great place to reinvent yourself." Don stopped to consider, then repeated, "If you were so inclined."

"I'm not sure I am," Josh said. "I'm not sure I'm ready for that kind of radical reinvention. I'm kind of an East Coast lifer."

"Oh, bullshit. There's no such thing. You need to crawl out of that dirty cesspool of a city and come out into the sunlight. Look at me. Who'd have thought I'd ever have become one of the beautiful people in Southern California?"

There was a long silence, and then Don started again, his tone modulating into something more serious. "I hear what you're saying about the kids, though. That's a rough one. When I left mine in OKC to come out to Hollywood, it was a tough choice. It cost me having any kind of real relationship with them. But I can't say I regret it all that much. I would have shriveled up and died if I'd stayed back there. Probably be working at a fuckin' Pep Boys or some such shit. Of course, that's just me."

They retreated to their own thoughts, passively surveying the action around them. The lounge had grown louder and more crowded. There were people standing close now, drinks in hand. Josh's chair was jostled from behind with increasing frequency.

"You know," Don drawled, breaking the lull, "if you ever did decide to make the move to L.A., you should call me. Maybe we could find a place for you with us. Who knows? The more I think about it, the more it occurs to me that your New York attitude and connections might be just the thing we need."

Under less lubricated circumstances, Josh might have been thrown for a loop as he struggled to process the significance of what Don was saying to him. But the alcohol had slowed his synapses to the point where it instead felt like a natural part of the conversation flow, as if this were simply the next segue in a script he'd already read. Still, true to who he was, Josh's instinctive default was to deflect rather than pursue. "I'm flattered," he said slowly, taking time to enunciate carefully. "But to be honest, I think I'm pretty tied down, as I said."

"Well, all it takes is a little imagination. I'm not going to twist your arm, though. You've got to want it. Look, if you are ever at all inclined to talk about this when we both get back, I'd be open to startin' the dialogue. Your call, my friend. The ball, as they say, is in your court."

Before parting, Don insisted on a last round. A couple of people Don knew from the convention found their way over to their table and chatted briefly, although later, Josh would find himself unable to recall much of what had been said. The chaotic scene in the bar grew increasingly blurry. Nursing the remnants of his third (or was it his fourth?) martini, Josh knew he had to cut this off before he woke up the next day and discovered someone had removed one of his kidneys.

He stood unsteadily, reaching to shake hands. Don opened his arms and Josh found himself enveloped in an enthusiastic, boozy embrace. "There you go, buddy," Don barked. "Bring it in."

As Josh stumbled from the table, he glanced back to see Don chatting with their waitress. Silver drink tray tucked under an elbow, she was eying Don with an amused, anticipatory expression. Josh watched her throw her head back and burst into toothy laughter, then she touched Don's arm and let it linger there. Swept up by the crowd, Josh was forced to turn away. Moments later, he found himself deposited out onto the casino floor. Clusters of meandering tourists, wild-eyed, clutching drinks, pushed past him. He started walking, searching for an exit, a means of egress. But it was futile. He stopped. He needed to focus, get his bearings, orient.

He jumped as a sudden roar exploded from a nearby craps table. A group of burly college-aged guys, flip-flops and backward baseball caps, exuberantly high-fived each other while loosely gripping the necks of sweating beer bottles in their other hands. The beefiest of them took a step back and glanced over at Josh. They locked eyes.

"Yeah," the guy bellowed at Josh from a few feet away, shaking his fist. "Fuck, yeah."

Josh shied away, unsettled. He had never been comfortable around hyper-testosterone fueled young men, even as a young man himself. Too much unchecked aggression. It made him nervous.

He continued to wander. Passing by a row of blackjack games, he stopped and held on to the back of an empty chair, woozy and listing. The dealer, in the midst of a shuffle, gave the newcomer a quick appraisal. The two players at the table, watching the dealer's eyes, followed with their own quick glimpses in Josh's direction. One, deeply tanned with tinted glasses, looked warily suspicious. The other, white-haired and older, appeared friendlier, even bemused. They turned back to their cards. The suspicious guy was dealt a blackjack. The other hit on a fifteen and received a six. They each happily collected their chips. On the next deal, both players won again. The first guy rubbed his hands together. Now they were both grinning. It was a hot table, apparently. Josh had a little cash in his wallet and could feel himself being pulled in. But he knew his addition to the mix could throw off the entire karmic balance of the game. A new player meant that the previous players would no longer be getting the cards they were originally destined to be dealt. If the table turned cold, Josh could be blamed. He'd seen it happen countless times. More importantly, perhaps, Josh still had just enough of his wits to remind himself that gambling while drinking never turned out well, at least not for him. He moved away.

He tried to concentrate, again seeking the direction of the lobby. He came to a massive field of slot machines and found himself trapped within rows upon rows of twinkling lights and clanging bells. The slots players sat impassively on their little stools, depositing money, pushing buttons, waiting for action. Had he already passed through this area? It felt vaguely familiar, but then again, everything was starting to blend together. Had he already seen that chunky middle-aged woman in the pink track suit at the machine on the end, plastic cup full of coins between her thighs? He couldn't be sure. He inched along to the end of one row, finally breaking free of the slots cluster and back into what passed for open space. But when he soon again encountered the beer-drinking, craps-playing frat boys, now subdued, hunched over, observing their game quietly, his worst fears were realized; this entire time, he had been wandering in circles. It dawned on him that the lounge where he'd parted from Don earlier was just steps away. He was dismayed. How could this be? How could he have been walking all this time and ended up right back where he'd started? With low-level panic welling in his belly for the second time that day, he sought out a somnolent-looking dealer at an empty table who, eyeing him questioningly, pointed toward a path that would, in theory at least, eventually lead outside and into the searing evening heat. Like Dorothy on the yellow brick road, Josh, head down, carefully followed the blue and gold carpet until, at last, he reached the hotel reception area. It wasn't exactly the Emerald City, but from there, he was able to cross the brightly lit marble floor and exit through the oversized glass revolving doors.

Though he had driven his rental car over to the convention center that morning, he was certainly in no shape to drive it now. He'd have to get back here early in the morning on his way to the airport, which was a total pain in the ass. But, he thought, this is what happens when you let Don Bieler buy you drinks. Actions have consequences.

Falling into a cab, Josh, calmer now, fuzzily tried to reconstruct pieces of his conversation with Don. Why did he have so much trouble separating truth from bullshit? Everyone else seemed able to parse these things. What gene was he missing? It was something certainly worth pondering, but he knew he wasn't going to find many answers while creeping along Las Vegas Boulevard, copious amounts of vodka sloshing in his bloodstream. The search for enlightenment would have to wait for another day.

In his room, Josh savored the silence, the smoke-free air, the sheer luxury of being able to move about without bumping into anyone. He swallowed three Aspirin, drank two glasses of water, and then another, lay down on the bed, and, still in his clothes, drifted into a dreamless sleep.

THIRTEEN

Claudia was in the middle of a tense edit session when she saw the number come up on her phone. Recognizing the prefix, a feeling of dread took hold. But she couldn't deal with it right away. They were on deadline, already way behind. The guy on the monitor in front of her was a well-regarded defense attorney who had become a bit of a celebrity, often opining on the cable news shows. The piece she was working on was to be shown at an industry conference the following week where this lawyer had been booked as the keynote speaker. The conference producer wanted to introduce him with a reel highlighting his work and accomplishments. But Claudia had been dismayed when she screened the raw footage. Unedited and unleashed, the guy was an unbelievable blowhard. He tended to speak in long, self-aggrandizing passages that meandered incessantly.

The field producer who had shot the piece, and with whom Claudia was now huddled in the darkened edit room, had warned Claudia that they'd spent hours trying to rein the guy in and get him to address the questions they needed him to answer. There was plenty of usable stuff buried in the reams of footage — they could fix it and make this pompous ass sound smart. But it was going to take a while. The whole thing was a hot mess. With the deadline looming, the anxiety level in the edit bay was oppressive. Claudia had received an email from the conference producer at five that morning asking where the finished video was and when they could screen it. She'd walked into the office already knowing it would likely be a late night. Caffeinated, stressed, but intensely focused, Claudia was pushing herself to work quickly. She had already snapped once or twice during the morning when she felt the rest of her team not keeping up.

She took the first chance she had, excused herself, and walked out into the brightly lit hall. The voicemail, from the school nurse, was about Amy. She had been inconsolable in her class and even the experienced special needs teacher had been unable to calm her.

"She seems out of sorts," the nurse reported in a matter-of-fact tone when Claudia reached her. "So we'd appreciate if you could just stop by and pick her up as soon as you can."

"Yes, okay. But I can't right now. I'm working and I'm in the city."

"I understand. So when do you think you can get here?"

"Did you hear what I said? I'm in the city. I can't get there. Are you sure she can't go back to her class? Or maybe wait with you in your office until it's time for the bus?"

"No, we can't do that, Mrs. Sherman. Your child is not well. We strongly advise that someone pick her up and bring her home as soon as possible."

"Okay, let me figure it out. I'll call you right back."

Claudia texted Anna but did not get an immediate response. That wasn't surprising. Anna tended to disappear when she thought she wasn't needed, especially when she knew she'd be working into the night. If past history was any indication, she would resurface soon. But Claudia couldn't afford to wait.

She thought of her mother, but that came with too many questions and complications, and she couldn't deal with that. Not today. Besides, if she remembered correctly, today was the day her mother was somewhere upstate at an animal shelter taking care of abandoned dogs and cats.

Reluctantly, she decided her best option was Marcus. He was taking his kids to a children's concert that evening, and, with Claudia knowing she'd be working in the city until late, they'd agreed to reconnect later in the week. For Claudia, this was actually a welcome mini-break from the intensity of the last several months. But now she needed him. With a sigh, she dialed Marcus's number at Iona. He sounded upbeat and delighted to hear from her. She asked him if he still had classes.

"Nope, I'm done for the day and no more office hours. Just finishing some grading. I'll probably head out of here soon."

A tattooed arm emerged from the other side of the door of the edit room. Claudia watched the door slowly open. A scruffily bearded face, silver rings hanging from one earlobe, followed. It was Matt, the intern.

"Claudia, sorry," Matt said, his face scrunched into something resembling pain. "Sorry," he repeated. "They need you back in there."

Claudia held up one finger and wagged it at Matt. "Can you pick up Amy?" she said into the phone. "I got a call from the school."

"Of course. What's wrong with her?"

"I don't know. Hopefully nothing serious. The school might just be hysterical. But she's having a bad day, and they won't let her go back to her class. We need to get her. You know how they get."

"Happy to do it." He actually did sound happy about it. For some reason, that annoyed Claudia.

Having to bring Marcus into this little domestic crisis pushed her buttons in ways she hadn't fully anticipated. As a rule, she hated being dependent on anyone. At the same time, she was self-aware enough to recognize that this feeling was kind of crazy. Irrational. This was an emergency, after all, and Marcus was available, willing, and fully capable. It was good fortune to have him as an option, and she should be grateful. What would she have done otherwise?

She was reminded how much she despised being a single parent. In the months since her separation, and especially since she'd started seeing Marcus, she had thought often about how parenting needs to be a two-person operation. Yes, there were countless moms and dads out there who somehow managed it alone every day. But she honestly had no clue how someone working at a demanding full-time job was able to be a halfway decent parent. And she was someone who was actually better at keeping her shit together than many other people — and she had Anna on top of it. There were too many moments like this where you just needed a spouse to tag team. Not that Josh would have been available either, she reminded herself; he was also working in the city. But at least he could have helped track down Anna or made other calls to find someone. As much as anything, it wasn't her automatically assuming that the other person could drop everything and run over to the school any more than she could. It was more just the idea of not being in this alone.

She called the nurse, then went back into the edit session. Nothing much had moved forward in her absence. The raw footage was so incoherent, no one was comfortable making decisions without her there. She was aware of the clock ticking. She forced herself to reorient, to concentrate on the task at hand. Marcus was on top of it, Amy would be okay. They'd finally found a decent stretch of video they could use when, a half-hour later, she saw Marcus's number on her phone. She excused herself again and went back into the hall. Again.

Marcus reported that Amy's condition, while not appearing super serious, was actually a little more of a problem than they'd initially assumed.

"I haven't tried to take her temperature myself, but the nurse said it's a little high and she feels pretty warm. And, apparently, she threw up in the nurse's office. I want to take her to the doctor. I'm sure she'd be fine if we just went home and I put her to bed. But since we're already out, I'd feel better stopping at the doctor's and getting her checked out. Just to make sure it's nothing to worry about."

"Okay, yes, please. Do it. Of course."

There was a pause. "I don't know who your pediatrician is." Another beat. "I guess that's something we should know about each other, right?"

Claudia didn't respond right away. Was she somehow at fault for not sharing this information? Was this something new couples with kids were supposed to disclose? How did information like this come up naturally in conversation?

Hi. Here are some things you need to know about me. I'm fond of Brussels sprouts, I have a thing about having my toes sucked, I've been checked for STDs, and here is my pediatrician's number, in case you ever need it.

The door to the edit bay opened, and the tattooed arm reappeared. Matt with the scrunched-up face. The pained expression. Again. "Claudia, sorry, really sorry, but...." A long intake of breath. "...They're waiting for you." A beat. "Sorry."

Stop apologizing, Claudia wanted to scream. *Just say it. Jesus. I'm not blaming you for the fucking semi-literate egotist we have on videotape or that my special needs daughter is sick or that the school nurse is an officious asshole or that my boyfriend is being so ridiculously patient and accommodating and kind that I can't even yell at him.*

"Hold on, Marcus," Claudia said. Then, to Matt, "Tell them I need five minutes. I'll be in there in five. If anyone needs coffee or a bathroom break, they need to do it now, because once I get this squared away, we're going to power straight through. Got it?"

She waited while he stood immobile, wrapped around the half-open door, unmoving. "Go, Matt. Tell them. Now."

Appearing a bit shaken, Matt snapped out of his trance. The tattooed arm slithered back behind the door.

Claudia told Marcus she'd text him the doctor's number momentarily. "I'm not too worried. Amy gets these bugs, and then they seem to pass quickly. But it's always anxiety-making. I feel so bad for her. It's so hard for her to process what's happening to her when she feels shitty. Ugh. I should be there for her." She considered whether she was a bad mother. "Let me know how she is, okay? Just text me as soon as you know something."

"Of course. Heading over now. Don't worry. I've got this. I'm sure I'm just being overly cautious. You should know that about me by now."

"Okay, yeah. I know. And Marcus?"

"Yeah?"

"Thank you for handling everything. I really appreciate you jumping in like this. It means a lot to know you're there for her."

FOURTEEN

Was that chance meeting with Don a random event, or was it a signal that his universe was pulling strings to make something happen? If he hadn't forgotten his phone, Josh would not have gone back to the convention center, and if he hadn't gone back, he would not have run into Don, and if he hadn't run into Don, the latter's semi-proposal would never have been made.

Since their Las Vegas encounter, Don's offer continued to hover somewhere out on Josh's horizon, not exactly real but not a total mirage either. He found the idea most enticing after a bad day, when he was fed up and ready to say *fuck it* to his whole dumb life as it was currently constituted. Which seemed to be occurring with some frequency.

The post-convention call Don had suggested had never happened. As Don had made clear, it was up to Josh to take the initiative and schedule it, and Josh had yet to do so. His instinct told him he should wait until he was more certain it was something he was sure he wanted to move on. Instead, he had sent a vague email to Don shortly after they'd returned to their home bases. He'd thanked him for the drinks but had made no mention of the possible job. Don's response had been similarly affable but ambiguous. With James's voice ringing in his head, Josh now found himself forced to contemplate whether this was the time to light the match to Don's offer and attempt to turn it into a truly legitimate Plan B. Running into him that day in Vegas certainly felt like fate, if one were inclined to take such things seriously. Could it be that his universe was finally taking pity on him, attempting to give him a shove in a particular direction?

One hell of a Plan B it would be. Reinvention indeed. What would James say? He wouldn't endorse anything involving Don, Josh was sure of that. But James wasn't making these decisions for him. Besides, James had done everything but tell him to go out and find another job. And this opportunity was practically hanging out there for the taking. It was the most — the only, really — Plan B-ish thing Josh had going.

And then there was something else holding Josh back; something he hoped the universe would perhaps also help him untangle. He desperately wanted to know what Erin had in mind. It seemed evident she was itching to get out of L.A. First there had been the culinary school idea, now this possible job in New York. If he knew she was going to stay put, he might consider L.A. as a more serious option. On the other hand, if she moved to New York at the very same moment he went west...well, that would be the exact kind of fucked-up thing that could happen to him. Everything could be set up perfectly, and then the universe would roll on the floor, laughing, having already long since determined that events in his life were all just one big cosmic practical joke. Josh needed to tell Erin what was going on, get a read from her. That would help him better understand his own next steps. But he had to be careful how he presented this to her. It would be a huge mistake to give her the impression his decision-making depended so heavily on hers. Even if he wanted to believe their futures could be linked, those feelings were something he had to keep locked inside. Maybe some of this would clarify when they saw each other again for the next Shoe King meeting in a few weeks.

FIFTEEN

For as long as Claudia could remember, her parents, Barbara and Marv, had hosted an annual all-day Thanksgiving open house at their spacious Bedford home. Guests were invited to drop by at any time throughout the afternoon or evening for a drink, a bite to eat or, if so inclined, to partake in the elaborate buffet for a more substantial holiday meal. The event was always highly anticipated by those who attended: old friends, relatives from both sides, and a select number of Marv's past and present business associates.

Though Claudia and Marcus had by now been out to dinner with her parents several times, Claudia had intentionally avoided bringing him up here, even though in the logical order of things, it should already have happened. She had fretted that seeing where she had grown up would color his perception of her. As an only child in this big house, some of her most vivid early memories were of her and her friends running through the many rooms, a seemingly boundless play area. At that age, the place had seemed enchanted, magical in some ways. But it had also been perfectly normal. It was where she lived. Later, the house had been the ideal place to bring her high school boyfriend. They were able to disappear with relative ease when seized by the urge for privacy.

She saw Marcus's eyes widen as she pulled her Honda Pilot into the circular driveway, the big white colonial with its colonnaded portico looming. The high school kid hired by her mom to handle valet parking for the day scrambled out of his sagging lawn chair to meet their car.

"Nice place," Marcus said, looking up with such deadpan understatement that Claudia, glancing over at him from behind the wheel, had to laugh. "This is really where you grew up?"

Marcus's youth, as he had described it for Claudia, had been starkly different. He was raised in a sketchy part of Philadelphia, and his father had been abusive and his mother what he characterized, rather ambiguously, as "nasty." He had worked hard over the years to ensure that those rough edges from his earlier days had been properly and appropriately sanded off. Yet there had been moments since they'd been together when Claudia had seen that scrappy, striving Philly kid break through the veneer of refined, middle-aged academic. It had happened as recently as Halloween night, when a group of teenagers had decided to use the street in front of Claudia's house as the staging ground for an upscale suburb's version of a rumble involving not knives or fists but instead a copious amount of raw eggs and shaving cream. Marcus, watching this impending face-off unfold from the living room window, was incensed, especially with his own car parked against the curb at what was essentially going to be ground zero. He marched outside and with bold self-assurance told the kids in an authoritative snarl to knock it off. To Claudia's amazement, they had quickly dispersed. It was not something Claudia could ever imagine Josh having either the temperament or the inclination to pull off.

They went up the wide stone steps, Claudia's nerves jangling, her stomach unsettled. She had been dreading the scrutiny and speculation today's outing would inevitably engender. She had been concerned enough that she briefly considered blowing off the whole thing, staying at home and making a low-key Thanksgiving dinner just for Marcus and the children. But then she remembered Marcus describing how Debbie, a splendid cook, would go all-out to prepare elaborate holiday meals. Claudia could never compete with that and had no desire to try. She knew whatever she did, no matter how much effort she put in, the final product would never hold up when measured against the memory of a sainted dead woman.

Besides, Marv and Barbara would never have stood for it. There would have been the inevitable family uproar, and, at some point, she would have had to relent to their pressure and make an appearance anyway. So here she was, just like any other year. Except this was completely unlike any other year.

When it came to sharing the details of her life with her parents, Claudia had always been careful about managing the information flow, even when she was young. Now, in the midst of so many transitions, this cautious approach became even more of an imperative. She had not as yet given them any hint of long-range plans with Marcus. Better for now for them to think of her relationship as more casual. There was no reason for them to know the reality just yet. She needed to present the next iteration of her life to her parents as a finished package, not a work in progress.

They were intercepted at the door by the speech pathology grad student Claudia's parents paid to work with Amy several afternoons a week. Jessica needed to get to her own family's holiday dinner later that afternoon, but at Claudia's behest, she had agreed to meet them here and take Amy off their hands for a couple of hours. On the threshold, Amy lingered, hesitant to enter and resistant to coaxing. She whined in protest and planted her feet as they tried to bring her inside. This was not out of the ordinary. Amy reacted poorly to too many people in one place at one time. Claudia could feel herself tensing as she watched her daughter's face begin to cloud over. But then Jessica, tall and solidly built, thick mane of red hair flying in all directions, swept her up, and they disappeared somewhere away from the gathering crowd.

Will and Daniel, both dark-haired and similarly stocky, ran ahead of the adults into the house without hesitation. Claudia saw Daniel, the younger of the brothers, turn and say something over his shoulder to Ethan, who was trailing behind. The two older boys stopped to let him catch up. Ethan pointed, and they turned the corner toward the room where Claudia knew the big-screen TV would be tuned to a day of football. A good-sized group, mostly men, would be there, quite settled in by now, with her father at the center of it. Marcus, observing his sons, strode purposefully past Claudia, following the boys down the hall, promising to return momentarily.

Barbara hurried over when she saw her daughter. Claudia's mother, elegant as always, wore a shawl draped over a black-lace, sleeveless cocktail dress, accessorized by a single string of pearls. Her shoulder-length dark hair was flipped, sixties style. Claudia marveled at how her mother never failed to pull off the perfect ensemble. Still, at that moment, Barbara appeared on edge. Even with the professional catering staff scurrying about, the Thanksgiving Day party always stressed her out. It seemed to take so much out of her, Claudia sometimes thought the whole thing should be scaled back — or retired entirely. But Barbara wouldn't hear of it. Even Claudia's modest hints in that direction were met with outrage and umbrage.

"Everything looks beautiful, as always, Mom," Claudia said, sweeping the high-ceilinged living room with her eyes. "Including . you." The florists had done their usual tasteful job, leaving an array of stunning colorful bouquets strategically placed around the rooms where the guests were gathered. Sunlight filtered in through the south-facing picture window fronting the big, sloping backyard with its sprawling lawn.

The set-up for the party never varied from year to year. To her left, Claudia could see through into the dining room. A partially carved turkey dominated the big table, surrounded by a variety of carefully curated side dishes that Claudia knew had been agonized over for weeks. A large man in a black dinner jacket and white shirt stood at the ready, wielding a scary-looking carving knife. Although unseen from where she stood, Claudia knew that the bar, a popular gathering spot, would be in operation around the corner in the next room.

Claudia was greeted by a young blond woman, also in black and white, holding a tray of stuffed mushrooms. Claudia smiled and waved her away politely. A moment later, another server appeared with white wine and Prosecco, the latter a favorite of her mother's. After a brief hesitation, Claudia decided a glass couldn't hurt. She lifted one and took a generous sip.

"The caterers were an hour late," Barbara hissed through clenched teeth. "I was livid. Same company we always use, same owners, but with different people now, I guess. I wasn't told that. They claim they got lost. Ridiculous."

"Well, it looks like it all worked out. It's fine now, right?"

"I was none too pleased." Barbara peered at Claudia with a critical eye. "You're still growing your hair out."

"For now. You like it?"

Barbara cocked her head and turned, assessing the back of her daughter's neck. "It could use a trim," she said after a long moment.

Claudia sighed. "I have an appointment next week, Mom."

Marcus reappeared, and Claudia raised her Champagne flute in a mock toast, prompting him to half bow as he neared. "They're in the TV room," Marcus reported as he joined them. "Ethan is showing them what I took to be his toy closet."

"That's a good sign," Claudia said. "Should keep them occupied for the next ten hours or so. Say hi to my mom."

Marcus leaned in, and Barbara reciprocated with a curt turn of her head. Marcus still hadn't fully grasped that Barbara only did air kisses. The result was an awkward half stab as Marcus brushed her at an angle that landed somewhere below her jaw line. They both took a step back, choosing to pretend that the little exchange had been executed flawlessly.

"How are you, Marcus?" Barbara said with that air of patrician remoteness she sometimes affected. It never failed to make Claudia's skin crawl. "Nice to see you again."

"The same to you. This is really lovely."

"Thank you. I'm glad it appears that way." To Claudia she said, "Jessica is upstairs getting Amy settled. And I saw Ethan fly through here." Barbara's coffee colored eyes tracked another of the catering staff as they went by. "I'm assuming those other boys were yours, Marcus?"

"Yes," Marcus said, appearing a little embarrassed. "Sorry you didn't get an appropriate introduction. Doesn't say much for their manners, I'm afraid. Or mine. I'll make sure they give you a proper greeting."

"It's perfectly fine. We'll undoubtedly have plenty of opportunity to get to know each other."

"You saw my dad?" Claudia said to Marcus. "Engrossed in the game, I assume?"

"I only waved. The room was pretty crowded. It's right before halftime, and something big seemed to be happening. From what I was able to gather."

"Perfect timing. We'll have his attention for fifteen minutes. We should go say hi now, then."

As they moved away, Marcus whispered into Claudia's ear. "Uh, am I underdressed?" he asked. She saw him eying her calf-length printed skirt and high-necked sweater. "I'm seeing a lot of people really going to town at this thing. You should have warned me."

Claudia took a quick glance at Marcus's gray pullover, corduroy blazer, and jeans. "You're a teacher. You look exactly the way you're supposed to. You're fine." She stopped to touch his shoulder and then kissed him softly on the mouth. Overwhelmed by a sudden surge of warmth, she let the kiss linger. "In fact, you're more than fine." She touched his cheek with her fingertips. "You're perfect."

They turned down the hall and were intercepted by a petite woman with short silver hair. Claudia made the introductions, explaining to Marcus that Elaine was one of her mother's oldest and dearest friends.

"Be careful how you say 'oldest,' my dear," Elaine said, wagging a few trembling fingers in protest. "One becomes sensitive about such things at a certain age." She turned. "So nice to meet you, Marcus. I've heard wonderful things about you." Claudia watched, amused and wary, as Elaine sized him up.

"The pleasure is mine," Marcus answered, taking her extended, mottled hand into both of his. For the second time since they'd arrived, he did the little half bow thing. What the hell was that? Was this something he only did at parties?

"It's so nice to see you again, Claudia. And," she repeated for Claudia's benefit, "it's delightful to finally meet the mysterious Marcus." Elaine had a lazy eye, which various treatments and procedures had as yet been unable to correct. It made it difficult to know where to look when talking to her. Claudia knew she was touchy about it; Elaine would self-consciously try to face you with only one side of her face. "But I must tell you," she continued, her one-eyed gaze settling on Claudia. "I was so deeply saddened to hear about you and Josh. Very difficult stuff."

"Yes, well, I can't argue with that. It *has* been difficult. But I think ultimately it will be for the best. I think we both feel that way. Josh and I, that is. Ultimately."

"When did you split up?"

"It was in the early part of the year." Claudia paused then added lightly, "I suppose we'll be celebrating our one-year break-up anniversary pretty soon." She saw her attempt at humor fall flat. Elaine had totally missed the sarcasm. Claudia looked at Marcus and pulled a face. She didn't want him to be uncomfortable with the direction this conversation was going.

"Yes, I guess you will," Elaine said. "But it's wonderful how the two of *you* have found each other. And so quickly. How long have you been together?"

Claudia's radar went up as she realized Elaine was trying to do the math. Was this seriously worth her effort? Claudia responded vaguely, saying, not exactly truthfully, that they had started seeing each other some time in the late spring. She was annoyed now and wanted to keep Elaine in the dark. She likened the situation to nineteenth century novels in which couples who had engaged in premarital sin would adjust the date of their wedding anniversary to ensure that the birth-date of their first child did not erupt into scandal.

"Barbara told me about your wife, Marcus." Elaine was saying now. "I just want you to know from my heart how sorry I was to hear it. I lost my husband. It's been about four years for me."

"Thank you. I appreciate that. And I'm sorry for your loss."

"Divorce is tough, often even brutal," Elaine said, looking again at Claudia. "I've been there too, as you know. It's impossible to minimize that pain, especially when young children are involved. And in your particular situation, it's even tougher, I would imagine. With Amy, I mean." She tapped Marcus on the arm and swiveled to turn back toward him, leaving Claudia staring into the bad eye. "But losing a spouse is something no one can understand except those of us who have been through it. We get each other in particular and meaningful ways. It's an exclusive club. Not that I would wish it on anyone, of course."

As Elaine moved away, Marcus said quietly to Claudia, "Have I ever mentioned how much I enjoy party conversation that's literally about life and death? It so lightens the mood. Is she always so upbeat?"

Claudia laughed. "She's a very sweet person, actually. She's been a good friend to my mother. But it's true, she seems to kind of revel in her status as a widow. Like it makes her noteworthy, distinctive somehow. I kind of figured it would come up. She wanted to make sure you knew she felt a bond with you."

"Hmm. Well, her exclusive club is not one I ever wanted to be a part of. There's nothing exceptional about a spouse dying except that's it's a really shitty turn of fate." A beat. "What was her husband like?"

"He was a great guy, actually. Significantly older than her. A second marriage for both of them."

"I do feel for her. And I'm sure she means well. But if she wants to bond, she should find a support group."

Claudia started and looked at him, taken aback a bit by his sharp tone.

"Sorry." He sighed. "But it just gets under my skin when people think that I'm somehow spiritually linked to them because we're both widowed."

"Yeah, I know. Just remember, she has a good heart. What can I tell you? How do you think I felt when she started trying to add up the number of months we've been together so she could subtract them from the months I've been separated?"

"Yeah, that was weird too."

Claudia lifted her chin and jabbed a finger at him. "People should stay the fuck out of our shit."

"Damn straight."

"Fuck yeah."

They continued along the path to the TV room, although it took a while longer to get there because they were waylaid by more rounds of greetings, introductions, and small talk. Everyone, naturally, showed great interest in meeting Marcus.

Finally, they arrived at their destination, a sizeable, wood-paneled room with built-in bookshelves and a large-screen TV facing soft-cushioned couches and chairs. More cushions were scattered across the carpeted floor, most of them occupied by football fans in various states of recline. Claudia spied Ethan at a card table in the back by the unshaded windows, playing a board game with Will and Daniel and appearing to be having the time of his life. Claudia took Marcus's hand as they picked their way past those sprawled across the floor. They reached her father, who sat surrounded in the middle of the couch, clutching a wine glass. Claudia bent to kiss him while Marcus, close behind, leaned in for a handshake.

Marv had a mop of curly white hair and small, bright eyes. His face had that jowly fleshiness along his jaw line and throat that men on the back side of middle age are often prone to settle into. He was unshaven, and though it couldn't have been for more than a few days, what had grown in appeared already neatly trimmed along the edges. With a playful tone, Claudia asked her father if he were planning an encore of the snowy, bushy beard that had last made an appearance several years earlier.

"Undecided," came Marv's gravelly though good-natured, reply. "You're welcome to check with me on Monday morning if you really want to know."

Marv was sunk into the couch, leaving them looming over him, awkwardly positioned for extended chatting. With an eye on the big screen, he offered a quick summary of the game, by this time well into the second half. After a short bit of this, Claudia decided she would check on the boys.

"Sit, Marcus," Claudia heard Marv insist behind her as she moved away. She looked back to see her father squeezing over to make a space where, a moment earlier, it had appeared there was none. "Watch the game with me."

Marcus peered over the top of Marv's head at Claudia and with a nearly imperceptible shrug eased his way into the narrow spot Marv had cleared. Claudia knew he'd be fine. Her father, a first-generation son of immigrants, was a natural raconteur. He loved to share his colorful recollections of growing up in The Bronx. These stories were ingrained in the family narrative and Claudia knew them all, though she had long understood there had been a degree of embellishment that had only grown over the years. If Marcus had, understandably, found himself unable to bond with an aging widow a few minutes earlier, he likely would have better luck with Marv, swapping stories of life growing up on the semi-mean streets of the urban northeast.

Claudia came up behind Ethan, kissing him on a plump cheek, one hand resting on top of his red corkscrew locks. He turned his face toward her. "I'm having fun, Mommy," he said before returning his focus to the action in front of him.

Claudia, observing, made a half-hearted effort to throw out a few queries about the game, but her comments were met with muted, monosyllabic replies. It was apparent that all the men she needed to be concerned with were accounted for and seemingly happily absorbed. She could quietly remove herself and for the moment at least not be missed.

She edged out of the room on the far side, along the wall lined with books. She lingered briefly, reminiscing about the hours she had spent there as a child, when she would randomly pick various titles off these shelves and thumb through them. Her father's interests ran toward biographies and histories, mostly of world leaders and mostly of men. Her mother was a fiction reader. When she was around twelve years old, Claudia had found her mother's heavily notated copy of *Mrs. Dalloway*. She had decided it would be her project to read the book, and she did, even though it had taken her weeks to get through it, and significant parts left her puzzled. But she'd thought it would be something she could discuss with her mother, something to share with her. She could still recall the moment she'd told Barbara she'd finished the book and wanted to talk about it. But her mother was either unable or unwilling to have that discussion, and Claudia's attempt to engage her went nowhere. Claudia had discovered only much later that Barbara had been a woman's lit major in college. It had been a startling revelation, and Claudia was again eager to hear about how that experience from a generation earlier had shaped her. But when she asked her mother, it was like a repeat of their stilted conversation from years before. Barbara was steadfastly reluctant to provide much insight into what she'd read, how her studies had reflected the broader political climate of the time, or even how she'd come to pursue that course of study. It was clear that that younger Barbara was destined to remain locked away, a mystery to Claudia.

The day had reached that point where there was a break in the festivities; much of the earlier crowd had moved on, and the bulk of the later arrivals had yet to appear. Claudia knew this lull wouldn't last long, so she decided to take advantage of the moment. She thought she might eat something. Or perhaps have another glass of Prosecco. She eyed one of the couches in the big open living room; it was unoccupied and looked inviting. She would recharge and then circulate again. She needed that second drink.

She'd only been sitting for a brief time when she became aware of someone locked in on her and drawing near. He had an awkward, loping gait, his entire body seemingly committed to his loose-jointed stride. The man was grinning, and his smile grew broader as he approached. It took Claudia a second to register Jerome, her father's one-time protégé.

Claudia's recollections of Jerome went back to when she was in high school; in those days Jerome had been a rising star at Marv's firm, and he and his wife Stacey were coming to their house for dinner with some regularity. Claudia's most vivid memories of those evenings were of Stacey and how kind she had been during those long dinners, invariably dominated by the men holding court at the big table long after dessert had been served. It felt like several lifetimes ago now; Jerome and Stacey had parted ways years ago.

"Look at you, lady of leisure," Jerome said, standing over her. "You look relaxed with your glass of wine. Don't you have kids to take care of?"

"I lost track of them days ago. I'm sure they'll turn up somewhere."

She felt herself bounce, her backside briefly lifted into the air, as Jerome fell ungracefully onto the couch beside her.

Jerome seemed delighted to see her and leaned in for a seated hug. They touched cheeks, his neatly trimmed gray mustache, though only slightly more than pencil-thin, somehow still managing to scratch her. The heavy scent of his cologne settled over her.

"I was wondering if you were going to make it here this year," he said after they'd exchanged initial pleasantries. "You know, with your changed status and everything."

"It's my parents' party, Jerome. I kind of need to be here. And besides, I don't have ebola. I still get out into the world now and again."

"Funny. You always did have a way of making me laugh." Jerome asked Claudia about her job, about Amy and Ethan, and, of course, about what had happened with Josh. Claudia began to feel she should have just printed out talking points. It would have been easier.

And then Jerome went there.

"I saw you come in with your friend. Marcus, right? What's his story?" Jerome's voice was ragged, apprehensive. "I mean, is this a serious thing, or just...." He stopped. He evidently hadn't thought through the rest of that sentence and now seemed unsure how to finish it. After a couple of false starts, though, he stumbled to his point. "I'm just saying, I've always liked you, Claudia. You probably knew that. So, if you're unattached, I mean if you are open to it, I thought maybe we could go out sometime. Just casual, you know? Maybe when we're both in the city?" Speaking in short bursts, he fingered the seams of one of the couch cushions. "But on the other hand, if you and, uh, Marcus are, uh, you know, exclusive, well then, I don't want to get in the way. I would never interfere." He shrugged with a weak smile. "I hope you don't mind me asking you this. I suppose I must sound a bit forward, but we've known each other a long time, and when you get to a certain point in life, you learn to just put it out there. If you know what I mean."

She couldn't say she was much shocked by the direction this conversation had taken. Like women everywhere, she'd been hit on by men of all types — appealing, not appealing, subtle, not subtle, married, not married. And like women everywhere, from the time she'd hit puberty, she had had to learn how to deflect unwanted advances. Granted, Jerome was easier to take than some. He wasn't completely gross. He was relatively intelligent, had all his own hair, and had been able to stay on her father's good side all these years, which was not always an easy thing to pull off. Marv was not someone inclined to hold on to business associates after their business together had ended. But did Jerome really think this to be appropriate? Did he think she would actually go out with him, even if she were available? It would be like dating your uncle. It was absurd.

Fortunately, he had provided her with a convenient out by mentioning exclusivity. She now played that card back at him, effectively squashing his budding romantic fantasies. She saw his face crumple though, she could appreciate, he at least made a minimal effort to cover his disappointment. They kept the mildly pleasant chitchat going for a few more minutes before he was struck by a sudden urge to check out the football game. In another moment, he was gone.

From her spot on the couch, as she observed the party begin to repopulate with the next wave of arrivals, Claudia thought about how strange her world had become that getting hit on by men like Jerome was now something that could just happen to her as a matter of course.

It made her think again about the viability of dating other people. As she continued to seek out the best strategies for navigating the fast-moving freight train that was Marcus and his long-term plans for them as a couple, this dilemma continued to eat at her. Granted, it was a little late in the game for this. She was already in plenty deep. They had discussed marriage, for God's sake. If she had had any intentions of pursuing an alternative path, it should have been well before now.

Marcus had the advantage of already having been down the dating road. That was one reason, he claimed, he was sure Claudia was the one. He was a big believer in chemistry. He knew when it clicked and when it didn't. But Claudia, a more recent arrival to the unsettled world of middle-aged single-hood, had had as yet no similar opportunities for comparison. She was still adjusting simply to being on her own. Was she making a mistake by jumping so immediately back into such a serious relationship? On the other hand, the idea of dating random men at this point in her life just sounded so horrendous, she couldn't really imagine it. Jerome being Exhibit A.

Soon after the Jerome encounter, Jessica came downstairs with Amy and informed Claudia that she would need to take off for her family dinner. Switching into mommy mode, Claudia assumed responsibility for her daughter. They hung out on the carpeted living room stairs for a while, Amy walking up and down, feeling the texture under her feet and occasionally peering down at the guests from over the bannister. Then Claudia took her into the backyard, where they strolled across the expansive lawn, crunching over the last of the fallen leaves.

Claudia recalled the day she and Josh had married. From childhood, she had always thought this backyard would be the perfect place for a wedding, and so, when she became engaged, it was natural for her to want the ceremony to be here. That spring morning had broken warm and bright after days of rain. She remembered how her gown had glinted in the midday sunlight. Jen had been her maid of honor, of course. The two of them, plus Claudia's bridesmaids, had stayed upstairs together on the eve of the wedding, too wired to sleep much.

The next morning, the bridal party had had their hair and makeup done by a stylist one of the bridesmaids knew from Fashion Week. At some point, a tray of mocha lattes had appeared.

Most of the guests, including some of the same people who were up in the house at this very moment, were from her side. Josh had had only James as his best man. He hadn't asked anyone else to be groomsmen. He had explained there was no one he felt close enough to. Josh's brother Sean, who was living in Singapore at the time, sent his regrets in a terse email. Claudia had thought this perplexing, even borderline offensive, but Josh had seemed unbothered. At the eleventh hour, Josh's mother expressed concern about how she was going to get to Westchester, casting doubt on whether she'd be able to make it at all. Marv had quickly arranged for a car service to ensure she would have no issues. Later, after Josh and Claudia had returned from their honeymoon and were settling into their new life, Claudia tried to gently point out to Josh that he could use a few more friends. "You're my best friend," she remembered him telling her. "I don't think I need anyone else." It had been such a sweet thing to say, she'd actually teared up. But now, thinking about that exchange all these years later, she was considerably less enchanted.

Claudia walked Amy across this lawn that held so many memories, trying to engage her by identifying the trees and shrubs as best she could. It was, as always, difficult to know how much Amy was able to comprehend, though she did repeat some of the names as Claudia spoke them. Amy was always happiest when outdoors, and Claudia's heart warmed to see her daughter making eye contact, smiling and relaxed, spinning her way across the yard. But as the afternoon went on, the weather turned threatening. The sky grew gray, the wind picked up, and the chill in the air deepened. They retreated back into the house.

Highly attuned to her daughter's shifting moods and sensitivities, Claudia had been concerned all day about getting Amy out of there before there were any massive meltdowns. Soon after coming inside, as afternoon stretched into evening, Claudia sensed her daughter's fussiness building. Claudia found Marcus standing in the dining room, eating turkey near the big table and chatting with a droopy-faced bald man. Apologizing for interrupting, her tone subdued but urgent, she told Marcus they needed to go. Wordlessly, he stopped chewing, looked at Amy for a long beat, looked back at Claudia, and nodded. She was relieved and deeply grateful for the ease with which Marcus communicated his assent. Josh had always seemed to have an endless capacity for making moments like these awkward and protracted. In a matter of minutes, the boys were gathered, coats were on, and they were saying their goodbyes. On their way out the door, Will turned, impulsively threw his arms around Barbara's waist, and told her he wanted to come back. Daniel, observing this, followed with his own rather inelegant but well-intentioned hug. Barbara laughed, surprised and a bit taken aback. But Claudia could see she also was touched.

* * *

A cold, biting rain had commenced; as they drove home, the rain transitioned to sleet. The headlights illuminated the wintery scene, frozen clumps beginning to stick to the wet streets and lawns. Claudia, now in the passenger's seat so she could keep an eye on Amy, listened to her daughter softly cooing, a sort of half hum, half grunt. Ethan, next to his sister, was quiet, while Will and Daniel, in the back row, were poking each other and laughing. Periodically, this would devolve into bursts of wrestling, until a sharp word from Marcus elicited a short-lived truce.

Staring at the blurred red brake lights spread out ahead of them, the windshield streaked and foggy, Claudia thought with a pleasing sense of anticipation toward Saturday, when she and Marcus would have the day to themselves. Josh was coming in the morning to pick up Amy and Ethan. Debbie's brother, whom Claudia had not yet met, had arranged with Marcus to take Will and Daniel, along with his own kids, into the city for the day.

As they made their way through the slick, whitening streets, Claudia again mused at how everyone at the party had seemed so interested in her current status. "It's like," she said, "they thought if they could find a way to ask the same question in enough different ways, they'd finally trip me up somehow, get me to admit that I was sleeping with you while I was still married."

"Well, technically you are. Still married, I mean. And sleeping with me."

"Oh my God, you're right. I'm a fallen woman."

"You're just realizing that?"

"I'm in denial." Claudia turned, extending her upper half into the back seat to rest a calming hand on Amy, who by now was rocking more vigorously. "How did it go with my dad?" she asked, craning her neck to look at Marcus.

"We seemed to hit it off pretty well. I know you said he can be irascible, but honestly, I have yet to see it."

"Irascible. Is that what I said? I thought it was something a bit earthier."

"It was. I cleaned it up. But either way, we had plenty to talk about. Well, actually he did most of the talking."

"Naturally."

"You didn't tell me he'd worked in investments before real estate development."

"Yeah," she said, turning back from Amy and getting herself resettled. "And he was a lawyer before that. My father gets bored easily, so he likes to change careers to challenge himself. He represented investment firms when he was a lawyer, and that got him interested in finance. Then, when he was working in investments, some of his clients were in commercial real estate. He becomes convinced he can do whatever his clients are doing better than they can. So he decides to try it out and see if he's right. And he usually is. My father has a knack for business."

"More than a knack, I'd say. It's a particular kind of genius." Marcus tapped the brakes, careful to keep a healthy distance between them and the car ahead. "I'm just a poor college professor. I have no talent for anything remotely like that. I guess the only way I'll be able to impress him is if my Thomas Paine biography becomes a bestseller and they make it into a movie. Which is none too likely. If I ever do finish writing the damn thing in the first place, that is." He sighed. "I'm sure your dad must be baffled by my career choice. I'm not in the game."

"Actually, don't be so quick to make assumptions about him. From what I can tell, he respects your intellect, which is no small thing, trust me. My dad doesn't value people by how much money they make. He judges them by whether they challenge themselves to reach their potential. He has no patience for underachievers. That's what baffles him. The whole idea of not pushing yourself is completely alien to how his mind works."

"I'll make a note of it."

"That's why he never really got Josh. You know, Josh has had the same job for twenty years and has never shown much of an initiative to move on to something better."

"But he's helping to run a company, right? So he's entrepreneurial. Your dad must respect that."

"I guess you could make that case. But the flip side is that James, the guy who's the actual owner of the company, has held Josh down and manipulated him into doing all this work while not being fair about the money. Josh looks up to James for some unexplained reason and is weirdly loyal to him. I've always thought of James as kind of a sleaze for the way he takes advantage of Josh. I think my dad's hope was that, at some point, Josh would grow some balls and tell James to fuck off."

Marcus flinched. "Hey, do you mind? Watch the language. We've got kids in the car." He glanced into the rearview mirror and adjusted his grip on the steering wheel.

"They can't hear us."

Ethan piped up from behind them. "What are you talking about, Mommy?"

Marcus shot her a side-eyed look. "Nicely handled. Go ahead. Let's see how you get out of this one."

"Are you talking about Daddy?" Ethan asked.

"No, honey. Someone else's daddy."

Marcus snorted with a shake of his head.

"Another daddy named Josh?"

"Maybe. There are a lot of daddies named Josh."

"There are?"

Ethan grew quiet. He was a smart and intuitive seven-year-old, and Claudia knew he understood his mother was playing him, that she was being intentionally illogical, even if he wasn't able to fully comprehend the reasoning behind it. *But*, Claudia thought, *at least it gives him something to chew on for a while.* And it seemed to work. The questions stopped while Ethan sat in the dark, the car plowing through the drifting wet flakes, and pondered a world full of daddies named Josh.

SIXTEEN

Josh awoke on Thanksgiving morning remembering those many afternoons he'd spent stuffing himself with hors d'oeuvres, watching football with Marv and making awkward small talk with Claudia's weird cousins.

Josh had never been terribly relaxed around his in-laws. Though he had gotten along with Marv well enough on the surface, it was an arm's-length relationship. Barbara, for her part, was tough to crack. She divided the world into two halves: family and everyone else. Anyone not within her very private and select inner circle was treated with a certain frigid civility. Josh had never been fully brought into the fold.

Over the last several years, Josh and Claudia had started taking two cars to the Thanksgiving party so that Josh could bring Amy home when she'd had enough. Josh always assured everyone he was fine with it but, in spite of his ambivalence at having to go to his in-laws in the first place, once he left with Amy and was sitting by himself in his house, he couldn't help but feel he was missing out on something.

Now here it was, another Thanksgiving Day, and he had a similar feeling. He didn't necessarily want to be forced to socialize with a bunch of people he barely knew, but he was equally uneasy being alone. He'd had no invitations and no options for the day. James and his wife, who were childless ("by choice," as James was fond of adding), had gone to their timeshare in Anguilla. There would be no Shoe King appearance at the homeless shelter to keep Josh busy this year either. Ryan and Courtney had made clear they had no interest in continuing that particular tradition.

It was ironic, of course. While living in the house with Claudia and the children, he had so desperately craved solitude; he would have killed for a single hour alone. Now, four empty days loomed, and it freaked him out. The only plans he had with other people were for Saturday, when he had agreed to take his children for the day. He realized belatedly he had yet to give any thought as to what he was going to do with them. It was always challenging — it had to be an activity Ethan would enjoy but that wouldn't overwhelm Amy. Sometimes he took them to the local airport to watch planes from the observation deck. Admittedly not the most inspired as entertainment options went, but reliable and cheap.

Josh thought about Erin, who was with her family in Denver. He had texted her earlier in the week, a rather tepid happy holiday greeting. He had yet to hear back. Still, a delayed response was not unusual for her, especially when she was away.

He sat at his little kitchen table, bright morning sunlight peeking through the thin muslin curtains, and thumbed through the newspaper while the big cartoon heads in the Macy's parade marched along, muted, on the TV in the other room. Josh spied the envelope from Claudia's lawyer on his table. Though the need to finalize the divorce was never far from his thoughts, leaving the envelope there as a constant reminder hadn't nudged him any closer to action. On the one hand, there had been plenty of moments when he'd felt like he should just sign the fucking thing and be done with it. But he couldn't bring himself to actually do it. James had torn into him, called him an idiot for not hiring his own lawyer. "Who does that?" his boss had bellowed one afternoon in his office. "You can't just handle this by yourself. Nobody does that."

But hiring a lawyer just seemed so unnecessary at this point in the process, not to mention wickedly expensive. There didn't appear to be much acrimony regarding terms. He knew what Claudia wanted, and he'd acquiesced. He'd agreed to give up custody of the children, which, admittedly, had left him queasy. The idea of submitting to such a thing, even the phrasing of it, had such an unseemly connotation. But he was looking at the situation in terms of cold pragmatics. He was in no position to have kids living with him right now, even part-time. He would have had to find a bigger place for starters. And then there would be the problem of child care. Bigger picture, his entire life was in upheaval. He had no way of knowing where he'd be or what he'd be doing in the coming year. So when Claudia had made clear she wanted full custody of the children, the issue seemed to have been settled. She had also pointedly mentioned to Josh that Marcus, that smug asshole, had been fully supportive of her decision. Her lawyer had written the custody arrangements into the agreement; Josh would have visitation, but the kids would be living with Claudia. Having skimmed through the pages of legalese, Josh had decided he was fine with it. Granted, the child support payments, as Don Bieler had so pointedly underscored during that drunken night in Vegas, were going to be a bitch. But it came with the territory, and he was resigned to holding up his end of the bargain. So why hadn't he signed yet? He knew his paralysis was preventing them from moving forward, but he just had not been able to pull the trigger.

Meanwhile, he had today to think about. About a week or so earlier, he had seen an ad for a prix fixe Thanksgiving dinner at a restaurant at a ritzy hotel in White Plains. Though it was pricy, he had, on impulse, gone online and made a reservation. It would get him out of the apartment and give him something to do. Better than staying inside all day pacing the floors. Or worse.

He had planned for a four o'clock arrival, thinking he would beat the crowd. By the time he walked out to his car to drive over there, the clouds had moved in and the temperature had dropped. Rain was coming, or possibly snow. There was very little traffic, and he knew he would be early. He took his time, opting for surface streets.

Working his way through the hotel lobby toward the restaurant, he could see even from a distance that the place was already packed. People were milling about outside the front entrance, kids chasing each other, parents standing with arms folded, checking their phones. Josh took his place at the back of the line and shuffled slowly forward. The restaurant had done its best to approximate the feel of holiday spirit. An array of colorful lights twinkled. A string quartet, heard but as yet unseen, provided a schmaltzy soundtrack. The heavy smell of roasted meats mingled with something cloyingly sweet.

As he inched ahead, it occurred to Josh that he'd never experienced the kind of traditional Thanksgiving dinner most people grow up with. It was not something his family had done. Oh, sure, his mother would usually make a turkey breast, and some years there would even be stuffing and mashed potatoes. But when the food was ready, his father and brother would serve themselves and then take their plates into the den to watch football while his mother would eat her dinner at the kitchen table and do a crossword puzzle. Confused by this, Josh would go back and forth between them, never able to find a comfortable place to settle, never able to shake the feeling that he was somehow intruding. As an adult, of course, after he'd met Claudia, he had gone to her parents' extended cocktail party every year. How odd, he thought, that he could get to this point in his life and realize he had never sat down to an actual, Norman Rockwell-style Thanksgiving.

The hostess, like a sentinel at her podium, button nose twitching, blond hair piled atop her head, observed Josh as he approached. "You are...Mr. Sherman?" she asked, pencil eraser pressed against her full lower lip, looking down at his name on the chart in front of her. She tilted her head to one side and raised her mascaraed eyes to meet his. "Just one tonight?"

"Just me," he replied, looking back at her.

She scribbled something and told him they were running a few minutes behind. She suggested he wait in the bar, pointing with her pencil. "We'll call you," she said, looking past him to the next group in line. "It won't be long."

The bar seemed intended to evoke one of those old gentleman's clubs from an earlier era, subdued lighting, wood paneling, and oversized leather chairs. There were large potted palms set about, fronds swaying as people went by. A fireplace burning fake logs dominated one side of the room. Half-empty bookshelves were tucked into the far wall. The place was crowded but not uncomfortably so. Josh crossed the room, having spotted a small table in a corner near the fire. He ordered a vodka martini from the waitress who appeared a moment later.

Shortly after his drink arrived, he was approached by an attractive woman, maybe thirty, in a modestly cut, knee-length black dress that accentuated her hips. Her light brown hair, bangs to one side, fell to her shoulders. She saw Josh, smiled, and with an open palm and extended arm, motioned to the empty chair across from him.

Josh smiled back and mimicked the same hand and arm motion, assuming she intended to relocate the chair to another table. But she left it where it was and instead slid in across from him. Leaning forward, she held his gaze and greeted him with an openness, a directness that threw him off. "Are you staying at the hotel?" she asked. "Here on business?"

"No, just dinner. I live in the area." Josh was tentative, wondering what this was about. Was she here in an official capacity? Were they going to offer him a cocktail on the house for having to wait? Or was this something else?

"Oh, so you're here with your family."

"Actually no, just me."

"Oh, okay. The food is great here, you're going to love it." She smiled at him. Josh was struck by her perfectly even white teeth. She asked him his name, and he told her.

"Hi, Josh," she said. "I'm Amanda." She offered her hand and held on to his, squeezing for a moment longer than necessary. Her almond eyes were large, her full lips lightly accented by a pale shade of lipstick. Her makeup was, if anything, understated. She could have passed for a young executive at an accounting firm. Well, way better-looking than your average accounting firm worker, he supposed, but otherwise she more or less fit the profile.

"What do you do, Josh?"

He told her he helped run a marketing company.

"Oh, cool, that sounds interesting."

"It can be."

"You work in the city?"

He told her he did.

"Nice," she said in her friendly, even tone. A moment later, there was this: "Say, I thought you might like some company later. I'm around all evening if that's something that you think might interest you. If not, that's okay too."

"Uh, okay."

"Yeah?" She seemed pleasantly surprised. "Hey, great. So give me your number, and I'll text you. Hit me up if you feel like getting together after your dinner."

"Uh, okay." And, as if in a trance, he did as she requested. He wasn't sure why. Was it because he wanted to have this option for later, even if the chances of his following through were remote? Was it because this modest interaction with Amanda was titillating on its own, even if it went no further? Or was he just trying to get rid of her, and this seemed like the most expedient way to do so? He became conscious of the other people in the bar and he wondered if he were being observed. Surely the bartenders and the waitresses knew who Amanda was, knew what she was up to. She had to be a regular. He had the sense they would go into the back, into the kitchen and laugh about it. *Did you see Amanda hitting on the guy with the vodka martini sitting by himself in the corner?*

He watched as she typed his number into her phone. A moment later, he could feel his own phone buzz in his pocket. Unfortunately, he thought with deadpan humor, that wasn't the only thing in his pocket that was buzzing. That would be a joke he'd save later for James, when he told him about this little encounter. James would appreciate it and laugh heartily. And then call him a wuss for not following through on the opportunity.

Amanda reached under the table, put a hand on Josh's knee, and slid it up the inside of his thigh. "Really a pleasure chatting with you, Josh," she said, maintaining that burning eye contact. Her hand edged a little further. He could feel pressure from her long, manicured fingernails.

Then she was standing. She leaned down to shake hands again, giving Josh a view of her modest cleavage, the border of a black lace bra peeking out. As she glided away, Josh watched to see if she had already spied her next victim. But she was too good, too clever for that. She knew how make him feel special, like he was the one man in this bar she had singled out as worthy of her attention. Whatever transaction was next on her agenda, she wasn't going to execute it in front of him. She faded into the shadows and did not reappear.

A few minutes later, the blond hostess found him and he was ushered into the dining room. Aroused now, he followed her sexy clipped walk, her backside swishing in her tight, narrowly cut business suit. Josh wondered how much the hostess was aware of. Again, he assumed they all knew each other. Did the blond know that he was one of Amanda's marks?

Unlike the bar, the main area was well lit, with more holiday lights strung throughout. He was finally able to locate the string quartet, intently doing their thing with great vigor in a roped-off corner. Josh was seated directly in the center of the big room. There was no place to hide. Everywhere around him were large families, as many as ten or twelve, from babies and toddlers in high chairs to really old geezers, white-haired and shriveled. There were a smattering of couples dotted here and there, but Josh appeared to be the only person dining by himself. Little boys, their hair slicked back, and little girls, in party dresses and bows, ran past him with gleeful, reckless energy and stared as they went by. A few stopped when they got to their parents and whispered, looking over at him. He wanted another drink; it would have relaxed him, but since he would have to drive home, he didn't think it was a good idea.

The prix fixe menu was elaborate and came with a long parade of courses. After the amuse bouche, there seemed to be a lag between each one arriving; when it did, it was delivered with a theatricality that brought further attention to his spot in the middle of the floor. The salad was made tableside, the soup served in a covered silver tureen and poured from a high arc into an intricately designed ceramic bowl. The dramatic flourishes worked well enough for the tables with the big groups. But when it was just one person, the production was ridiculous and way more than he desired. It was too much attention, too over-the-top, too much time. At a certain point, somewhere between the pumpkin ravioli and the turkey dinner with all the trimmings, he had a tremendous impulse to be done with the whole show. He'd already prepaid, and it would have been simple to stand up and walk out, get in his car, and drive home. But then, it occurred to him, this would cause an entirely new scene. So he stayed where he was. He pulled out his phone and looked again at the text from Amanda. She hadn't written anything — what was he expecting her to say? — just her name. Still, he could hardly deny it. Their brief encounter had gotten under his skin. It was audacious, illicit, dirty.

When the main course had finally been cleared, Josh told the waiter he would pass on the multistoried dessert cart that was poised to be wheeled over. He added a tip to the check, relieved to finally be on his way. He loitered for a moment in the hotel lobby thinking he might spot Amanda, but she wasn't around. He went through the big glass doors and handed his ticket to the parking attendant. He looked for her again as he stood under the brightly lit covered awning and waited for his car. Probably upstairs with another client, he thought glumly.

The weather had indeed turned while he had been inside. Snow was falling, or maybe it was actually sleet. The way home was messy and slow, the roads slippery. Driving required his full attention. He felt himself relax when he finally reached his apartment. Inside, he took off his coat and looked again at his phone. His adrenaline surged. Amanda had texted a new message.

Hey, I'm around for the next couple of hours. Hit me back if you want to get together. Really liked chatting with you. A.

Josh was beguiled by her sign off. "A." There was an intimacy to it, as if they were already lovers, like they were sharing something known only to them. There was, he decided, an air about her that was sweet and understated. Classy. Josh stood in the middle of his small living room and weighed the urge to text her back. He could get in the car and be in White Plains again within the hour. He began to rationalize. There wasn't really anything morally wrong with this. Yes, of course, he recognized that what she was doing was illegal, technically, but that was irrelevant as far as he was concerned. They were consenting adults. He was no longer married, at least not in any real sense. So it wasn't like he was cheating. And she certainly seemed to be operating on her own free will. He knew about human trafficking, but this was far from that. She was probably just moonlighting, a kindergarten teacher or a yoga instructor by day. Amanda was someone he could see himself legitimately dating under other circumstances.

He hadn't been with anyone since his separation, and even for a while before that, since he and Claudia had essentially been celibate. So, yeah, duh, big surprise. He craved female company. Up until this moment, he hadn't realized just how desperately he felt that.

He finally convinced himself he would do it. He would text her and drive back over there. But as he considered the actual effort it would take to go through with it, the logistics seemed overwhelming. Driving through the slick, frozen, unplowed streets, getting to the hotel, meeting up with her, getting a room, all of this was daunting. Not to mention having to stop at the ATM on top of it. Not having had much experience in this area, he didn't have a clue what she might charge. Whatever it was, he knew he couldn't afford it. And then there was the energy and stamina required to go through with the act itself, of course. If he just went to bed and jerked off, he would break the spell. And self-abuse would certainly be less complicated, less time-consuming, less expensive, and less morally ambiguous. The more he thought about it, the more that seemed like the appropriate course of action. Tomorrow he would wake up and laugh at himself for his foolishness, his idiocy, over this ridiculous close call.

But then he reread her text, and as he did, he became aroused all over again. He remembered the feel of her hand on his thigh, those nails. Ah, what the hell. He'd had a rough year. An hour or two of fun with a sexy woman he was paying to be nice to him? It didn't sound bad at all. On the contrary, it sounded like exactly what he needed.

Now that he had made his decision, he was all in. He tingled with nervous energy, his shallow breath coming in short gasps. He felt incredibly awake. He brushed his teeth, wiped his mouth, then brushed them again. He decided he would get in his car and text her just as he was leaving so he could give her an accurate estimate of when he might arrive. He knew enough to know he shouldn't ask her about her rates via text. He'd have to get enough cash to make sure he was covered.

He went downstairs and, hands shaking, pulled his keys out of his pocket. When he reached the street, he could see that the sleet or snow, or whatever it was, was falling harder. Driving in this was not going to be fun. He carefully lifted his feet through the slush, his steps muffled and heavy. As he clambered in and settled behind the wheel, his phone buzzed again. *Jesus*, he thought, *she's nothing if not persistent.* He wondered what she would say now. Maybe she had sent him something a little suggestive, to prime him, get him in the mood. He started the engine, turned on the defroster, and looked at the message.

He was staggered by what he read. The text wasn't from Amanda. It was from Erin.

Hey, thanks for the holiday greetings. Happy T-Day to you too. Don't overdo it on the turkey. C U in a few weeks. Getting excited to blow R & C's minds!! R U ready??? Consider it done!!

He sat in the blackness, the wet snow dropping all around. It was thick enough now that he couldn't see much beyond the arc of his headlights. He sighed. In an instant, his moment had passed. He was both let down and relieved.

Back upstairs, he tried to think of an appropriate response to Erin. It had to be warm and witty, but it couldn't appear that he'd put too much thought into it. Something breezy, off-the-cuff. And funny. Definitely needed the humor. Now was not the time, though. He was suddenly exhausted, and he had nothing clever to say. He'd wait until tomorrow to respond. He looked at his phone again and smiled at something he'd missed the first time he'd read Erin's text. It was the way she'd ended it: *E.*

ALAN WINNIKOFF

PART TWO

SEVENTEEN

Chunky fingers like little sausages clasped around the back of his neck, elbows akimbo, eyes nearly shut, James tilted in his chair and exhaled. Something resembling a smile tugged at his thin lips. Observing this moment of repose, Josh mused silently that this was as close to meditative as James was likely capable of. And, indeed, it didn't last long. After a few seconds, James snapped back, flicking his fine, straight hair away from his forehead, a signature gesture Josh knew so well, though that hair, once the color of straw, had, over the years, gone mostly white. *God*, thought Josh, noting the crow's feet around his boss's eyes, the vertical lines pulling at the jowly skin around his mouth. *We're getting old. Funny how that works. Age kind of creeps up on you incrementally, so gradual you don't even notice. Until suddenly, one day, it just totally kicks your ass.*

With a conspiratorial look, James opened a drawer at the side of his desk, lifted out a small stack of red plastic Solo cups, and, with great deliberation, lined them up, as if preparing for a game of three-card monte. Silently, with that same impish smirk, like a kid getting away with something, his hand disappeared into the drawer again, this time emerging with an amber bottle that he gripped by its neck. Still taking his time, he unscrewed the top and poured generous shots into each cup.

"We've earned this," he said with his crooked smile, breaking the silence. He handed a cup to Erin, lifting his own to her in a silent toast. Then, turning to Josh, arm extended, half rising, he said in a beckoning tone that was vaguely challenging, "For you, my friend. And don't tell me you don't drink Scotch. You're in."

It was true Josh couldn't stand whiskey of any kind, which James, of course, was well aware of. It was also true that it was not yet three in the afternoon, and Josh still had work to do. But he knew better than to protest. This was a command performance. Opting out was not an option.

On the one hand, there was just cause for this celebratory moment; the Shoe King presentation had concluded minutes earlier, and LAKreativ had nailed it. Yet, at the same time, a murky, worrisome uncertainty hung stubbornly in the air.

Shoe King: The Game was Ryan and Courtney's vision brought to life. It had multiple levels and rewards, and the players, or more precisely their alter-ego shoe avatars, were able to compete directly against, and engage with, other avatars in real time, just as Ryan had envisioned it at that earlier meeting the day of Bob's passing. Erin had set up iPads around the conference room so everyone could livestream with her team back in L.A. Looking fetching in a sleeveless mid-length, lightly patterned dark green dress that complimented her eyes behind her distinctive black-rimmed glasses, Erin was the MC, narrating as they went along. Josh thought her masterful — engaging, charming, authoritative.

Though Courtney had demurred — "I'm not a gamer," she had insisted in a way that made clear her declaration was not up for debate — Ryan had been excited to play.

Once you decided on your avatar, the app prompted you and provided the necessary tools to name it, write its backstory, and design its look. Erin's lead programmer, Chris, blond, sun-bleached dreadlocks, white t-shirt and thin, scruffy beard, had dubbed himself Spidey Power Sandal, a superhero surfer with the ability to tame the awesome-est of waves. Kerry, petite with big eyes, in a tank top and a lot of tattoos and piercings, was Open-Toed Ophelia, a beat poet and rapper who spun rhymes that dazzled and amazed. And Greg, bearish and hirsute, a mass of red hair covering his head and face so that only his eyes and mouth appeared uncovered, was Re-Boot, survivalist, outdoorsman, and conqueror of the sheerest cliff faces and mightiest mountain peaks.

Josh was initially puzzled by these avatar personalities; they were so cheesy and goofy. But then it dawned on him what Erin was going for. If these L.A. hipsters had gone all in and been true to their full-on, cooler-than-thou hipster-ish instincts, they would have come off as, at best, remote and off-putting. And smug and superior didn't win over clients. Instead, by making their avatars silly and ridiculous, rather than trying to be ultra-cool, the intensity level in the room dropped precipitously. It allowed everyone else to be equally silly, to relax and feel as if they were all on the same side. Watching Erin orchestrate this whole thing, Josh found himself shaking his head admiringly. It was quite brilliant, really.

The start of the demonstration was delayed for a few minutes as Ryan pondered options for his own avatar name. He self-consciously threw out a couple of ideas, looking pleadingly to his sister for help. Finally, under pressure to come up with something, he fell back on his roots, settling, rather prosaically, thought Josh, on SKNYC Ryan. One hand resting against his cheek, fingers digging into his ever-present three-day stubble, Ryan hunched forward, leaning over the iPad, absorbed, grinning, and, on occasion, cackling loudly.

James and Josh, exchanging glances, hung back, observing the scene as it played out. Beaming from under her black bangs and heavy eyeliner, Courtney seemed happy to see her brother happy. The chair at the far end of the table, near the windows, where Bob had always sat, was left empty. No one said anything, but no one had to. It struck Josh that Bob was more present in his absence than he'd been when he'd been present, at least in recent months.

The players in L.A. had been well coached by Erin. They obviously knew their game; they had built it, after all. But they were also fully prepared to engage Ryan. They came across as laid-back, at times nearly somnolent, but they were also, perhaps deceptively, hyperfocused on the task at hand. They made Ryan feel that he was a welcome part of their crowd. "Dude, you're awesome," one of them had burst out with a nasal bellow when Ryan had successfully achieved another level. The development team made little attempt to disguise that their apparent bursts of spontaneity and bonding were, in reality, well-coordinated and rehearsed, a carefully planned setup. The entire room, Ryan included, quickly picked up on this. But he ate it up anyway. He didn't seem to care, or perhaps he simply couldn't resist.

After the gameplay had wrapped, Erin reminded everyone that the app was still in beta and not yet ready for prime time. Chris and the other designers offered further details about how it would play when all the bugs were worked out, applications added, and the final build launched. Ryan, adrenalized, foot tapping under the table, now deferred to his sister who, with chilly efficiency, took center stage, peppering the team with questions. She kept coming back to timing and deadlines. She wanted specific guarantees on when they could actually go live. Erin assured her they'd be working straight through over the Christmas holidays. But, she added cautiously, in the interest of total transparency, she couldn't promise delivery by the January first deadline the twins had mandated.

"As you can see," Erin said. "There are a lot of layers. We're close, but we don't want to give you anything that is less than perfect. If it takes a couple of more weeks than we'd planned for, I think we'd all agree it's worth the wait."

"That's okay," Ryan blurted, looking up from the iPad he was still exploring. He glanced across the table toward Courtney and added, "We're both going to be away anyway. I'm going skiing in Banff starting on Monday, and my sister will be in Italy. Why don't we touch base that first week back after New Year's?"

But Courtney wouldn't let it go. Her face tightened, and she pursed her lips. "We need a hard deadline from you," she insisted, gray eyes narrowing. "We have to be able to promote the live date. Our in-house promotions team needs lead time. We need to coordinate with all of our stores. We can't let this slip. You've known we've been aiming for a first of January launch for quite a while. You've known that. I'm confused. I don't understand why you would wait until now to tell us that you won't make it in time."

Erin blanched and swallowed, momentarily thrown off by Courtney's aggressive stance. But she took a breath, nodded, and quickly regained her equilibrium, confidently assuring Courtney she would take another look and see if they could shave some days off the development schedule.

The meeting was turning, an edgy tension swiftly escalating. Courtney, unappeased, continued to push while Erin diplomatically refused to commit, unwilling to be locked into something she knew she likely wouldn't be able to hold to. Someone else might have handled the situation differently, Josh considered, watching, but that wasn't Erin's style. Alarmed by this shift in tone, James took control, the adult in the room, moving with authority to reassure, smooth over, and wrap up. There had been such strong positivity during the demonstration of the app; they couldn't allow that to dissipate.

"We'll figure it out," Ryan said, pushing away from the table, pulling on his sheepskin coat, suddenly the reasonable one, the conciliator. "As long as it's as awesome as it appears to be, we'll find a way to make the dates work."

Courtney turned to Erin. "Let's talk later," she said curtly. "I'll call you."

Now it was Josh who had reason to be alarmed. This was not protocol. The clients didn't do calls directly with the creative team. That wasn't how it worked. The James Gang was the agency of record; they were the ones who subcontracted LAKreativ. They owned the client relationship, and Josh was the project manager, the point person. Everyone had always understood that and had always respected that it was the order of things. Otherwise there would be chaos. Josh was forced to intervene.

"I can talk to you about it, Courtney," he said with a forced glibness. "Happy to go over the launch calendar with you. Maybe we can speak tomorrow?"

Courtney stared at him blankly from under her dark bangs. "That's okay," she said after a long beat. Then, echoing her brother, she added, "We'll figure it out."

In the doorway of the conference room, clearly anxious to be done, James nodded toward Josh and Erin and told them he'd do a debrief with them in his office. "I'll join you there in a minute. Just let me walk these charming folks to the elevator first."

And so there they were, reveling in some version of a victory lap, drinking Scotch in the middle of a Tuesday afternoon. Josh remained unsettled. He had assumed he wasn't the only one feeling this way. But now he wasn't quite so sure.

"Don't get the wrong idea, Erin," James said as he sipped from his plastic cup. "This is not a daily occurrence around here. But today deserves special recognition. They gave us a ridiculous assignment with an impossible deadline, and you fuckin' killed it."

Erin ducked her head, thick hair falling across her face, and said, with a small smile and a quick glance toward Josh, "It's a team effort."

"Nah," Josh said, breaking into a grin in spite of his unease, warmed by Erin's look. "She's just being modest. She gets all the credit."

"Well, I love all the humility," said James. "It's very endearing. But honestly, I don't really give two shits who gets what. All I know is that what I watched just now fucking rocked. I haven't seen Ryan that aroused since I took him to the Victoria's Secret fashion show when he was eleven."

Josh put his cup to his lips and held it there. He would have liked to have diluted it with some water, or at least an ice cube. But James drank his Scotch neat, and so, for today at least, did everyone else. His party, his rules.

Already falling behind, Josh watched James pour out second shots for himself and Erin. Josh was somewhat relieved when Erin held up a hand. "This will be it for me," she said with that same half smile. "I have a couple of conference calls and some other stuff I still have to do."

There was a knock on the door, and Ashley breezed in with James's mail. She eyed the bottle on the desk as she handed over a small stack of envelopes wrapped in a rubber band. With an apology for the interruption, she told James there were a couple of the things he'd been waiting for. "Thought you'd want to know they came," she said with her usual dry efficiency.

"Thanks, Ash." James quickly riffled through the letters, pulling out one and tossing the others aside. He called to her as she was crossing the room. "You want to join us for a drink?"

Ashley stopped as she was reaching for the door and turned back around. "Sure," she said, her sharp features softening. "I won't say no if you're offering." Her eyes touched on the three of them with their plastic cups in hand. "Am I safe to assume this means it went well?"

Ashley was small-boned, with a long, straight nose, thin lips, and close-set eyes. She reminded Josh of a bird, though with her multihued hair, dangling silver jewelry, and thrift shop chic sensibility, she was a bird with a singular style. Cradling her cup in both hands, she settled in, leaning against the credenza behind James's desk. The framed photo of James and Bob laughing, arms wrapped around each other, loomed over her shoulder.

James peered into his own cup for a long time. He swirled the contents, as if he might find some answers there. Finally, he lifted his head. "To be honest with you guys, I'm way beyond trying to predict what those two — our poor little orphan waif clients — are thinking. I don't even think they know what they want. But that's to figure out later. Right now we're celebrating this moment of triumph. You know how Ryan was saying we're cookie cutter and not creative and all of the rest of that bullshit? It pissed me off — as I know it did the rest of you." James turned the cup again in his hand. He took a long, thoughtful swallow before continuing. "You know, at a certain point, it stops mattering if Tweedledee and Tweedledum out there can't recognize that that demo was totally kick-ass. We know what we're capable of. And, really, right now, for me, that's the most important thing. In this business, sometimes you wind up doing this shit more for yourself. Sometimes that winds up mattering more. If you want to keep your sanity, that is. And when you pull it off, it's worth taking a moment."

"Yep," said Erin, appearing a bit heavy-lidded. "Totally. There are definitely times when that's the best way to look at it. Today was a good reminder."

But Josh's unease was unabated. Though this self-congratulatory back-patting was all well and good, it didn't sit right with him. He thought James sounded resigned, fatalistic, checked out. It was so unlike him, it was deeply troubling, not to mention deflating. Was this some sort of thinly veiled valedictory message as James prepared to ride off into the sunset to embark on his grand Plan B? Had he stopped caring? Josh couldn't accept it, not here, not from James.

Though they were close in many ways, Josh had learned to maintain a certain wariness around his boss. He knew James could be touchy when challenged, especially if there were other people around. More often than not, Josh held back. But now he was irked. The little bit of Scotch seemed to have been enough to loosen his tongue.

"I understand where you're coming from," Josh began. Aware he'd been slouching, he pulled himself up in his chair and leaned forward before continuing. "And sure, it's a satisfying fuck-you to a client that undoubtedly deserves a poke in the eye. At the least. I'm not going to say it doesn't feel good. But don't you think this celebration is a bit premature? I mean, what are we doing here?" He paused and gestured toward the bottle on James's desk. "What is all this anyway? Feeling warm and fuzzy about ourselves doesn't pay the bills. We still need to eat."

There was a stillness in the room, the air heavy with anticipation. Josh could sense Erin watching him steadily. He shot a quick look over at Ashley, cup resting against her lower lip, her blank stare unreadable. Shifting back to James, Josh saw his eyes flatten, one side of his mouth twisted. There was something Josh found validating about this particular expression, as if he sensed James taking a certain satisfaction, perhaps even amusement, in hearing Josh so out of character, so defiantly contrary.

On the other side of the wall, they heard a sudden short burst of laughter, then footsteps fading as the front door slammed. Then the office grew quiet again.

James lifted his cup toward Josh. "This is also true," he said finally with a low growl. "Give the man credit for keeping it real. For shining a light" — a beat — " —into the darkness."

* * *

They had set up Erin at an empty desk at the far end of the open floor, and she spent the remainder of the afternoon there, head down, buried in her laptop or on her phone. It was well after seven when she finally reemerged, rapping gently on the door jamb of Josh's small, un-windowed office. It was just the two of them by this point, Ashley and the rest of the James Gang's small team having packed it in an hour or so before. James had departed even earlier, not long after the Scotch-infused debrief had broken up.

"Are you staying?" Erin asked, computer bag on her shoulder, hooded gray parka already buttoned. That same colorful scarf, the one he remembered from their dinner all those months ago, flowed out from the top of her coat, covering her throat.

"Nah. I'm out of here too. I think we've done enough damage for one day." Josh's shoulders lifted, then dropped. "It's been an interesting one, that's for sure. I'll walk you out." He asked where she was headed.

"Going back to the apartment, I guess. Take my time. Meander. You know me, I love just walking around when I'm here."

Erin had mentioned earlier that she had lucked into an available apartment on lower Fifth, near Washington Square Park. The tenant was a friend of a friend of a friend. Somehow, through connections, the place had fallen into her lap. All Erin knew about the guy who lived there was that his name was Russell, and he was a photographer on extended assignment in India.

"I have that meeting in Brooklyn tomorrow about the new job," she said as Josh turned off his computer and pushed away from his desk. "So I guess I should prep a bit for that."

"Cool," Josh said. "Did you ever get any more sense of those guys, the company culture, all that stuff you were wondering about?"

"Not so much, to be honest. I've talked to a few people, but it seems mixed. We'll see what happens. I'm not meeting with them until tomorrow night, actually. They're taking me to dinner." Erin looked at Josh. "Do you think that's a weird way to do a job interview?"

"No, not really," Josh replied. "On the contrary, it probably means they're serious about you. Otherwise they'd just wedge you into an open half hour at some point during the day. You should take it as a good sign."

"I guess. I've never done a dinner interview before."

"At least you'll get a good meal out of it," he said with a hopeful grin.

"I should be so lucky. There's so many Brooklyn restaurants I've heard about, read about, that I've always wanted to try." Erin watched Josh lock the office door. "I'm thinking of heading out there early tomorrow, giving myself some time to explore, play tourist," she went on. They reached the elevator. "I'm kind of just looking forward to seeing where the day takes me."

For a tantalizing moment, Josh was swept up by a desire to invite himself to go along. He ached to explore Brooklyn with her and thought for a long moment about how he could make it happen. But reality quickly set in. He had a packed schedule, and there was no way he'd be able to get away. He said instead, "Let me know if you need suggestions.

Don't want you wandering into some sketchy areas that have yet to be pacified for the tourists."

Erin laughed. "I think I'll manage. I have this really great app that tells you everything. I'll be fine."

Out on the street, Erin suddenly stopped to face him.

"How are you doing with your kids, Josh? Your daughter? I've been wanting to ask you."

"Um, you know, it's okay. It's hard. One day at a time, as always, I guess."

"Are you getting to see them as much as you want?"

"Oh, yeah, of course. Claudia and I have it worked out. I'll always make sure I'm, you know, a part of their lives. They stay over with me sometimes. I miss them, though." There was a long silence, and they started walking again. "It's hard," he repeated. "But it's reality. At least as reality is currently constituted. "

Erin angled her head and shot him a puzzled look. She started to respond but then seemed to change her mind. They reached the corner of Fifth Avenue, and Josh hesitated. But Erin, barely breaking stride, turned south and kept going, and so, though neither of them said anything, it seemed natural for him to accompany her. They continued quietly for a block or so. Erin was distracted, looking up, studying the triangular Flatiron Building on its triangular piece of Manhattan real estate.

"Orphan waifs," Josh said after they'd crossed 23rd Street.

"What?"

"I was just thinking. He called them orphan waifs. James. He called Ryan and Courtney orphan waifs. But they're not orphans. They have a mother, and she's still alive and kicking."

"This is your takeaway from the day we just had?"

"Well, it kind of got stuck in my brain when he said it. I knew it wasn't right. You didn't pick up on that?"

Chuckling, Erin pushed playfully against his shoulder. "All right, Josh. I'm glad we got that straightened out, at least."

A few moments later, Erin's tone changed. "I actually am a bit worried about Courtney, though," she said. "She can be fairly unreasonable about those deadlines. Expecting us to build a gaming app in three months...it's been a bit crazy."

"'Unreasonable' is a kind way to put it, I'd say. James thinks they're in over their heads, that they're panicking."

"It's hard to argue with that. I know you don't agree, but I think James has the right attitude. At a certain point when it comes to crazy clients, you have to let it go. Otherwise it will eat away at you until you're as crazy as they are." Erin peered at Josh from under her hood, wide, dark eyes flashing behind her glasses. "Sometimes I have to just remind myself that people like Courtney are so wrapped up in their own shit, they don't even see us as people. We're just a vessel — there to provide a means to an end."

"You're right. Of course. But that's still so depressing. I don't know. The way James was in his office today...it was deflating. It was so unlike him. Dealing with crazy clients is what we do every day. Letting it go, as you say...it just feels like giving up, like we're letting them win. James has always looked at business as an intellectual challenge, like deconstructing and then solving some really complicated puzzle. That's always been the fun part for him, the part that he's really good at."

Below 14th Street, the graceful curves of the white marble Washington Square arch began to come into focus, partially obscured by gray, leafless tree branches hanging over from the sidewalk's edge into the avenue. A few blocks later, Erin stopped and turned to Josh. "Oops. Almost walked right by it. This is it. Pretty nifty, right?"

A moderately sized apartment house with a red brick facing, the building was not much different than countless others in New York. Still, it wasn't difficult to imagine the appeal for someone like Erin, with her outsider's highly charged, romanticized notion of New York City.

They stood under a beige awning, faded and discolored from its years of absorbing whatever the city had to throw at it. "Do you want to come up and check it out?" Erin asked. "Russell has — how shall I put this? — very specific tastes in décor. He's got this whole Asian thing going on. Kinda cool in its way, but a bit thematic for my tastes." She had turned away from Josh and was staring into the lobby. A doorman in a burgundy cap, hands behind his back, observed them impassively from the other side of the glass.

"Does he have any Scotch?"

Erin turned back. She studied Josh's face, then slowly broke into a wide grin. "Seriously?"

Josh shook his head and laughed. "No. Definitely not. I'd probably puke."

"Not in Russell's apartment, please. I might have a hard time explaining that one."

Huddled in their coats, hands buried deep in their pockets, they lifted their feet and stomped in place once or twice as a dry winter wind kicked up and cut through them. The endless New York street scene churned all around; wide-eyed NYU students blended with tourists taking pictures with their phones, while a few ragged, aging hippy denizens of Washington Square shuffled past. They could hear music, a guitar and some sort of hollow percussion, drifting faintly out of the park.

"Could I entice you with a glass of wine?" Erin asked after a minute.

"Russell's wine?"

"Why not? Let's live dangerously."

Josh thought about her offer for a long moment.

She waited.

"You sure you don't need to get ready for tomorrow?"

"Like I said, it's a dinner meeting." One eyebrow lifted. "I could stay out until dawn and totally rage and still be good to go."

"Is that the plan?" he asked.

"Not unless you're offering to be my escort."

"I'm old, remember? A quiet glass of wine in Russell's nifty Asian-themed apartment might be more my style."

EIGHTEEN

Just past sunrise, on a frigid, cloudless morning not long before Christmas, Claudia set out for a drive that would take her across New Jersey, nearly to the Pennsylvania border. She was to interview a retired boxer who, still in his forties, was showing signs of early dementia. Claudia's company had been hired by a medical nonprofit that was fighting for better regulations and protections for athletes in violent sports. Claudia was apprehensive about the meeting; though by now she'd spoken several times by phone with the man's wife, she had been unable to get a clear read on how functional the guy was. The woman had sounded tentative, taciturn. Claudia's assignment on this first encounter was to assess how well the boxer could handle an on-camera interview. The plan, if all went well, was to return after the holidays with her video crew to shoot a piece that their client intended to use as the cornerstone of their advocacy program.

For a long while, she plowed slowly ahead, edging farther west until she was finally able to pick up speed, breaking free of the thick traffic that seemed to flow endlessly in every direction through suburban New Jersey. Claudia kept her focus on the physical act of driving. She watched the exit signs flash by, attuned to the voice of her GPS prompting her with its next set of instructions. Long drives were never easy for her. Over the years, she had developed coping mechanisms. She had learned to compartmentalize, power through, go on autopilot as much as possible. It was the best way for her to overcome the inevitable anxiety that would grip her as soon as she got out onto the open highway. It had been this way for her since college.

During her junior year at Brown, Claudia had accepted a last-minute invitation from her roommate Meg to accompany her on a spring break trip to Nashville, where Meg planned to spend the week with her friend Olivia at Vanderbilt. Claudia had never met Olivia and knew nothing about her but, as it happened, she had no other spring break plans. Claudia had done the sloppy drunken thing on South Padre Island the year before and, while she'd had fun and had no regrets, once was enough. She had no particular urge to relive the binge drinking, the relentless, aggressively swarming boys, and the overcrowded hotel room that by week's end stank of sweaty bodies, sex, and vomit. So she eagerly took up Meg on her offer, and they spent the week in much more comfortable surroundings, exploring Nashville, listening to live music and hanging out with Olivia, who Claudia discovered she liked very much; they bonded over their common interest in literature and the arts. Meg, a pre-med major, was more inclined to view the world through the eyes of a scientist. Before the visit ended, Claudia and Olivia pledged to see each other again.

On their way back to the East Coast, somewhere in the middle of West Virginia, while Claudia dozed in the passenger seat, Meg lost control of the car at what the state police would estimate to be in excess of ninety miles an hour. They slid off the highway, rolled down an embankment, and smashed into a tree. Claudia woke up in a local hospital with a concussion, a shattered hip, and a lot of painful cuts and bruises. After surgery and a couple of days to emerge from the shock and the anesthesia, it was left to her mother, who had been keeping a bedside vigil, to break the news that Meg had been killed instantly. Claudia had no memory of what had transpired at the moment of the accident. Had Meg swerved suddenly or looked away for a moment or just been spacing out? Had something spooked her? There was no way to know, not then, not ever.

Claudia went home to recover and did not return to school until the following fall. By then, of course, everyone knew who she was and what she'd been through. Some people went to ridiculous lengths to avoid any mention of her ordeal, while others were extremely direct and asked pointed, at times almost comically awkward unfiltered questions. Claudia's senior year was a struggle as she was forced to cope with her unwanted notoriety as "that girl." She mourned for her friend, as well as for the loss of a major part of her own identity; her injuries, among other things, had put to an end any aspirations she might have had for continuing her dance career.

After graduation, Claudia moved to the city with Jen; to her great relief, she was able to regain her anonymity and, to some degree, successfully reinvent herself. Yet there were those times when she did find herself talking about the accident. It wasn't often and it was never without pain, but if she felt sufficiently close to someone, at some point it seemed necessary. As much as she wished it hadn't, the accident had forever put its stamp on her, defined her. There was no way around it. If you wanted to know Claudia, understand her soul, you needed to know that this had happened to her.

As time went on, Claudia became aware of a troubling pattern to these conversations. Invariably, it seemed, at some point the other person would nod knowingly and say something to the effect of: *Life turns in an instant. You just never know how much time you have.* Then that person would snap their fingers for emphasis. Claudia came to dread the moment of the finger snap, to the point where she found herself holding her breath and cringing as she waited for the sharp click and pop. Only when she heard it did she allow herself to exhale.

And so it came time for Marcus to hear her story. It was on that Saturday after Thanksgiving when they had the day to themselves. They could have done any of a million things, but as it happened, they wound up spending the afternoon in bed, their heated bodies intertwined as a cold rain splattered against Claudia's bedroom window. This was extraordinary in itself, she marveled at the time — and again later. How long had it been since she had had sex in the afternoon? Years? Decades? Certainly not since her kids had been born and likely not for a long time before that. There were, clearly, certain tangible benefits to a new relationship that simply couldn't be replicated.

Claudia lay across Marcus, eyes closed, breasts pressed lightly across his hairy chest, listening to his steady breathing, inhaling his musky scent. She was drowsy, at peace, dare she say content, trying to hold on to this feeling, though she knew even while in it that it would be fleeting, ephemeral, like trying to catch water.

Musing lazily over ideas for places they could travel to together, they amused each other by conjuring fantasies about getting on a plane and exploring some far away locale. This led to reminisces of memorable trips they'd taken. Marcus told of his extended pre-grad school trek through the Rocky Mountains, where he and several friends had explored the backroads of Colorado and Utah, hiking and climbing fourteen-thousand-foot peaks. Claudia was reminded of her South Padre Island adventure, and they both laughed as she described the disgusting hotel room that somehow, at that point in her life, had seemed perfectly adequate, even normal. Finally, with some reluctance, Claudia came around to the ill-fated drive with Meg. She spoke slowly, in broken sentences, choking up at points as she always did. When she stopped talking, she waited for Marcus to say something about seizing the moment and how life can turn on a dime. She tensed, waiting for the finger snap.

But it never came. Marcus held Claudia tightly and was silent for a long time. Then she heard him say, in a soft mumble, "It hardens you."

Claudia lifted herself up and looked into Marcus's eyes, at that moment a particularly vivid robin's egg blue. No one had ever responded to her story in this way. Many years before, when she'd told Josh about the accident, he also hadn't snapped his fingers or proffered platitudes — thankfully. But, typical of Josh, he hadn't said much of anything else either. He'd explained later he hadn't replied more forcefully, more vocally, because he was processing. He needed time to think about what she'd told him. Not good enough, she remembered thinking at the time. Not good enough. There are some instances in life when you don't process; you react. His response, or lack thereof, was maddening and wholly inadequate, but as she would discover in the ensuing years, that experience pretty much summed up what it felt like to be married to Josh.

Now, here was Marcus with a response Claudia had not anticipated but instantly knew was exactly the right thing. Sensing a breakthrough, she needed more. Pensive, but with a note of urgency, she pushed him to elaborate.

"I just mean, you go through something like that, you are going to go one of two ways," Marcus said, facing her, propped up on an elbow. "You can break down and no longer be able to cope with the world. Hopefully that doesn't happen. So instead you get tougher, so stuff can no longer pierce you as easily. Which is good in some ways, maybe. But it also means it's harder to let go, to allow yourself to feel."

"Is that what happened to you?"

"Sure, of course. I'm still fighting it. After Debbie died, I was so acutely conscious of that shell settling on top of me. It takes a lot to make that fall away. To allow it to happen. If I didn't have my kids to take care of...I don't know what would have become of me. I might have shut off the world completely. But I couldn't afford to do that. And I'm grateful I didn't because, if I had, I might not have found you."

Warmed by this, Claudia kissed him, then pulled back so she could see his face. "I guess it can also mean, hopefully, that you no longer sweat the small stuff," she said. "You gain perspective. The little things don't matter as much, you don't let those things aggravate you."

Marcus replied, "Perhaps. Unless you become so subsumed by the annoying small stuff that each micro aggravation feels suffocating and overwhelming. It can just as easily turn in that direction."

"But there's also the good small stuff," Claudia countered. "Those little life moments of grace, of beauty. Those are the things we need to pay attention to, right? The small good things you experience every day that can't be taken for granted — or shouldn't be. They're so easy to overlook."

"Or to dismiss as being self-indulgent, not worthy of our attention somehow," Marcus added.

Now, as she drove across western New Jersey's barren, snow-splotched winter landscape, hands on the wheel, part of her brain intent on the strip of road in front of her, the other part somewhere far away, she thought about that fateful drive with Meg, but also about Marcus feeling his way through his grief in the weeks and months following Debbie's passing. She wondered, not for the first time, where the line was. How do you stay resilient but still remain open to what you want to feel, what you need to feel, those small life moments? She was well aware her tough skin had toughened further since Amy's diagnosis. In her experience, this was true of most special needs parents. You're thrown into something that cuts to your core. Your child is damaged, but you need to keep going. The shell descends. It becomes protection, a way to prevent the pain of daily life from seeping in. If you didn't have that default, you'd be a wreck, a nonfunctioning basket case. To Marcus's point, there was also the risk of becoming either numbed or overwhelmed by the thousands of tiny details. Even today, on her way to meet a man who was suffering from brain damage, Claudia had to search within herself to find that balance, that formula for putting it all into boxes, for staying coolly professional while still keeping her heart open.

She knew Marcus well enough at this point to be able to recognize that his wounds extended beyond losing Debbie. He'd once told Claudia, almost casually, that getting punched in the face by your father before your tenth birthday left you with a stark choice — it forced you to either fall apart or grow up. She had been horrified at the time, but now she was better able to see how his chaotic, at times terrifying upbringing was an essential part of making Marcus the finished product he had ultimately become — or at least to the extent that anyone can ever be finished. His adult self bore the imprint of his experience with his father and then, later, the loss of Debbie. Claudia's imprint was Meg, and now Amy. And, of course, the divorce. Claudia and Marcus hadn't been through exactly the same things. And yet they shared something. And, thankfully, it was light years from her mother's friend Elaine and her widow's club to which she had so morbidly and clumsily welcomed Marcus on Thanksgiving.

"We have to do this for each other," she'd said to Marcus after a long silence on that rainy afternoon while they lounged in her bed.

"Do what exactly?" he'd asked, sounding distracted, or perhaps just extremely relaxed. He was tenderly, absently, stroking the white, jagged scar along the curve of her hip. Claudia was, for a moment, self-conscious of her stretch marks, patches of cellulite. But she made herself let that go.

"Oh, you know," she said. "Chip away at those shells. Each other's shells." She snorted a small laugh. "Crack those motherfuckers into a million pieces. Allow ourselves those moments of grace. We have the right to take some happiness out of this screwed-up life."

As it turned out, the interview with the boxer went better than she had anticipated. Claudia's nervousness about the man's level of cognition had proven to be unfounded. He was charming and funny, his warm smile lighting up a round, puffy face, dark, knowing eyes crinkling under thick, scarred brows.

But later, as Claudia was saying her goodbyes to his wife, the two of them standing close together on the creaky, weather worn wooden porch, the woman expressed concern.

"He seems to slip a bit more each day," she said in a low, distracted voice, staring off across a stubbly field toward the narrow strip of highway beyond, specks of cars sliding silently by. The woman had walked out of the house wearing only a thin sweater. She tugged at it, wrapping it tighter around her shoulders. "I don't know if I can handle the long-term care. Long-term, that is."

Claudia heard a bitter, mirthless chuckle. The woman seemed to want to open up; it occurred to Claudia that she probably didn't have many people to talk to.

"You don't know what you can handle until you have to handle it," Claudia said. "You find strength. Besides, right now he seems to be doing pretty well. Better than I'd been led to believe."

"He has his good days. He was excited that you were coming. But I pick up on things in him other people don't."

"I'm sure that's true." Claudia was growing uncomfortable. She didn't want to be sucked into an emotional conversation. It wasn't that she didn't feel empathy. She did. Perhaps too much.

"Tell me how you do that. How do you make yourself stronger than you are?"

"I can't answer that," Claudia said. "You have to find it in yourself. But what I can tell you is that you have no idea what you are capable of until it's right in front of you."

"You sound like you speak from experience," the boxer's wife said, her small eyes searching Claudia's face. The woman wore her dark, shoulder-length hair parted in the middle; the late afternoon winter light caught gray roots against her scalp.

"Somewhat." Claudia thought again that she didn't have the bandwidth to do this. She had enough of her own shit to deal with. She couldn't take on someone else's, someone she didn't even know.

"Look," Claudia said. "The whole reason I'm here is that we want to try and get your story — your husband's story — out there. So that people can learn from this, and we can protect others, other athletes who are at risk. That's why you agreed to be interviewed, right? You said you wanted this, that you wanted your voice to be heard."

"I do. I want to...to help. I know how important it is. But it doesn't do anything for us...for our own...situation."

"You're doing a good thing. Both of you are. It's important. It's meaningful. Not everyone is able to contribute like this, in such a tangible way, to the...the greater good."

A sudden gust rattled the house. Claudia impulsively took the woman's small pink hands in hers, holding them there for a long beat. Then she stepped off the porch and crunched across the gravel driveway. She reached her car, looking over as she slid into the front seat; the boxer's wife was leaning against the house, back pressed against the dull eggshell tinted siding. Above her, just below a second-floor window, one of the rain gutters dangled at an awkward angle. The woman put a hand on the flimsy screen door, turned back toward the driveway, and waved, a diminished, nearly motionless gesture. From behind the wheel, Claudia returned the wave. Then she picked up her phone, punched in her GPS, and started the car. It was a long drive back, and she needed to focus.

NINETEEN

In the days that followed, his inner voice was harsh, stinging, brimming with contempt, with ridicule.

Oh, Josh, little man, man of limited imagination, of lowest expectations. You know it's only a matter of time, and likely soon, before she finds you out, your weaknesses, your shortcomings, your dull spirit and dulled soul revealed. How long do you think you can keep this up, this charade, this pretense?

That was the voice that predominated, that rang in his head, tormenting him mercilessly. And yet, in the midst of this relentless onslaught, there were also those occasional brighter moments. If he'd had enough sleep and was fully caffeinated, perhaps after a hard hour of cardio in the gym, his fog of self-loathing, his absolute conviction that this ill-advised romantic venture was doomed to an ugly end, would temporarily lift. It was during these times, infrequent though they were, that a certain buoyancy took hold and he began to believe that perhaps there was a way after all, a path forward. At these moments he was renewed, reborn to the possibility that life, even his small, prosaic life, had a capacity for enchantment, for that bit of magic he had long simply assumed, in his middle-aged malaise, had become as unattainable as fairy dust. Who would have imagined that fate, his unflagging nemesis, would allow even this bit of light to shine through?

When summoning images of their night together, he would invariably return first to the moment of the sleeveless green dress slipping from her shoulders, dropping in slow motion and coming to rest atop the cream-colored Chinese rug dotted with finely drawn leafy dwarf trees. It seemed implausible that this could be the same dress Erin had worn when presenting the Shoe King app to Ryan and Courtney hours earlier, the dress she'd worn while sipping Scotch in James's office. She had been clothed then, and now she was not. That alone was an astounding thing to contemplate. And yet there she was, standing before him in Russell's Asian-themed bedroom with the blue and white porcelain lamps and the platform bed, bare-shouldered, bare-bellied, white skin illuminated by a thin shaft of light spilling in from the living room through the open doorway. Josh gently touched those wonderfully wide hips, then slid his hands underneath the thin elastic band that ran along her waist, to something softer, smoother, warmer. She leaned into him; he tasted wine — Russell's wine — on her tongue.

For so long, his entire breadth of experience had been Claudia's slim, boyish figure, those small breasts that fit easily into the palm of his hand. Claudia had a way of oozing sexiness; even the way her breasts would almost disappear when she lay flat on her back, virtually unmounded, dark nipples pointing upward, was always, to Josh, astoundingly erotic. For so many years he had loved and made love to that body, and, while he knew every mole, every crevice, every line, her scent as familiar as his own, he had never tired of it, never failed to take pleasure in its gifts. Until more recently, of course, when sex between them, for reasons simultaneously hopelessly complex and readily identifiable, had ground to a halt.

But now Josh was transported, not just to another country but to an entirely different planet, a distant galaxy, one with topography stunningly alien to anything he'd ever known, or could at least recall. He was an explorer setting off into uncharted new worlds, truly a stranger in a strange land.

Erin's body was an endless landscape of high peaks and rolling valleys, an impossibly vast array of wonders spread out before him. Even her smell, a sharp, pungent earthiness, was from a world with which he was not familiar; he breathed deeply as he ran his mouth along her skin. Erin's response to his touch was true to her nature; she reciprocated with uncomplicated, warm enthusiasm and an easy confidence that relaxed him and excited him even more.

He was chagrined then, mortified really, when their first attempt started and then concluded in little more than an eyeblink. Though ashamed, he wasn't all that surprised. It had been such a long time, and he had been so aroused, it seemed inevitable. Erin, again in keeping with her temperament, appeared unfazed; she seemed to take his ineptitude in stride. Josh couldn't help contrasting Erin's reaction with Claudia, who would at times seethe in frustration, wired and on edge, when he would finish too soon.

Though greatly tempted, he somehow resisted the impulse to apologize. After a short intermission, in which they distracted themselves with good-humored snarky comments about Russell's taste in decor, they tried again, and this time, more in control, he held out until he felt Erin arch her back and moan softly beneath him. They clung to each other for a long time as they both shuddered to their climaxes. And then, after dozing lightly for some number of minutes, he'd lost track of how long, something miraculous occurred, and they went for it yet again, this time concluding as he lay on his back, Erin straddling him, rocking, eyes closed, momentarily far away, the magnificence of her body on full display above him.

The universe had certainly looked favorably upon him this night, or perhaps it had simply decided to take pity. And even though he was fully aware that this same universe could just as easily take away what it had proffered, Josh willed himself not to think beyond the moment; if anything, he was transported back in time, to his youth, when a night like this, while by no means a common occurrence, was at least more plausible. Who would have thought that at his age, in his situation, with what he had become, he would ever experience anything like this again? It was inconceivable. And yet there he was.

Later, well past midnight, half-sleeping and groggy, he became aware of her lifting herself out of the bed. He opened his eyes and watched her pad across the room, that fleshy nakedness, her full, rounded ass, the wide waist, those smooth, solid thighs, receding into another part of the apartment. Her strut was unselfconscious, unabashed, unapologetic. *This is who I am*, her body seemed to be telling him as she slipped away. *This is what I look like. Love me, love all of me.* And indeed he had.

After a few minutes, now wrapped in a thin gold silk robe that stopped just above her knees, Erin returned to the bedroom with several cartons of cold Chinese takeout.

"Leftovers from the night I flew in." She handed him a set of porcelain chopsticks, smooth and cool in his hand. Her voice was husky, raspy. "Russell does not appear to own silverware," she explained with her half smile and a minimalist shrug. "Just these."

As sleepiness melted away and his head cleared, Josh was overcome by a ravenous, consuming hunger. He dug in, half sitting, half lying, nestled against Erin's thigh, the smell of sex heavy in the air. Opening the containers, he allowed himself to be swept up by the pleasure and anticipation of small surprises. He discovered sesame noodles, a broccoli dish with black bean sauce and a few other things he couldn't readily identify. Not that it mattered.

A post-coital appetite is like none other; they ate greedily, with immense satisfaction, alone together in the dim in the dead of night in the big city. Finally, after they'd had all they wanted, Josh picked up the empty cartons and moved them onto the night table, away from the bed. Crawling back under the covers, he looked over at Erin, trying to read her thoughts. She smiled, eyes heavy and half shut, and reached gently to touch his face.

And then they slept.

TWENTY

Anyone who happened to catch sight of them that frigid January morning, perhaps a school official taking a break from her day to gaze out her upper-story window at the crowded parking lot below, would have had little trouble decoding their body language. Even without knowing their conversation, without knowing anything about them, that administrator peering down through the dank gloom would have quickly surmised that these were two people at odds. Claudia, knitted ski hat pushed down almost to her eyes, wrapped tightly in a thick, lavender wool scarf, held herself stiffly, nearly motionless, arms folded, ankles crossed, pressed against the squared back of her Honda Pilot, her primary gesture a minimalist wagging finger. Josh, by contrast, was in constant motion, pacing in small circles, sometimes gazing overhead at the dull, heavy sky pushing down upon them, sometimes staring off at the piles of graying snow that had been plowed off to the edges of the blacktop and left to melt and refreeze as fickle weather dictated. He would pause to issue a comment or response and then resume his looping walk, long black overcoat flapping around his calves whenever the wind kicked up, leather gloves not quite sufficient to keep the tips of his fingers from slowly going numb.

Josh could feel Claudia's eyes tracking him with each step. He knew what she wanted, why she had insisted on facing off in this icebox of a parking lot when they both had other things to do, other places to be. He knew she meant it to be a continuation of the discussion about Amy that had begun with Marcus on Christmas Day. But as Josh had made clear then — and was resolved to do again now — he wanted no part of that conversation.

In theory, he supposed their plan made a kind of sense. He got it. He was able to see the logic, the value, in what Claudia and Marcus were proposing. But the idea of Marcus having so much influence over Amy's care was intolerable, untenable. It was a capitulation, like submitting to the dark side. The ferocity of his own reaction had come as a surprise to him. It had emerged from somewhere deep, feral. But now he felt he had no choice but to hold firm. Anything originating from Marcus needed to be rejected out of hand. On principle.

They had just emerged from their long-scheduled meeting with Amy's teacher and therapists. These twice annual get-togethers invariably left both parents frustrated. It wasn't that those working with Amy were indifferent or incapable. On the contrary; Josh was often touched by how so many in the school led with their hearts. But by this point, it was evident even to him that these well-meaning, empathetic professionals could accomplish only so much. Institutionally speaking, the public school and the system were simply not structured in a way that would allow Amy to thrive to her fullest potential.

What she required were around-the-clock therapies, consistent and seamless, and engagement designed to meet her specific needs. That was why, in a rare moment of comity in the months before the breakup, both Claudia and Josh had agreed, albeit painfully, that Amy needed to move to a residential facility, sooner rather than later. The challenge, of course, was finding the right place and then getting approval and funding from the school district and the state agencies. Adding to Josh's feeling of guilt and disconnectedness, the burden of navigating this bureaucracy had fallen squarely on Claudia. It had been left to her to find a way to break through to a human being who knew the secret code for unlocking the process and moving it forward. Josh had only a vague sense of the mysterious acronym-laden agencies Claudia had become familiar with and was now able to discuss with remarkable fluency. Meanwhile, the reality of the moment — Amy's reality — was as uncomplicated as it was unsatisfying. As long as she remained in the public school system, it was essential that she have access to the full scope of resources available, such as they were. What ate at her parents was the recognition of how limited their options were and how little power they really had. And now, on top of it, thought Josh, you had Marcus entering the picture, sticking his nose into a place, a situation, in which it did not belong.

Josh had arrived at the school that morning stressed and anxious. Driving over, he had been preoccupied by the nagging dread he would find Marcus among those sitting around the long wooden table, with his little pointy ears and his little square glasses and his all-knowing little chinless smirk. As he clenched the wheel, Josh cautioned himself not to react, not to show his feelings on his face. He had worked himself into such a state that he was momentarily thrown off balance when he arrived and realized Claudia had come alone.

Josh saw his wife look up from her phone as he entered the cramped, windowless room. Dressed casually in leggings and a baggy gray wool sweater, she nodded at him wordlessly, the lavender scarf hanging loosely around her neck. Her dark hair, Josh noted with a quick, disapproving glance, had grown out past her shoulders. She was surrounded by a table full of women: Amy's teacher, her speech therapist, occupational therapist, physical therapist, school psychologist, parent advocate, and the supervisor who ran the special needs program for the district.

There were no empty seats at the crowded table; Josh stood uncertainly near the doorway, all eyes on him expectantly. Then someone, the speech therapist, popped up and, tottering slightly in her spiky heels, took a few steps toward a shadowy corner of the room. The therapist squatted, her dark skirt, a size too tight for her short, chunky body, pulling up along her thighs. She lifted a metal folding chair, brought it toward the table, and opened it, then smiled at Josh broadly from under thick black curls, red nails and red lipstick glistening. She gestured with an extended palm that he should sit.

Each of the women took their turn reporting on Amy, periodically referring to the neatly typed pages in front of them. These reports were generally upbeat, citing the progress she had made since the beginning of the year with language, cognition, and basic living skills. She was now brushing her teeth independently, with minimal prompting, a breakthrough, they all agreed. Claudia, eyeing each speaker closely, scribbled in a small notebook, at times interrupting to fire off a question or observation. Several times, she tried to pin down specific behaviors and approaches. A discussion would then ensue — earnest, thoughtful, well-intentioned.

Josh stayed quiet for the most part, his mind drifting. He had a conference call with a client scheduled for later that morning; conscious of his train schedule, he kept one eye on the time. He mused at how strange it was to be in the situation in which he found himself, listening to his wife who wasn't really his wife anymore, talking about his daughter with whom he no longer lived. Physically removed from Amy's daily life, he was more of a bit player than ever.

About halfway through, it dawned on him that when Claudia said "we" or "our," she wasn't necessarily referring to him. First-person plural pronouns, when spoken by one half of a couple about the other half, could be intimate, even sexy. But now that he was outside that bubble of coupledom, it was chilling, sickening, to realize that those pronouns Claudia was using more likely pertained to Marcus. For some reason, this line of thinking conjured up thoughts of Erin. He forced himself to refocus, redirect.

As the hour grew short, the administrator looked at Claudia with a careful smile. "Let's hear from the parents. Why don't you tell us how Amy is doing at home."

"Well, we've covered a lot of it already," Claudia began in a measured tone. "She doesn't always carry over what she learns at school to similar behaviors and skills at home. We need to generalize her progress. Which, of course, is why our ultimate hope is for her to receive the residential placement. Different people using different therapies and approaches is not effective for her."

"Understood," said the supervisor. She was a large woman with short, graying, curly hair. Her navy dress hung on her formlessly. When she shifted in her chair, her movements appeared labored — heavy and ungraceful, yet she spoke with a commanding presence, curt and to the point but not without warmth. "Do you mind if I ask," said the woman, glancing down at her laptop. "How is Amy handling the, uh, the changes in the household?"

Josh saw Claudia wince. She peered over at him, the first time he'd felt she'd acknowledged his presence since he sat down. "You mean our, uh, our separation?"

"Yes," said the woman.

"Well, it's been difficult. For everyone." Claudia stopped to make eye contact with those around the table, eliciting some small nods and a couple of soft murmurs. The speech therapist who had gotten Josh his chair was the only one who looked his way. She shot him a half-smile he wasn't sure how to read. He smiled back.

"With Amy, it's hard to tell what she's thinking, of course, what she knows," Claudia continued, swallowing hard. She cleared her throat and studied her notebook. "She knows her daddy's not there. She knows that much. It's an adjustment."

"Have you seen this play out in her behaviors?" pressed the administrator.

"As I said, it's hard to know. We have...fortunately...we have support. My, uh, my boyfriend." Claudia grimaced again and paused. She spoke in choppy bursts, picking her words carefully. "He has been spending a lot of time at our — my — house and he has two boys who are a little older than my — our — children. They've been great with Amy. As has, uh, Marcus himself, of course. It helps. It eases the transition. I guess. But yeah, the whole thing has been difficult, I'm not gonna lie."

"Do keep us updated on this, Mrs. Sherman." The supervisor looked briefly at Josh. "It will be extremely helpful for us to know what's going on at home and how Amy's dealing with everything there. We've also been observing her for behavioral changes at school, of course, which we'll share with you as well."

Claudia nodded and swallowed again. "Of course," she said with a tight smile. "I appreciate your concern. But, um, I just want to add, I think that, considering all the upheaval, I think things are going relatively smoothly at home. Relatively. We're figuring it out."

As the supervisor closed her laptop, the usual assurances were made that a comprehensive program was in place for Amy "to continue her progress."

Claudia mumbled her thanks to the group. Josh, taking her lead, did the same. There were more nods and sympathetic looks as everyone rose. The meeting had gone past its allotted time, and the women quickly said their goodbyes, gathered their papers, and rushed out. When the door opened, another couple was standing just on the other side, waiting, arms folded, appearing tense and looking anxious.

TWENTY-ONE

On Christmas Day, some weeks before the school meeting, Claudia had woken to find a text from Josh saying he had gifts for the children and that he wanted to bring them over. She was initially annoyed he'd waited until it was actually Christmas to tell her this. A little advance planning would have been nice. But as she thought it over, she decided it was important that the children see their father on this day. Then there was something else too. For some time, Claudia had been trying to plot out when best to speak with Josh about an idea Marcus had that could help Amy. Knowing that anything involving Marcus and the children was bound to be fraught, she had been procrastinating. Now, it seemed, that opportunity had unexpectedly arrived. As Claudia texted Josh back, letting him know he was welcome to stop by, it occurred to her that this could be the fortuitous opening she'd been looking for.

When they were first married, neither Josh nor Claudia had put a lot of effort into Christmas. Neither of them cared much. They'd exchange gifts in the morning without much fanfare and then head over to her parents in the late afternoon. But after the children were born, Claudia had decided they should have a tree. She still seethed when she recalled how Josh had flung hurtful accusations at her, declaring her a hypocrite, citing her outspoken stance on organized religion. Claudia had stood her ground, countering that for her, as for many others, Christmas could be considered a benign cultural event, not a religious one. She didn't feel she was compromising her principles or her values. And anyway, it was for the kids; she didn't want them to feel weird or ostracized. Besides, there was no rulebook, no reason to be dogmatic about any of it. It was a pragmatic decision. Circumstances changed when you had kids. This disagreement escalated, turning into one of the biggest blowout fights of their marriage as they both staked out maximalist positions. They didn't speak for days.

Eventually, as couples must if they wish to remain a couple, they cooled off and reached an accommodation. In the ensuing years, the Christmas tree had become an annual tradition, and, eventually, from Claudia's perspective at least, it seemed that even Josh had come to grudgingly appreciate it on some level. Now, this first Christmas without Josh in the house, Claudia was determined to keep the tradition going. Ethan looked forward to helping with the decorations, and Amy reacted with her own version of glee, responding enthusiastically to the flashing lights and hanging ornaments.

For Marcus, Christmas had deeper spiritual significance. He was raised Catholic, and in spite of the roiling turmoil he'd endured growing up, he had held on to a good chunk of his religiosity. For better or worse, as he liked to say, it was in his DNA. He and Debbie had agreed that their children would be enrolled in CCD; they still were. Claudia, while maintaining her antipathy toward religion, could feel Marcus pulling her, gently but steadily, in that direction. She could see this was one of the many things they were going to have to sort out going forward. Even their wedding, still a hypothetical at this point, would be colored by the decisions they would need to make about a ceremony. A lot of compromising lay ahead. It was difficult not to be daunted by it.

Josh arrived shortly after ten. He rang the bell, which somehow, observed Claudia, felt both appropriate and weird. He came through the door with a large stuffed lion, unwrapped, tucked under one arm.

Spying Amy near the sparkling tree, torn bits of wrapping paper strewn about the wood floor, he crossed the room and handed the gift to her. Claudia watched as he squatted in front of their daughter, speaking quietly, hands resting lightly just above their daughter's hips. Claudia remembered, though grudgingly, how gentle, how patient Josh could be with Amy. Of course, as she also reminded herself, he had rarely been the one taking care of her constant, minute-to-minute needs.

Amy embraced the lion and carried it around with her for a few minutes before dropping it onto the coffee table and wandering away. Ethan's present, also unwrapped, was a truck with sound effects. Still in his pajamas, Ethan hugged his father, then began driving the truck along the window sills throughout the house. The adults could hear beeping and simulated engine roars emanating from unseen corners. Will and Daniel, prompted by Marcus, emerged shortly after Josh arrived. They made eye contact, offered limp handshakes, and said their hellos before quickly retreating to what had been turned into their shared bedroom — Josh's former office.

Josh perched on the edge of a chair in the living room while Claudia and Marcus sat close together on the couch across from him. The lion remained crouched low on the coffee table, a silent observer.

"Are you going to your parents' later?" Josh asked without enthusiasm, looking around the room, hands hanging loosely in his lap. His eyes landed on the tree with its tinsel and ornaments and glittering lights.

Claudia glanced toward Marcus. "That's the plan. Probably just a quick dinner and get the children back here. It's a lot of stimulation for them. And four kids is a lot for my parents."

"Right."

"What about you?" she asked, immediately regretting the question.

"I've got some plans," Josh responded.

She was sure he didn't, but she wasn't about to press him on it.

"Good," she said. "I'm glad you won't be alone." She watched Josh shrug with open palms. He reached out for the lion, turned it toward him more directly, and stared into its glassy eyes. For a second, Claudia wondered if they were about to witness him attempt to engage a stuffed animal in conversation.

Groping for topics, they chatted for a few minutes more, forced banalities about the weather, the holidays, that no one wanted to pursue but that were clearly necessary since a prolonged silence would have been so much more awful.

Marcus thought to ask Josh about the upcoming football playoffs, adding that he still rooted for the Eagles, even after living in New York all these years. Claudia knew that Josh, a lifelong Giants fan, hated the Eagles. She worried for a second that these polarized team loyalties would heighten the tension between the two men still further, as if that were even possible. But as she listened to them bat their sports allegiances and opinions back and forth, they sounded almost normal. You could almost imagine them arguing as friends over beers in a bar somewhere. Amazing how sports could do that for men. The great common denominator.

Eventually, though, even the vigorous sports conversation failed to sustain itself and tailed off. Claudia knew Josh so well, his rhythms, his patterns. He had a clock in his head and was undoubtedly counting down the minutes until he could exit in a way that would be marginally less than totally awkward. She knew if she wanted to bring up Marcus's idea, it had to be now. There was no telling when she might get another opportunity.

"We need to talk to you about Amy," she said finally, stiffly, as the conversation lulled again.

"Okay." Josh was immediately guarded, shooting a quick look in the direction of Marcus before returning to Claudia. "What about her?"

Claudia mentioned, hesitantly, Marcus's connection to his colleague at Iona. She stumbled, watching Josh's face. "You tell him," she finally said, turning to Marcus, hands fluttering. "You can explain it better than I can."

Marcus leaned forward, staring hard at Josh. His gaze, though intense, was not unfriendly. Claudia had a glimpse into what made him a good teacher. Josh was like one of those problem students who, while bright, needed an assignment clarified in a very particular way for it to click. "Here's the story, Josh. There's a guy who teaches some courses at Iona who I've become friendly with. He's a special needs lawyer by training. He used to work in Albany, he was a legislative aide, and he dealt a lot with the special needs agencies. He's an older guy, semiretired now, actually, just teaching mostly to keep himself busy, and because he enjoys it." Marcus reached to put his hand on top of Claudia's; she reflexively pulled away, uncomfortable, conscious of Josh watching them. Marcus took a breath before starting again. "This guy, he's been around a long time, and he knows a lot of people in state government. He knows how to navigate the system. He, uh, knows where the bodies are buried, so to speak. Actually, come to think of it, you might even recognize his name. Paul Morrissey? He's in the news once in a while." They watched Josh lift one shoulder unenthusiastically. "Anyway," Marcus went on, "he says he might be able to connect us, cut through some of the red tape, get us a more preferred level of attention. Basically do us a favor. He says he's willing to try." Marcus paused again, then repeated, "As a favor, just so you understand. You wouldn't have to retain him. That is, pay him."

Claudia saw Josh's face cloud over, crumple. He shuddered, and his face twitched.

"I know what retain him means," Josh said.

Marcus's mouth twisted downward. He fell silent while maintaining steady eye contact. Though she had an overwhelming urge to lash out at Josh for his childish petulance, Claudia knew it would be a mistake to be baited, to sink to his level, as doing so would only derail the purpose of this conversation. The truth was, she and Marcus didn't need Josh's approval for any of this. It wasn't a legal matter; they had every right to move forward without him. It was just that it would be so much easier if he would just acquiesce, if, just for this one thing, they could all be on the same side. She wanted everything out in the open. She wanted his support. She also, she had to admit to herself, didn't want him to be able to throw this back at her later in case something didn't work out.

"I don't know if this is necessary," Josh said in that same flat monotone after a prolonged silence. "We can handle Amy's placement."

"Josh," Claudia said. "We're not getting anywhere, and you know it. We've been spinning our wheels. Why not see where this goes? It can only help. It can't hurt."

"I want to do whatever I can," offered Marcus. "For Amy. For all of us. That's all this is. There's no other agenda. I hope I'm being clear about that."

But Josh shook his head and grimaced, steadfastly refusing to support the idea. Their efforts to engage him further were rebuffed with terse, short retorts that got them nowhere. The room fell silent. Shortly after, as Claudia had anticipated, he looked at his watch and told them he needed to go, he had somewhere to be.

TWENTY-TWO

In the days and weeks that followed, Claudia had held on to the hope that once Josh had had the opportunity to process, he would realize how recklessly impulsive he had been, and, more to the point, how the only person he was hurting was Amy. Surely, he would eventually come to regret being intractable on Christmas Day. Claudia tried her best to be fair, to see the situation from his side; indeed, there was a part of her that actually could kind of understand his reaction. They had sprung this idea on him. He probably felt blindsided. There was so much emotion surrounding all of it. But by this point, surely he must have calmed down and would be able to be more rational, more objective. More of a grown-up.

Now, here she was, facing off with him in the school parking lot after the meeting, already strung out from the intensity of the morning, and they were right back where they'd left off at Christmas. Yet she felt she had no choice but to bring up Marcus's offer again. It was too important. It felt like her last best chance. She leaned against her car, Josh pacing in front of her, and pointed out again, tentative, prodding, how their only concern had to be Amy. Claudia was dismayed, baffled as she realized Josh had still not come around, was still as obstinate as ever.

Claudia's frustration began to boil over and, without Marcus beside her as a calming influence, she could feel it getting the better of her. She had tried to be nice, and it hadn't worked. "Can you just please not be so weird about this?" she snapped, pleading, exasperated. "Okay? This is for Amy. It has nothing to do with anything else. You need to try to put your personal feelings about Marcus aside. Please don't be weird? Please?"

"I don't want him involved. She's not his responsibility."

"He's *already* involved, Josh. He lives with Amy. You don't."

"Yeah, so I heard. I didn't know you were going to air our dirty laundry to those teachers in there." Josh nodded in the direction of the building they'd just departed. "I'm not sure that was entirely necessary."

"It was — and it is. Our situation, yours and mine, affects Amy. In all facets of her life. Whether you want to admit it or not. The school needs to know what's going on at home. Did you think our separation was supposed to be some big secret that we should keep from them?"

"I don't know. Whatever. I just don't want Marcus's help with the placement thing."

They waited as a long white delivery truck thundered by, leaving a trail of exhaust, grinding gears as it passed. The interruption allowed Claudia to gather her thoughts. She stared ahead as the truck stopped at the end of the parking lot and slowly began to back into the school loading dock, a gaping hole at the rear of the red brick building.

She wanted resolution, one way or another. Josh's fixed determination to be so incredibly petty, so self-indulgent, to turn this into something that it wasn't, left her with only one option.

"I want us all to be in agreement," she said. She searched for that tone that sometimes served her well when conducting video interviews. Engaged but with the necessary degree of detachment. "I really do. But I'm also not going to wait any longer. I'm going to tell Marcus to talk to Paul Morrissey. If he can help us, I want him to try." She could feel herself slipping further, the edge creeping into her voice. "It's not about you, Josh. It's for our daughter. Whom I assume you still care about."

"I wish you wouldn't," he said. "But since you've already decided, I guess there's nothing left to talk about. My opinion apparently doesn't matter."

There was no point in trying to push him further. They were at an impasse. And she had no intention of bringing up the idea again. She'd tried. She was so done. "I need to go," she said, feeling for the car door handle through her mittens. "It's too freezing to stand out here any longer arguing with you about this."

She climbed into the Pilot, started the engine, and cranked the heat. In spite of her wool hat, her ears stung from the cold. She waited a minute to thaw out before shifting out of neutral. She saw Josh a short distance ahead of her, shaking his head from side to side, muttering, as he walked toward his own car. She was so fed up. How had she ever been married to this man? He seemed to be getting stranger. In the meeting that morning, he'd appeared only half present, so obviously distracted, not really listening, checking his phone constantly. It was as if he had only minimal interest in the well-being of his own child. And then the way he'd ogled Janine, the speech therapist, as she'd bent over to get him a chair. What was that about, flirting with her from across the table with his little creepy grin? It was gross, sickening.

Claudia had to ease the Pilot past him to get out onto the street. As she came closer, he unexpectedly wheeled around and put up a gloved hand. She thought he was waving goodbye, maybe a sign he was willing to be slightly less hostile. But then she realized he was signaling for her to stop. She thought about just continuing on, waving back as she drove by, as if she were unable to comprehend his gesture, like someone who understands a foreign language but pretends not to. Still half frozen, she was also reluctant to crack the window. In spite of her misgivings, however, she tapped the brakes. She looked at him blankly as the cold air rushed in.

"What now?" she sighed.

Josh moved toward her, his head, like a floating balloon, partway inside the car. Suddenly very near, those sleepy chameleon eyes, those eyes she'd once found so alluring, were right on top of her. Today they looked very green. There was a spot on his chin, raw, the color of brick, a tiny fresh scab, where he'd nicked himself shaving. His face was flushed.

"This is probably not the best time to get into this, but I kind of need you to know something else," Josh said. "About me, I mean. I figure I might as well mention it now while we're here."

Claudia felt her shoulders tighten. "Oh, yeah? Okay. Let's hear it." She waited, resigned to whatever he was going to throw at her.

"So...yeah. Okay. Uh, well. It looks like I might be moving to California."

Though she'd had no idea what it was he'd wanted to tell her, this bit of information would not have been her first guess. And it had the effect he'd clearly desired. She was stunned, thrown for a loop. But she couldn't let him know that. She concentrated on not reacting, staying silent, simply letting him continue.

"Yeah, things seem to be moving in that direction," he went on in that oddly detached way he sometimes had. "And rather quickly."

Josh started to explain further. Perhaps sensing her impatience, he rushed through some of the details, making it difficult for her to entirely follow his story. Something about a guy in Las Vegas offering him a job in L.A. He emphasized more than once that he expected to soon be out of work. "I'm not sure what's happening with the James Gang," he said. "James might very well be shutting down the agency and going into the movie thing full-time. That's looking pretty certain, actually. I've known it was a possibility for a while, and now it seems to be happening. So I've been working on other options. My Plan B. I have this opportunity out in L.A. It's a good one. I'd be foolish to pass it up."

"Your Plan B?" Claudia finally said.

"Yeah. You know? I've been trying to figure out my next moves, to listen to what my universe is telling me."

His Plan B? His universe? Where the hell did he come up with this shit?

"Okay. And what about, uh, this?" Claudia fanned her hand in the direction of the school building.

"What's *this*? I have no *this*, Claudia."

"What about your children? How are you going to stay involved with them? What are you going to tell Ethan? Or do they not matter?"

Josh set his lips tightly, shifted sideways and took a single step away from the car. Claudia wondered if he was going to do that annoying thing from earlier where he'd started walking in circles. "I don't know yet," he said, turning back to her. "I haven't gotten that far yet. There are still a lot of things to figure out. But I can assure you I will stay involved with our children. If I have to fly to New York every other weekend or something, that's what I'll do. You might think a lot of shitty things about me, Claudia, but that's one thing you don't have to worry about. I'm committed to our kids."

"Okay, fine," Claudia said, maintaining her minimal affect. "You've got it all figured out. I'm sure you'll be able to fly across the country for every holiday, every recital, every soccer game, every therapist meeting. Of course you will."

"I'm not abandoning my children, Claudia. In spite of what you" — Josh hesitated — "you and your boyfriend may want to believe."

Claudia waved at him dismissively. She had heard enough. She needed to get out of there. "Why don't you just let me know when all your details are firmed up, I guess? We'll need to...to...and, yes, we'll have a lot of things we'll need to work out."

As she watched the window close, Josh put his hand up again. *Seriously?* thought Claudia. *What the hell is he doing? Either he's losing his mind, or I am.*

The window opened again. He hesitated once more before speaking, and, again, she waited. "There's something else. You might as well know the whole thing. I mean, what the hell, right? Just lay it all out there? Right?"

Claudia still refused to engage him. He looked so stupidly happy with himself, with his asymmetrical twisted grin, dumping all this shit on her. It irked her further to see how much he was enjoying this control as he parceled out his bits of news in slow, measured spoonfuls. She focused on the steady idle of the Pilot's engine; the low rhythmic rumble soothed her somewhat.

Finally, Josh plunged ahead. "I've met someone. She lives out there. In L.A." Another long beat. Then, cocking his head questioningly, "You're not going to say anything? I'm getting the silent treatment now?"

"You've met someone." It was a statement, not a question.

"Yeah. A woman."

"I get that it's a woman."

"Yeah, so, well, I needed to tell you that too."

"And so you have."

"I need to do this, Claudia. I was hoping you'd understand."

"You need *me* to understand?" Claudia's voice rose an octave, and she heard herself laugh, an involuntary guttural bark. "You don't find anything odd about saying this to me after the conversation we just had two minutes ago about Paul Morrissey?"

"They're not the same thing."

"Well, that's certainly true. That's probably the first thing you've said today that we can actually agree on."

They stared at each other. From somewhere in the building, Claudia heard children, a dozen or so high-pitched voices talking over one another. She spoke up. "So you're moving to California."

"Possibly. Probably. It's not one hundred percent sure. But yeah, probably. Most likely. The guy with the job just got back into town from vacation. So I'm flying out there on Monday morning. I'll meet with him Monday afternoon. So hopefully I'll know more soon."

She could see how he was trying to dent her composure, how he wanted to see her squirm. And yet, except for one or two flashes of anger, she had been mostly able to maintain her outwardly placid demeanor, the discipline to remain unreadable. She hoped her minimalist reaction was getting under his skin. The idea that this was frustrating to him was fleetingly satisfying.

She asked him, "Are you going to sign the papers?"

Josh hesitated and looked down. "I'll sign the papers," he said, barely above a mumble.

"Before you take off for California. I want that done. It's enough already."

"Assuming James shuts down the James Gang," Josh pressed on, grinding his teeth, "I'll have no income, and that doesn't help either of us. This situation in L.A., it actually seems to be coming together. It's the chance for me to reinvent myself. California — L.A. — is the perfect place to do that." He paused, and still she said nothing. "You've got a life. You can't make me feel guilty for wanting one too, for wanting to move on too."

"We *had* a life, Josh. For better or worse," Claudia said, finally allowing the emotion she'd been holding down to rise to the surface. She heard the venom in her voice and hesitated as she attempted, not very successfully, to recalibrate her tone. "As you fly off to reinvent yourself in Los Angeles and write your revisionist history as the aggrieved party, the tragic hero rising from the ashes, just try to remember whose decision it was to break up our marriage. I'll give you a hint," she spat out as she put the car into drive and started to roll forward. "It wasn't mine."

TWENTY-THREE

As seemed to be so often the case, the details of the move to Los Angeles, his Plan B, had begun to fall into place not so much because of anything he was actively making happen, but instead because of external events that seemed to be conspiring to steer him in a particular direction. For now, at least, he was riding that wave, waiting to see where he might land.

The week between Christmas and New Year's had been quiet, as it always was that time of year, the office operating at half speed. Other than rushing to get the Shoe King app finished, which was really now in the hands of LAKreativ, there wasn't much going on. Everyone took advantage of this time to recharge. Josh was coming in late and leaving early, and James was barely around at all.

So Josh was apprehensive when, late one night that week, checking his phone to see if there was a text from Erin (there wasn't), he instead saw a message from James telling him to meet at the diner near their office first thing in the morning. The diner was hardly a random choice, and it certainly wasn't because of the quality of the food; the place was James's location of choice when he had something significant to share with Josh and he didn't want to arouse suspicion or alarm in the office.

Lying in bed, no longer sleepy, Josh speculated on how the conversation was going to go. Though he had a pretty good idea what it was about, he was holding out hope he might yet be proven wrong. He tried to tell himself conjecture was futile and only served to contribute to his insomnia. It didn't help. That all too familiar feeling of queasy adrenaline had taken hold, running through his veins and settling in his belly.

Arriving heavy-headed at the diner the next morning, Josh pushed his way through the glass doors, shook off the damp cold, and spotted James in a corner booth, half rising, phone to his ear, beckoning impatiently. Josh took this uncharacteristic punctuality as another ominous sign. James wasn't inclined to show up on time to anything, to say nothing of being early.

James looked particularly large that morning, dressed in a loose-fitting blue and white ski sweater dotted by cartoonish snowflakes drifting across a wide expanse of knitted wool. His gray overcoat lay in an untidy heap beside him. He set the phone down on the table's worn Formica surface, the color of dirty dishwater, and knocked back a slug of coffee as he watched Josh approach.

Shrugging off his coat and sliding in across the table, Josh was rattled by James's disheveled appearance: unshaven, hair hanging limply across his forehead, eyes heavy and bloodshot. The harsh overhead lighting served to heighten the effect of a man under duress.

Josh thought it best to try to lighten things up by defaulting to the needling banter they often used to destress each other at moments such as these. "Rough night?" he asked.

"I might have had a round or two," James responded, his voice nasal and even deeper than usual. He tilted his head and peered at Josh with one eye while rubbing the other with a closed fist. "Then I remembered I said I'd meet you here at eight. What was I thinking? I should have made it ten."

"You've turned over a new leaf — a whole new you."

"If only that were true. My alarm clock is an asshole."

Josh gestured toward the plate glass window, a cold gray drizzle casting a fuzzy, metallic gloss over the crowded sidewalk dotted with umbrellas. "Of course, then you would have missed this lovely morning. The most beautiful part of the day."

"Fuck you."

"So you just summoned me here to watch you have a hangover and complain?"

"I wish." James nodded to a waiter loitering nearby, a hollow-cheeked young man in a cheap black dinner jacket. The waiter, with his high-pitched, indeterminate accent and perky demeanor, was eager to please; Josh could see this was immediately irritating to his breakfast companion.

"You eating?" James asked, ignoring the waiter. He continued to squint, as if trying, and failing, to bring Josh into focus.

"I'll have something."

James ordered oatmeal, paused, then told the waiter to bring a side of bacon. Yet another disruption from the routine — James ordinarily ate little of anything before noon.

"You're having bacon?" Josh asked, unable to suppress a smile. "The oatmeal's too healthy on its own? You need to dilute it?"

"I'm indulging my baser impulses. I'd prefer not to be judged."

Josh asked for a well toasted bagel, then sat back in anticipation. He knew better than to try to jumpstart the conversation by throwing out a lot of questions. James would start talking when he was ready. Josh watched the big man pour sugar into his coffee, stir and taste it, before placing the cup back in the saucer. His hand trembled slightly. He looked at Josh again with great consideration.

"Spoke to Ryan last night," James said finally with a heavy sigh, his voice gravelly. "He called me kind of out of the blue." Another sigh. "Ah, what the fuck. There's no easy way to say this, so let me just tell you straight out. They're not going to keep us on. We're getting shit-canned."

"Like, totally? We're off the account?"

"You don't fire someone halfway, Josh."

"I'm just trying to understand." This was, of course, what Josh had assumed — and feared — this impromptu breakfast would be about. Still, hearing the news said aloud shook him. As it had James himself, apparently. It was one thing to speculate, to think that you knew how you were going to react to bad news you'd been bracing for. It was something else entirely to plunge into it, to go from supposition to reality. Josh took a breath. "So how did it go down?"

"Well, now, there's an interesting question." James paused to check out a young woman in a tight-fitting black dress as she went by. Josh was oddly reassured that, even in this dark mood, James had the presence of mind to stop what he was doing and eyeball a pretty girl. There was still some small bit of normalcy in this world.

"Ryan says they love our creative," James explained, lowering his voice. "But they want to go with someone more aligned philosophically to their sensibilities." His hands lifted from the table, and he shook his head. "Whatever the fuck that means."

"More aligned philosophically," Josh repeated, turning the phrase over on his tongue.

"To their sensibilities," James repeated, eyeing Josh closely. "I don't even know what he's fucking talking about."

"I guess I understand it. I know what he's trying to say," said Josh slowly. "But then again, not really."

"Yeah, yeah, I get it too," James said. "Obviously. We all get what he *means*. But it's just so..." He trailed off, then started again. "My favorite part is that he told me he thought it might make more sense to just work with LAKreativ directly. Cut us out. I had to remind the little shit that their contract is with *us*. The James Gang employs LAKreativ, and we own the IP. Jesus, it's so fucked up it's really beyond belief. I can't honestly believe I had to explain that to him."

"What are you going to do if they try to go around us?"

"What do you think I'm going to do? I'll sue them for every last ugly fuckin' shoe they own." James paused and added more calmly, "Not that I'm really much worried about that part of it. LAKreativ has our back. They would never do that to us. At least I don't think they would." He shook his head. "I'm not sure who's out to screw who at this point. It's just the idea that Ryan would even bring it up. I guess I'm going to have to tell LAKreativ to stop work. Immediately. That should be another fun conversation."

"Yeah," Josh said, frowning. "Erin's team is almost wrapped. The app, the game, it looks great, by the way. For what that's worth at this point. You're supposed to, or were supposed to, review the final next week. So fucked-up."

"Fucked-up does not even begin to describe it, my friend."

When the food arrived, James put the oatmeal aside and gnawed thoughtfully on a piece of bacon. The salty-sweet, woody smell of cured meat, something Josh had never cared for, settled over the table.

Josh was quiet; he concentrated for a few moments on the simple act of spreading cream cheese evenly across half a bagel. He took a bite then said as he swallowed, "I've gotta say, though, James, I mean, if we're being totally transparent about all this, I guess I'm just slightly surprised you're this upset, this angry. I'm just being honest. I mean you made it seem like...."

James's cold glare, red-rimmed eyes narrowing, prevented him from continuing.

"Made it seem like what?" James stabbed toward Josh with the bacon. "What were you going to say? Let me explain something to you, in case you're not getting it. I've put my life into this shitty little company. This is not easy for me. I don't want this."

"Okay, okay. That's not what I meant," Josh said, taken aback. He tried to think of a way to start again, to rephrase. They'd lost plenty of clients over the years, and James always had been able to take it in stride, move on, maintain forward momentum. *There's always something else* was his reassuring response to setbacks. And there always had been. It was Josh who tended to obsess and take their losses to heart. Still, even as he had played out this potential scene in his head while lying in bed, sleepless, a few hours earlier, even as he understood the deeper consequences of losing the Shoe King, Josh had not expected quite such an agonized reaction from his boss. In some ways, in many ways, he'd come to terms with the idea that James *had* wanted this to happen. He had wanted a reason, an excuse, to make a radical change in his life. And now the opportunity was upon him. Or so Josh had thought.

"It is kind of overwhelming," Josh said, trying again. "Hard to even process. All I meant was you told me after Bob died that you wanted to do your film thing. Besides, you said the Shoe King was running out of money."

"They are. They have. Or they will. Soon enough. One of these days, in the not too distant future, Ryan is going to have to pay a visit to Bob's original investors, his Long Island posse, asking them for yet another bailout. I'd love to be a fly on the wall when that happens. Those guys have gotten used to getting checks, not writing them." James was quiet for a long time. Josh waited. "But you know," James said with an indifferent shrug. "Typical Ryan bravado. He made it sound like they're doing just fine."

What Josh really wanted to know was what Ryan had told James about the money already owed to the James Gang. In light of James's foul mood, however, now was not the time to bring that up. He knew if his boss had had something positive to report, he would already have done so.

James continued to stare across the table, his perturbed expression unwavering. Feeling compelled to fill the void left by the silence, Josh kept talking, even as his inner voice cautioned he'd be better off if he would just shut his mouth.

"And what was that whole Scotch-drinking debrief with Erin about?" Josh asked. "You sure seemed resigned that day. You and I have never discussed it, but it certainly looked like that was some sort of a farewell. Was I wrong about that?"

"If that's what you thought," James growled, "then, yeah, you got the wrong impression. Don't assume you can read my mind. Because you can't." He poured sugar into the oatmeal, studied it for a long second, then poured some more and stirred. "Next time just ask me. I'll save you the trouble."

It was suddenly — perhaps belatedly — obvious to Josh that what was killing James was not so much that the cord was being cut, but rather his impotence in dictating the terms for the cord cutting. James had always assumed he could string along Ryan until the last possible moment. When, and only when, James decided the timing was right would he then tell Ryan to fuck himself. Instead the tables had been turned — James was the one who had been played. James couldn't bear being the rejectee instead of the rejector. It was all so clear now. Not being in control of the break-up, being powerless, was what was really making him crazy.

"Okay, so maybe I misread you, I guess," Josh said, raising his eyes to look at his boss.

James retrieved the bowl of oatmeal and gingerly sampled a spoonful. He dumped yet more sugar into it, swallowed another spoonful, and shook his head slowly, as if the oatmeal had let him down somehow. He put the tips of his fingers together. "I'll give you this, Josh, if it makes you feel any better — you're not totally wrong. I did tell you I wanted to take my shot at producing my movies full-time. Which I do. But the truth is, if you really want to know, and this is the only time you're ever going to hear me say this, I was never one hundred percent sure I had the balls for it. I kind of like my life the way it is. Now my bluff appears to have been called. It would appear that my universe is telling me to go and fucking figure it out. So, yeah, I'm going to give it my best shot." James stopped and looked around the diner as if suddenly realizing where he was and wondering how he had gotten there. "It's never wise to ignore your universe."

Listening to James sent Josh reeling yet again. He had always assumed that, like anyone, James had his moments of self-doubt. But in all of his years working at the James Gang, he could never recall him sounding so insecure, so uncertain.

"I'm going to take Ashley with me," James continued, sounding more sure. "I don't want to lose her. I'll give her some big title, and the two of us will see if we can make a go of it. I'm going to stay in our space, at least until the lease runs out. And you, by the way, are welcome to keep using your office. If you want it. For your own projects, or whatever. Gratis, of course," he added with a toothless, grim smile.

"So you're shutting down the James Gang." Josh shook his head and stared down at his half-eaten bagel.

"Unless you can think of a way to keep it going. It doesn't look like some big deep-pocketed client is walking through the door throwing out wads of cash any time soon. Believe me, I've been out there looking. I've beaten every bush there is to beat."

"As have I. I haven't given up either, you know."

"How's your Plan B looking?" James asked, eyebrows lifting. "Did you ever do anything after we talked about it? Or have you just been waiting to let fate make the call for you?"

Josh hesitated before acknowledging that he did have a Plan B and that it did appear to be coming together. "But you're not going to like it," he said. He had been dreading this conversation too. "This might not be the best time to get into it. Maybe we can talk when things settle down a bit?"

"Josh, when you go to jail, your worst fear is getting fucked in the ass. After that, anything that happens to you is not so bad in comparison. So whatever you've got to tell me now could not be worse than what I've just been through. Just say what you're going to say. I can take it."

"Well, okay, if you really want to hear it." A beat. "It involves Don Bieler."

James raised one hand to his chin, rubbing his lower lip thoughtfully with his index finger. "Huh. Well, that's up there. I'll give you that." He nodded slowly, his voice rising. "Don Bieler? Seriously? Did I miss something? First Ryan, now Don Bieler. Is this National Shitheads Day? Did I miss a memo?"

"I told you you weren't going to like it."

"It's just that...Don Bieler? Well, look, you need to do what you need to do. But Don Bieler? Seriously? Jesus, Josh. He's just..." James looked pained. "He's just kind of a...a lowlife." He paused, studying Josh's face. "You don't think so?"

"He's really not such a bad guy. He's always been good to me, straight with me. You don't really know him. I know him better than you do at this point."

"I'm not sure that's true."

"I don't know why you have such a problem with the guy, and honestly, I don't need to know. But whatever went down between the two of you was a long time ago. Everyone changes, learns from their mistakes. Give him a little credit. Give me a little credit, for God's sake."

"If you say so. What exactly is Bieler offering?"

"He says he has a job for me."

"Yeah, I got that much. Doing what exactly?"

"That's the part I still need more specifics on." Josh could hear uncertainty creeping into his voice. "But it sounds like a good opportunity. Something senior. Something involving helping him manage his YouTubers business."

"Uh-huh. In California?"

"Uh, yeah."

"So you're moving out there?"

"It's looking that way."

"And I suppose this also has something to do with Erin."

Josh could feel his face start to redden. "What's Erin got do to with it?"

"Oh please, Josh. You get a hard-on every time her name comes up."

"I don't think that's exactly true."

James shot him that flat look that never failed to push Josh's buttons. If this was indeed the end, if they were truly splitting up, that condescending expression was the single thing Josh would miss least.

"And that day she did the presentation for Ryan and Courtney?" James continued. "You walked in the next morning looking like, I don't know what. Pretty ragged. Like something the cat had dragged in and then puked up. Plus, you were wearing the same clothes two days in a row. It didn't take an Einstein to figure out there was something up between you two."

Josh thought about that morning in Russell's apartment, the morning after. Having had no other option but to pull it together for the work day ahead, he'd dragged himself out of bed, legs aching and feeling shaky, and gotten going while Erin was still sleeping. He'd showered and even found one of Russell's disposable razors. He'd made sure to stop for coffee with a triple shot before coming into the office. But none of it had had much of an impact on his overall presentation. He remembered Ashley eyeing him curiously, almost smiling, her look lingering, as he walked past her into his office.

When he'd kissed Erin goodbye, her soft sleepiness drawing him toward her, he told her to be sure to message him as soon as the dinner interview was over. Later in the day, he texted to wish her luck; her reply back was upbeat and warm. She'd had a great day poking around Brooklyn and was at that moment at the restaurant, waiting to meet up with everyone. But he didn't hear from her later as anticipated, so the next morning he texted again.

Her return message, sent while waiting for her plane, had been brief and somewhat cryptic: *Didn't go well. Weird. Boarding in a minute. Will explain later.*

In the ensuing weeks, as Josh learned the details of Erin's dinner interview, and as it became clear that her proposed move to New York would not be happening, Josh's options for his Plan B narrowed further, slowly but steadily coming into focus.

He looked across the table at his bleary-eyed, stressed-out boss, gnawing on bits of greasy bacon.

"Okay, okay, great." Josh could feel himself starting to break into an embarrassed grin. "Congratulations. You've outed me. Yeah, it's about Erin, too, alright? Guilty as charged."

"Look, whatever there is between the two of you, I fully endorse it. She's a great girl. And you're essentially single at this point. So go for

194

it. I know I would. That body alone could keep you busy for a good long while."

"Do you mind? Jesus."

James leaned back against the booth's cracked vinyl, the strip of bacon still clutched tightly in his fist. "So when is all this happening?"

"I don't know yet," Josh said. "I still have to arrange the meeting with Don. He's out of the country, away for the holidays, and won't be back until the middle of January. So I'm waiting. But I'm looking to plan a trip out there soon so that I can get a firm read on the what and when."

"So you've been in touch with Bieler?"

"We email back and forth."

Josh saw James grimace again. He realized this level of detail was something he probably should have, could have, held back.

"Okay. The idea of relocating to L.A. makes a certain amount of sense in its own weird way," James said, sounding as if he were evaluating one of their campaigns. "Love the idea of you and Erin. She might actually be good for you. The Don Bieler part, not so much. But it's your call. I'm not going to tell you how to live your life. Just be careful with Bieler, though, okay, Josh? A word to the wise. Go into it with your eyes open. On the other hand, if you can go out there and build a life, why the fuck not?"

"Thanks, I appreciate that," said Josh. "I'm feeling pretty good about where things are headed, all in all. L.A. is a great place to reinvent yourself." After a moment he added, with a drop less conviction, "So they say."

"So they say," James echoed. Josh could see James's gaze veer off. "You're going to have to figure out your family shit, though," he said, refocusing on Josh. "Your kids and all that. That could get messy. Have you said anything to Claudia yet?"

Josh admitted he hadn't. "I know it's going to be messy. I realize that. And I'm not proud about leaving my kids. That part sucks. But you know, I don't think I've ever in my life said for once I just need to be selfish and do what's best for me."

"Uh, yeah. Not that I have any particular desire to sit here and judge you, but I'll just point out that you did move out of your house. Which effectively ended your marriage. So there was that." James held out his hands. "Some might contend that that was done out of, uh, self-interest."

Josh wagged his head back and forth. "I'm not disputing that. You're right. It happened. But that just validates what I'm trying to tell you. This is all connected. Don't you see?" he insisted, his voice rising. "It's all one narrative. Why doesn't anyone understand that? It started with moving out, then the separation, the divorce, and now I'm moving onto the next phase in California. But it's all part of a single narrative — me finally doing something for me." Josh stopped. He wanted James to understand him and perhaps even to empathize. That mattered, his endorsement mattered. "I need to change things up, James. You're doing it. Claudia's doing it. This may be my last best opportunity. I don't want to spend the next twenty years living in some crappy apartment in this cesspool of a city regretting not acting when I had the chance. This is my chance."

"Is it really a cesspool?" James asked, the smirk returning to his face. "I hadn't noticed. Though I've been wondering what the smell was."

"I'm just sayin'." Josh waved a hand toward the crowd of pedestrians on the other side of the picture window, scurrying through the wet, gray murk, wrapped in their heavy coats. "I mean, look at it out there. You don't get that shit in L.A."

This was beginning to sound uncomfortably reminiscent to the conversation Josh had in Las Vegas. Except now he seemed to be playing the Don Bieler role. And in spite of his having just defended Don's character to James, he wasn't sure Don's life choices were something one should aspire to emulate. While it could be argued that Don was a success story, at the same time he was also a cautionary tale. Since that night in Vegas, Josh had occasionally thought about Don's adult kids, the ones he had decided to leave behind in Oklahoma and now had no connection to, didn't even know. As a parent, how do you rationalize doing something like that? Don seemed to have been able to make the hard choices and not look back. Indeed, he appeared to have had little remorse. That was hardly Josh's nature. He regretted everything, second-guessed every decision, beat himself up over every misstep, real or perceived.

Still, he was in so deep by now. His universe seemed to have its own ideas, and he was fully committed to following its lead. Besides, what other options did he really have at this point? He was going to ride this wave wherever it wound up taking him. Plan B or die trying.

TWENTY-FOUR

Claudia hit the accelerator and exited the ice-dappled school parking lot, the motionless figure of her almost ex-husband, gaping, hands at his sides, growing smaller in her rear-view mirror. With a final look back, she made the turn and merged into the flow of traffic onto the main road through town.

Seething, Claudia was overcome by the urgency to escape from Josh as fast as possible. Gripping the wheel tightly, she took a couple of deep breaths as she tried to steady herself. She needed to find a way to process their conversation. In some ways, she tried to reason, it wouldn't be the worst thing if he actually were to move to the other side of the country. He'd be out of the way, and she wouldn't have · to deal with him as much. Or at least not in the same way. But she worried for her children, for Ethan first, of course, but for Amy too. Though he wasn't inclined to articulate it, she knew Ethan continued to miss Josh terribly; how was Claudia going to explain that Daddy was now living three thousand miles away? Knowing Ethan, he would likely blame himself, somehow believe it was something he'd done. Just the thought of that hurt her heart. As was so often the case, it fell to her to pick up the pieces and manage the consequences of Josh's childish solipsism.

What pissed her off most at this moment, however, was not what Josh had said so much as the way he had said it. He had been so smug, so righteous, so happy with himself. Plan B indeed. It made her want to scream in frustration. And then she decided she would scream, needed to scream, and so she did — a primal shriek that echoed in her ears, reverberating within the confines and isolation of her well-insulated Honda Pilot. When she was done, she felt marginally better, raw, scratchy throat notwithstanding, a small measure of her anxiety having momentarily abated.

Claudia continued heading through the village toward home, only to abruptly reconsider when she remembered that Marcus would be at her house. He didn't have classes that day and had decided to spend the morning working on his Thomas Paine book. She wasn't ready to face him just yet; she needed a better handle on her emotions. Maybe it was silly, stupid really, this desire to hide her unfiltered self from him. Surely, getting to know all sides of each other — the good, the bad, the ugly — was an essential part of the process, a necessity in any relationship. And yet she couldn't abide him seeing her this way, so close to the edge. Not yet, not now. Not today.

She parked near the coffee house off the town's commercial strip, the local gathering spot for the refugees who had decamped to the suburbs from hipster Brooklyn or similar environs and were trying to hang on to whatever shred of cool they were still able to muster. The sudden rush of sticky warmth as she went through the doors soothed her after so long standing outside in the cold. But the place was oppressively crowded: tattooed moms at long wooden tables, phones against their ears, tending to fussy, cracker munching toddlers in designer strollers as bearded guys in black T-shirts hunched over their laptops, spread out across sagging, mismatched couches in the back. The windows were heavy with condensation, and the mingling aromas thickening the air — coffee, pastries, cloying perfumes, baby powder — made it difficult for Claudia to breathe, as though a weight were pushing on her chest. She paid for her coffee, scanned the room

in a last, halfhearted, and fruitless search for an empty seat, and
returned to her car.

* * *

Claudia dropped her coat, scarf, and hat onto the living room couch,
left her shoes in the middle of the floor, and continued through to the
kitchen. She leaned forward, palms pressed against the gray granite
countertop, eyes closed. When she opened them again, there was
Marcus, standing near, observing her. He hadn't showered or shaved,
and she was momentarily startled; his dark stubble gave him a swarthy,
vaguely menacing countenance. Barefoot, he wore a faded Grateful
Dead T-shirt — two skeletons dancing joyfully across his chest — and
dark sweat pants that hung loosely on his hips. He'd been working since
before she'd woken that morning; she knew when he got on a roll with
the book, he could be intensely focused. It was one of those details she
had learned about him, filling in another of the many blanks as to who
he was and how he ticked.

"Was it that bad?" he asked, eyes tracking the trail of clothes she'd
dropped behind her. "You look really stressed." Hearing the concern
in his voice confirmed for her what she already knew: her effort to pull
herself together on the drive home had failed miserably.

"It was infuriating," she replied through gritted teeth, her voice still
ragged from her earlier screaming session. She cleared her throat once,
then again.

Marcus nodded sympathetically and put a hand out to her. But when
he asked about the teacher meeting, Claudia realized he was assuming
that what had upset her had something to do with Amy. So, no, she
was now forced to explain, that part of the morning went about as
expected. Frustrating but predictable. Right now, she told him, this
was about Josh.

"Ah, okay, I probably should have figured that," came the response.
"Let me guess. We're still forbidden from speaking with Paul?"

"No." She stopped. "Well, yes, actually. There's that too. He's still being a total dick about that. Giving him time to think over your offer didn't make him any less of one, apparently. But that was also predictable. Sadly. Besides, we're just going to ignore whatever Josh says about that and move forward anyway. That *is* what we finally decided, right? So, it's not really that either." She exhaled and folded her arms. "Are you ready to hear the latest? Josh has decided to move to Los Angeles. Apparently, he's got a job. And a woman. Sounds like a country song, doesn't it? All he needs is a pickup truck and a bottle of whiskey."

"Glad you haven't lost your sense of humor over this."

"Trust me, I have."

"So that's what's eating you."

And then, in a rush of half sentences, it began to tumble out. "Does Josh not realize he still has children he needs to take some responsibility for? I mean, what the fuck? Also, the way he presented the whole thing to me. He was just such a...a..."

"A dick."

"Yes."

"Yeah. You might have mentioned that."

"Well, you asked. It seems like it bears repeating."

"He's had a rough year," Marcus said. "I'm sure he feels like he needs to blow everything up and start over again."

"He's not twenty-two anymore. It's not that simple." Claudia reached for the cup that had grown cold on the counter and peered dubiously at the remnants of the foamed milk floating listlessly atop her mocha latte. She set it down with a grimace and pushed it away. "What is it with middle-aged men wanting no strings? No accountability? At a certain point, you guys need to get it together — learn to grow up."

With a small smile, Marcus ran a hand along her upper arm with short, gentle strokes. "We're not all like that, you know."

"I know. I don't mean to lump you in with your maladjusted brethren. Believe me, don't think I don't appreciate your relative normalcy."

"Thanks. I think. Though I'm not sure it's much of a compliment. You make it sound like it's a low bar."

"It is. Try not to take it personally."

"How could I?" Marcus paused. "Look," he added, "I think Josh is just trying to figure out how to survive."

"Survival is not a solo proposition. Whatever he thinks he's doing, he's not doing it in a vacuum. That's what's so maddening." Claudia could feel her teeth grinding. "He doesn't have a fucking clue there are other people he needs to take into account. Like his children, first and foremost."

"I think he probably does. He's just decided his own needs are more of a priority right now."

"Really?" Claudia's eyes widened. "And how do you know this? Have you guys been sharing secrets? Sneaking out for beers late at night after everyone's gone to bed?"

"Yeah, we totally get each other now. Did I neglect to mention that?" Marcus was still touching her arm. He looked at his hand as if it were not attached to him. But he made no effort to pull away. "I'm just trying to, uh, conjecture where he's coming from. It's not that complicated." Marcus chuckled. "Josh is not that hard to read."

"Yeah, no shit." Claudia sighed. "Do you think you could just stop being so goddamned insightful where Josh is concerned? And empathetic? You're on my side, remember?"

"I didn't forget." Marcus continued to eye her closely, that same tight grin framed by that same unwavering composure.

What are we doing here? Claudia thought. *What exactly is happening right now?* There was a lightness to their banter, a good-natured teasing hovering along the surface, their small smiles fixed and determined. But what was this underlying compulsion of hers to poke him, to provoke him? Was she trying to elicit a reaction, to goad him into snapping back at her? Claudia usually appreciated and had even come to depend upon Marcus's unfailingly reliable self-possession, his steadiness. But then she remembered there were moments like these when she found herself wishing there might be some sort of middle ground between his uncrackable unflappability and Josh's careless, self-absorbed fecklessness.

She studied Marcus's face behind the scruffy stubble. Without his glasses, his eyes appeared softer, more accessible. Still, that placid demeanor, so even, so frustratingly impossible to read at times, was at this moment having a weird effect on her, pushing her toward a darker place. She was wound much too tightly right now.

"I need to work," Claudia declared, moving toward the stairs. "And so do you, I'm sure." She found her laptop where she'd left it on the night table next to her bed. A few days earlier, she had gone back to the dementia-stricken boxer's house in New Jersey, this time with her video crew. Now she needed to screen the footage they'd shot. Though unmotivated and distracted, deadlines were looming. And once the children got home from school, there would no longer be much chance of getting work done. When she returned to the living room, Marcus was on the couch with his own laptop.

"Look at the two of us," Claudia said with a lopsided smirk as she plopped down next to him. "What a cliché we are."

Marcus grunted, eyes fixed on his screen. She plugged in her headphones and clicked on the video. The shoot had been intense; even her tough-as-nails tech guys could be seen biting their lower lips and turning away. The boxer, likeable as ever and remarkably devoid of self-pity, had spoken emotionally and with great clarity of what he termed, with impressive self-awareness, his "long decline." But even as he made his plea to protect the next generation of athletes from a similar fate, he simultaneously and unselfconsciously expressed a genuine love for his sport. He spoke of how it had given him opportunities he never would have had otherwise, and, most movingly, at least to Claudia, about what it felt like to be in the ring, one on one against his opponent, to persevere and win a fight, that exact moment when he felt the ref raise his arm high in victory and the crowd went nuts. The man's authenticity was impossible to resist.

The wife, for her part, her hands intertwined with her husband's, spoke of their life together, how they shared both the highs and the lows, and how proud she was of the man, how she loved him for his courage and unblinking toughness. There was still that vulnerability, that fragility, that Claudia had witnessed in the wife that day on the porch. But there was also now a resoluteness, a clear-eyed fierceness, that she had not seen earlier. She was struck by how the woman seemed to have found that elusive reservoir of strength she had been searching for. Or maybe, Claudia thought cynically, she was giving her too much credit. Maybe she just had a knack for pulling it together for the camera. Claudia had not had the chance to speak with the woman alone during that second trip. There were too many people around, and they'd had an ambitious shooting schedule they'd needed to get through. At various moments during the long day, Claudia had caught the woman eying her. Now, watching the footage, Claudia had the sudden impulse to give her a call and check in, see how she was doing, see if she wanted to talk.

Claudia had been working silently, absorbed, for a good while. When she stopped, she lifted the headphones away from her ears and turned, quietly observing Marcus as he went back and forth between the yellow legal pad with his scrawled notes and the manuscript that filled his screen.

Finally, she spoke. "I want to go ahead with it, Marcus."

"I know. I understand," he responded. She watched him press *Save,* though his eyes were still on his screen, fingers still poised above the keys. He looked over at her. "Paul teaches on Tuesdays. I'll see him then. We just need to send him Amy's history, whatever records you have of her therapies that you can get hold of."

"That's great. Awesome. I can't wait to see what he can do. Please tell him how grateful we are — I am." Claudia stopped and thought maybe she shouldn't continue, maybe she should wait for a better time. But this *was* the right time, she felt certain of it. So she kept going. It wasn't Paul, she explained in a subdued tone. That wasn't what she was talking about.

Marcus let himself fall against the back of the couch. She finally had his full attention. "What *are* we talking about then?"

"You know. Don't you? About us? About our future?"

Marcus was tentative, cautious. "Our future?"

"Yeah. You know? You and me? You proposed to me? It was a while ago, so I can see where it could have slipped your mind." She shrugged. "Shit happens."

"Seriously?"

"Yeah. Seriously." A beat. "The big seriously."

"That's great. Wow." Marcus seemed to need a moment for this to sink in. He shook his head. "Really? That's not what I was expecting to hear from you right now. That's amazing."

"Yeah. I kind of think so."

"Wow," he repeated.

"Yeah. Wow."

Then there was what felt like a long silence as they stared blankly at their screens. They both seemed to want to look anywhere but at each other. If there had been dancing bears on the other side of the room, thought Claudia, they would have happily allowed themselves to become totally distracted by the display of ursine agility in front of them.

"You seem weirdly underwhelmed by this development," Claudia said. Worry crept into her voice, which to her own ears sounded distant and hollow, like it was coming from far away, like it sometimes feels when you have a head cold or too much to drink. "This is breaking news I'm giving you here."

"I understand the magnitude. Trust me."

"So what is it then? You're supposed to be jumping up and down wildly, take me in your arms, shriek to the heavens, and twirl me around the room."

Marcus hesitated, then let his shoulders fall. "Maybe I'm just not the jumping, twirling, shrieking type."

"So what is it then?" she repeated.

He closed the laptop and scratched at his unshaven face. He continued to stare straight ahead. The house was still. Claudia felt a chill run through her. "You're scaring me," she said.

"I just want to make sure this is happening for the right reasons," Marcus said with a heavy sigh after a long time. "That this isn't just a reaction to Josh."

"Josh? What does Josh have to do with it? With this? With us?"

"Do I really have to explain it?" There was an edge to Marcus's voice, a rawness Claudia did not often hear from him. Perhaps, Claudia, thought, she'd finally succeeded in locating his cracking point. The tough Philly kid, the kid with attitude who grew up not taking shit from anyone, who fought back against anyone who got in his way, the alter ego Marcus normally kept well hidden, was perhaps now seeping through.

"Look, Claudia," Marcus continued. "For months you've made it clear you've thought it was too early for us to move forward with the... with our plans, that we weren't ready, that we needed more time. And I became okay with that. I'd accepted it, that this was how it was going to be. That we would move at your pace, not mine. Now, after seeing Josh this morning, you suddenly burst in here and declare yourself ready to spend your life with me. Do you not see the cause and effect? It's right out there, so I'm pretty sure you do. So let's just cut to the chase. It feels like you are reacting to something that doesn't directly involve me. Am I happy? Sure. I am. I want us to be together. But the particular circumstances give me serious pause."

"I'm glad you feel like you can, you know, be so direct with me." Claudia felt herself going numb. "I'm not used to that and, you know, I do much better with direct. But on the other hand, you're totally reading me wrong. What you're saying is really hurtful, to be honest. My commitment to this relationship is not some sort of reaction to Josh. Yes, he's being an obnoxious little weasel. But what else is new? I can't control whatever shit he decides to pull on any given day. I have no control over that."

"No. But you can control how you react to it."

"The truth is, I've been thinking about this — about us — for a long time. Way before I knew anything about what Josh was cooking up. It's practically all I've *been* thinking about. And I finally realized I'm ready to commit. And now you're going all negative on me. I mean, this is one of the biggest days of our lives, or potentially could be, is supposed to be...you're kind of...I don't know, you're definitely killing the moment."

"I don't think it's about being negative," Marcus responded. "But if I sound wary, I'm completely justified." His voice dropped as the cerebral, academic Marcus began to reassert itself. "You know how much I've been wanting this. You know how I feel about you — about us. The timing just strikes me as a bit odd. And hardly coincidental. It does take some of the joy out of it, I can't argue with you there."

"I'm sorry. I don't know how to convince you otherwise."

Marcus shook his head vigorously and pursed his lips. It was a gesture Claudia didn't exactly know how to read, but the intensity of it was enough to rattle her further.

"I'm going to take a shower and get dressed," he said. As he walked across the room, he stopped and turned. "I know you probably think I'm walking away mad. But I'm not. So don't take it that way. I just need a few minutes to clear my head, let everything settle. Just give me a few minutes. Don't go anywhere, and don't freak out because I'm leaving the room. Sometimes a shower is just a shower."

"Okay," said Claudia in a small voice. She watched him go up the stairs, then heard the bathroom door close and then the water in the sink running. That would be him shaving. A few minutes later, there was the sound of the shower. The pipes vibrated in the quiet house.

There had been that part of her that had wanted to push Marcus, to test the limits of his remarkable equilibrium. And now she had succeeded. But this wasn't how it was supposed to go. Getting up and going into the shower was, for Marcus, the equivalent of someone else going from room to room smashing the furniture.

The real truth — a truth painful to admit, even to herself — was that she *hadn't* been entirely straightforward. It had taken Marcus about a nanosecond to see through her attempt to convince him otherwise. It made her realize she was going to have to up her game in this relationship. Marcus was not Josh. Still, she would continue to dispute the cause and effect, at least the way he had posited it. In recent weeks, she'd become more certain than ever about where they were headed, and she *had* been pondering when to assert her readiness to go forward. Yet if she were being completely honest with herself, and as Marcus had so quickly homed in on, the conversation with Josh that morning *had* been the final nudge, the last straw. But why? What was with this nagging remnant of doubt, and why did it insist on lingering so stubbornly? Was there still something, somewhere in some overlooked part of her brain, that had needed to be absolutely certain there was no longer even the sliver of a chance of reconciling with her husband?

She looked up to see Marcus in the middle of the room, one of her oversized blue terrycloth bath towels wrapped around his waist. He stood in silence, eyeing her. Water drops glistened on the thick black tufts matting his chest.

"So," he said after a minute.

"So," echoed Claudia.

"Any further thoughts?" he asked, as if there had been no break in the previous conversation.

Claudia shook her head. "Just that you have to trust me. I want you to trust me. I want you to know you can."

"I do." Marcus chewed thoughtfully on a thumbnail. "I have faith in us. Faith and trust. That's a pretty solid base to build on, I'd say." He sucked in his breath and then let it out. "And, as far as Josh goes, that's a whole other thing. Let's—"

Claudia held up a hand. "Stop. Let's just stop talking about Josh. Okay? Every time his names comes up, it becomes toxic. *He's* toxic."

"That's an interesting way to put it."

"You know what I mean. All that matters from this point forward is us. I believe in us too. And I love you. I really do. I want to be with you." She could feel herself beginning to well up. "We're going to be great together. That's all that matters."

"All right then," Marcus said, still sounding a bit tentative. He took another breath before continuing with more conviction. "Let's do this thing then." He snorted out a one-syllable laugh. "Let's do this fucking thing. As you would say in your eloquently Claudia way."

Rubbing her eyes, Claudia laughed too, and the tension that had been weighing her down all day began to lift. "Fuck yeah," she said. "Now you're talking my language."

She rose and went to meet him in the middle of the living room floor. With a single sharp motion, she pulled at the towel and gave it a little snap, letting it drop to her side. For a moment she stood admiring his nakedness. Then she lifted his arms and put them around her waist. She felt herself melting into him, and it felt right, it felt natural, the post-shower sultry-sweet scent of his skin, the fine dark hairs across his shoulders and back, the even rhythm of his breathing.

"I still haven't brushed my teeth," he said after a few minutes. "You're very brave to be kissing me."

"It evens out." Claudia put her hand to her mouth. "I've got coffee breath, and you're kissing me back."

"What do you say we both take care of our personal hygiene and meet in bed in five minutes? How much time before the kids come home?"

"Not much, I'm afraid. And Anna will be here any second."

"Shit." He touched a spot below her chin with his mouth and ran his fingers over her sweater, along the outline of her breasts. She bit her lower lip as she put her hand between his legs. She heard him moan softly. "Can you text Anna, tell her to take them to a playground somewhere?" he said, his breath coming quicker. "Maybe somewhere deep in Connecticut? In the woods? With a lot of confusing back roads?"

Claudia laughed again. "Sorry. Not likely."

"In that case," Marcus said with a sigh, "I'm going to take another shower. A cold one this time."

"I promise I'll make it up to you." Claudia stroked his hardness again, then let her hand fall away. She took a step back, again sizing up the picture in front of her. "Just stay exactly like that, okay? Just as you are, and we'll pick it up where we left off."

"I'll do my best." He kissed her again. His look, part lust, part amusement, added to her own rapidly intensifying affection and arousal. She wanted him so badly at that moment.

They heard the screen door open and the front door lock rattle.

"Hate to tell you," said Claudia, eyes widening. "But I believe Anna has arrived. She's about to get a view she's likely to remember for a very long time."

"Perfect." Marcus bent to pick up the towel and disappeared quickly up the stairs just as the front door opened. "Timing is everything," he said over his shoulder as he fled the scene.

A flash of dark hair, stocky body, overflowing grocery bags obscuring her face, Anna came bustling in from the cold. With a quick hello, she hurried toward the kitchen. Claudia listened to the sudden burst of activity, cupboards slamming shut, refrigerator opening and closing, water running. She went to the window and stared out at the weak winter sunlight, dense patches of snow as yet unmelted across the shaded sections of the front lawn. Claudia took a moment to reflect upon her new status as an officially engaged person. She was excited, if a bit overwhelmed. There were a lot of plans that were going to need to be made and a lot of people to call. They had to figure out a date and find a place for the wedding. A wedding! Holy moly. This shit had suddenly become real. She had to call her parents. And Jen. She and Marcus would have to figure how to talk to their kids about their new blended family.

And then there was Josh. He would need to be handled delicately. In spite of everything, she resolved not to tell him her news in the same shitty way he'd broken his to her earlier. She didn't need to be an asshole about it just because he had been. This wasn't a quid pro quo. She was better than that.

For the first time, practically since the day Josh had walked out on her, she started to feel a fraction more generous toward him. She hoped his future plans — what was that dopey way he had phrased it? Plan B? — would work out for him. Why shouldn't she? She had her new life. Fuck it. Let him have his. While things between them might never be what one could call relaxed, it would be a whole lot more pleasant for everyone if they could just find a way to ease some of the oppressive tension they'd been living with.

He'd told her that morning he would be flying out to California in a few days. She would wait until he got back and then meet him over coffee. She decided to text him right away and tell him this — that she wanted to get together as soon as possible after he returned. They would meet, and then it would be done. This was, in so many ways, the best possible outcome. Everyone would move on with their new lives, Claudia with Marcus and Josh in California. They should both be happy. And then she could let it all go. And then she would be free.

TWENTY-FIVE

The carousel shuddered to life with a low mechanical groan. The new arrivals who had been gathering in languid anticipation, marooned in the no-man's land of baggage claim, were instantly on high alert. If they'd been dogs, their ears would have shot up. Josh watched each piece of luggage freeze for a fraction of a second as it emerged at the top of the silver metal chute before tumbling ungracefully onto the spinning belt. But after a few minutes his focus began to attenuate as the same items repeated themselves: green army duffle, hard black suitcase with the Ireland sticker, gray garment bag with the purple ribbon. Each appeared before him, slid past and then, a minute later, reappeared. How was this possible? Where were their owners?

This was the most stressful part of flying for Josh — not the crawling traffic on the way to the airport, not the layers of security, not the amped-up Type As jostling through the plane's narrow aisle to claim that last bit of open space in the overhead. None of those moments, all essential parts of the air travel experience, filled him with this kind of anxiety. He never failed to assume it was his bag that was destined to be lost. He could imagine it even now halfway to Tokyo and, indeed, he was already scanning for the location of the shabby little office he would soon be forced to report to. This feeling of hopeless despair intensified each time someone nearby would, in a moment of bliss, snatch at their luggage and, reunited, happily scurry away. The number of passengers still waiting had thinned rapidly. Whereas a few minutes earlier, Josh had been barely able to squeeze up to the edge of the low metal barrier, he now had ample room to spread out as he continued to watch the luggage (*not mine, not mine, not mine*) fall down the chute and begin its rotation.

Fortunately, he rationalized, in an effort to tamp down his welling unease, he wouldn't need his bag right away anyway. Not knowing quite what to expect on this trip, he had packed for a week. But he had been sure to wear his standard work uniform on the plane — jacket, dress shirt, black loafers — so that he could go straight to Don's office if necessary. He looked at his phone again to see if there had been a response to his email. Still nothing.

Then, just as all hope was lost, miraculously, there it was, his tan folded suit bag, emerging out of the abyss, innocently making its way toward him, seemingly oblivious to the stress it had unleashed. Josh glanced over at the handful of travelers who remained, looking glum, their eyes searching, empty, devoid of hope. For a short moment, he felt sympathetic. But their plight was quickly forgotten as, finally free, it was his turn to exit giddily, buoyant, practically floating into the bright, embracing Southern California sunshine. He threaded his way between the thick line of cars, taxis, and buses cruising along slowly outside the terminal and edged under a green rental car sign to wait for the shuttle. The palm trees dotting the airport grounds swayed in the slight breeze. A smell of jet fuel — and what else was that, maybe smog? — tickled his nose. The heavy coat he'd worn that very morning — *was that just this morning?* — as he had left his Yonkers apartment in the predawn darkness, stepping carefully across the cracked frozen sidewalk toward a waiting town car, was now draped awkwardly over his arm. It felt superfluous, ridiculous. Why would anyone need a coat this heavy, ever? It was January, the sun was burning through the late morning haze, and, in this alternate world, the outfit of choice was shorts and flip-flops.

He peered out through the shuttle's clouded windows, his first glimpses of L.A. life beginning to reveal themselves along the fringes of the airport: a taqueria fronted by an oversized cartoon dancing tortilla, a car wash, a check cashing store, a billboard for a nearby strip club, enormous tasseled boobs looming fifty feet off the ground. In the far distance he could see mountains, partially obscured by a ring of gray haze. He rummaged through his carry-on bag for his sunglasses.

He bumped along, briefly troubled as he considered how he hadn't been totally truthful with either Claudia or James. Not that he had exactly lied. But he was, perhaps, guilty of misdirection by making certain details appear more definitive than they actually were. His primary embellishment had been in giving them both the impression that his meeting with Don was to be little more than a formality, that they simply needed to sit down face-to-face to wrap things up and seal the deal. In reality, he didn't even have the Don meeting scheduled yet. That was why he continued to obsessively scan his phone.

What was one hundred percent certain was the leap he had made in his head. There would be no more hedging, no second guessing. In the days leading up to his getting on the plane, he'd informed his landlord that he intended to break his lease. He'd made an appointment with a company to ship out his car. Most significantly, he'd finally signed those goddamn papers and sent them back to Claudia's lawyer. So that was done. And, as of about thirty minutes ago, the moment his plane had touched down, Plan B, what he was now calling Josh 2.0, had officially launched.

The key to ensuring its successful execution, Josh continued to remind himself, was in making sure both Don and Erin believed they were not his sole reason for coming to L.A. It was the first rule of negotiation, and it applied equally well to business or romance — if you appear to have no other options, you appear desperate, and if you appear desperate, you are liable to spook the party you are pursuing. So, yesterday, before he'd left his office, he'd emailed Don and told him that, after mulling it over these past months, he had come to the conclusion that reinventing himself in L.A. was making more and more sense. He, of course, referenced their meet-up in Vegas and Don's hint at an opportunity with his firm. He then added the crucial, though wholly fabricated, detail that he had several job possibilities already lined up in L.A. He also made sure to mention — he knew Don would appreciate this — that there was a woman involved.

Josh had employed a parallel strategy with Erin. Shortly before getting on the plane, he had texted her that he had just secured an interview in L.A., that it had come up suddenly and unexpectedly and that — hey! — as long as he was going to be out there, they should get together.

In the six or so hours it had taken for him to be transported from one coast to the other, there had been, dishearteningly, no response from either of them.

* * *

During one of their late-night phone calls some weeks earlier, Erin had told Josh of the dinner she'd had in Brooklyn. They'd met at a steakhouse, and of the half dozen or so attendees, she'd been the only woman. There had been considerable drinking and, as the evening wore on, they began to make comments about her, right in front of her. She wouldn't give Josh specifics, but she said she had been both offended and creeped out. "And I'm not a person who gets like that easily," she'd insisted. "I'm pretty good at tuning out the noise, at letting things bounce off me." At first she tried to ignore what was she was hearing, but at a certain point, she'd had enough. She excused herself to go to the restroom and stayed there longer than necessary. When she finally returned to the table, she knew she didn't want anything more to do with these guys, these techie Brooklyn bros, and she certainly didn't want the job. She finished dinner, thanked them and, feigning exhaustion and citing her early flight, skipped dessert and got on the subway back to Russell's apartment. She had decided to wait until she got to L.A. to let them know that she was withdrawing from consideration. But by the time her flight landed, they had emailed their offer. And it was a good one — for starters, they were doubling her salary. She politely declined and even managed to muster a bit of cheer. They were still a client of LAKreativ, so she still had to be nice to them. But she had been disgusted, nauseated. Lying on his bed that night, phone pressed against his ear, Josh, listening sympathetically, expressed appropriate horrified outrage at their behavior. He told her she'd done the right thing but that she was also smart not to burn bridges. Inwardly, of course, though he felt badly for her, he was also secretly relieved. Knowing she would not be moving to New York simplified things. Plan B wouldn't work if Erin was not going to stay in L.A. And now all indications were that she was. Another piece of the puzzle that his universe had conveniently dropped into place for him.

Meanwhile, it had been nearly a week since he'd last heard from her. He reminded himself that it was not unusual for her to drop off the radar at times. It was also true that once the Shoe King project fell apart, there had been less reason for them to be in constant touch. He shakily assured himself that her radio silence meant nothing. He tried not to dwell on it.

* * *

In the enormous car rental parking lot, Josh traversed several endless aisles before finally tracking down the numbered spot that had been assigned to him. He opened the trunk, then stopped, distracted by a plane about to land, coming in low and loud, right over him. When he looked down again and checked his phone, he caught his breath. Don had replied. With great deliberation, stomach turning, he put his stuff into the red Nissan and climbed behind the wheel. The air inside the car was stuffy and stale, made worse by a generous application of perfumed air freshener. He opened the windows, squeezed his eyes shut, blew out some air and read Don's message.

Hey buddy,

Great to hear from you! Sorry for not responding earlier. It's been a shit show, haven't had a minute to breathe. I guess that's good, business keeps blowing up. But fucking stressful, for sure. You know how that is!

Anyway, good to know you are finally taking my advice and deciding to relocate to my fair city. I wholeheartedly endorse the idea! Also good to know that there's someone of the female persuasion in the picture. That always softens the landing!

You should definitely call me when you get here, and we'll make a plan. You'll come out to my place in the Valley — we're right over the hill. I have a smoker in the backyard. I'll introduce you to some good old-fashioned Oklahoma BBQ! The best in all of Sherman Oaks, lol!

Oh, and you mentioned our convo in Vegas. Honestly, I can't remember what I said to you that night. I can't really remember much of that night at all, to be honest, except I kept the party going after you left. So you know how it is — I tend to get a bit enthusiastic after I've had a few pops.

Anyway, yeah, but no, unfortunately there's nothing here that would be a fit for you. That might be my bad if you got a different impression. I might have gotten a little ahead of myself on that one. With that said, I'm happy to make some intros for you, whatever I can do. Now that I know that you are definitely relocating, I'll put out some feelers and I'll keep my eyes open. Though from what you tell me, it sounds like you might not even need my help. It's great that you already have job interviews lined up. Awesome — way to work it!

Anyway, give me a call so we can make a plan. Looking forward to hanging out! And, BTW, I have Dodger season tix, so when the season starts, we'll go to a game or two. Maybe when your Mets are in town. You're going to love living in LA. Land of opportunity! And no snow!

Josh leaned his forehead against the hard, warm vinyl of the steering wheel and concentrated on steadying his breathing. He didn't know how long he stayed like that, but it must have been a while. He became aware of one of the red-jacketed parking lot guys, hands on knees, leaning into the open window.

"You okay, buddy?"

He turned his head and peered at the man from behind his sunglasses. Slightly built with dark skin and dark hair, the guy had a thin mustache and pockmarked cheeks. "You need help?" he asked earnestly. "Directions, maybe?"

Josh mumbled that he was all right, and the man nodded slowly and backed away, still eying him. Josh saw him a minute later chatting with another attendant in a similar red jacket. They looked over toward Josh, and the first guy tilted his head in his direction and pointed. They both shrugged. The next time Josh looked up, they were gone.

He read Don's email again, looking for hidden clues, a silver lining, something he could grab hold of. Don had said he would help him. So there was that. He needed to be firm and hold him to his offer of introductions. It occurred to Josh how few people he actually knew in L.A., how few truly valuable contacts he had out here. If Plan B was falling apart, he needed to find a way to pivot, to move directly into Plan C. He was used to working through obstacles, setbacks. He knew the best thing he could do was to keep moving forward, keep readjusting, find new pathways. Always maintain forward motion. It was a skill he'd learned from James, the master at it.

He soothed himself with thoughts of Erin. After all, wasn't she the real point of his being here? Job offers came and went; a good job was a lot easier to find than a good woman. There was a reason people wrote cheesy love songs, not cheesy jobs songs. So as long as he didn't screw up what he had with Erin, do something stupid to chase her away, then the core of Josh 2.0 was still intact. Don's email had been a shock, a body blow, but already he began to feel the first stirrings of recovery. He'd be okay. Maybe this was for the better. He started to see how James may have been right about Don all along. Josh should have listened to him. It could be a blessing in disguise. There was so much in his head right now. His universe was in full chat mode, and he strained, trying to pay attention to everything it was telling him.

He wanted to go to LAKreativ right then, see Erin right away. But showing up like that would be stalking. You don't just drop in on someone at their place of work without giving them a heads-up. He checked his phone again. Still nothing from her. He could text or even call, just casually, to let her know he had arrived. But even that felt too aggressive. He had to let her respond to his first message first. After her Brooklyn experience, the last thing he needed right now was to give her another reason to feel creeped out by the male species.

Before driving off the rental lot, Josh emailed Don back. He thanked him and told him he appreciated the offer of introductions. He suggested, again, that he could stop by later that afternoon.

He had made a reservation at a hotel in Santa Monica, right on the beach. The place was way more than he could afford; it made him a little ill to think about what he was spending. But this was no ordinary trip — it was a life-altering event. And, frankly, he was hoping that after his first night here, he'd be invited to stay with Erin and would no longer need the overpriced hotel room. Though under other circumstances that might have sounded wildly presumptuous, in this case it didn't seem so unreasonable. They'd already slept together; they were almost like a couple already. Or, sort of. Whatever they were, was it really that much of a leap of logic to assume she might offer to let him crash at her place, at least until he got more settled?

He thought about checking out Erin's apartment before going to the hotel. After imagining it for so long, he had an overwhelming urge to see where she lived. That was stalking too, in a way, also vaguely creepy, but since she would be at work, it wasn't really. He began the drive over, taking surface streets instead of the freeway so that he could immerse himself in the life of the city. He wanted to see people, stores, restaurants, houses. The freeway would give him none of the flavor he was looking for. Morning had transitioned to afternoon, and the air had turned warmer. He closed the car windows and turned on the air conditioning. AC in January, he thought as he navigated his way slowly through L.A.'s west side traffic toward the ocean. What a marvelous thing this was. Right now, in New York, people were wrapped in thick layers, reluctant to even step outside.

He left the car in a lot near the Venice boardwalk. He would proceed on foot toward Erin's apartment, which, according to his phone, was about six blocks inland. If this were soon to be his new neighborhood — and, ultimately, that was the idea, right? — he might as well start exploring, get to know his way around.

Before setting out, he went toward the edge of a grassy park that fronted the vast stretch of beach. Women and men in skimpy swimsuits, with lean, tanned bodies, were hefting weights at an outdoor gym. Rollerbladers, bike riders, and skateboarders flew across paved pathways. Beyond it all, in the distance, he saw waves breaking against the long strip of coast. He had a notion to stroll across the sand and dip his toes into the Pacific; he liked the symbolism of it. But that could wait. There were other things he wanted to do first.

He had had some preconceived mental image of Venice residents living in low-rise bungalows, strung out on stilts along the sand, hugging the water's edge. Now he saw how stupidly wrong that was. The beach was the beach, meant for recreation. He turned around and started walking and soon found himself in a neighborhood of boxy apartment buildings and compact, tidy houses. He was awed by how verdant the place was. The streets were lined with L.A.'s ubiquitous palm trees, the flowering gardens bordered by neatly trimmed hedges and blooming plants. Bursts of reds, blues, purples spilled across the sidewalks.

Keeping an eye on his GPS, he navigated toward Erin's block. His body was vibrating, his heart racing. Her building, two stories, squat, square, and gray, appeared to have only one deck, so he assumed what he was looking up at had to be hers. The deck was smaller than he'd envisioned. There was a bicycle propped up against a wall, but not much room for anything else. It looked like all of about two steps from a sliding glass door to the other side. Still, a deck was a deck and this was Venice Beach. And it was hers. He conjured an image of the two of them after work, standing close with their glasses of wine, looking serenely at the sun slowly sinking into the ocean. But wait, where *was* the ocean? Remembering the picture she'd shared with him, the one with the potted plant in her bedroom, he was confused. He couldn't see how the water could possibly be visible from this spot. And yet he remembered it so clearly. He clutched his phone and quickly scrolled through his photos.

He was stunned when he found the image she'd sent those months ago. There was no swath of ocean in the shot. It was just trees and buildings, an extension of the neighborhood he was now standing in. How could he have misremembered so egregiously? He had viewed that photo so many times, studied it so carefully, been certain of every detail. But there was no denying what he was looking at — his memory had been totally wrong.

His phone buzzed. It was Don, emailing back. He was in Chicago until Friday, but, he said, Josh should definitely call next week, and they'd set something up then. So there was that.

Josh decided he would check into his hotel. He needed downtime; adrenaline had been pumping through him for hours, his nerves were depleted. Back in the parking lot, he leaned against the rickety attendant's shed, shifting impatiently from foot to foot, as he waited for his car. His red rental was right there, he could see it clearly, only a handful of spaces down from where he stood. Still, protocol required that he wait for it to be driven up to him.

Josh heard his phone in his pocket again, alerting him to another new email, this one from a Gmail address he didn't recognize, the letters EW followed by a string of numbers. He stared dumbly for a long moment, then was jolted, as if by an electrical current, as it clicked belatedly in his malfunctioning brain that EW had to be Erin.

Josh stabbed furiously at the phone. He had no patience to wait the second or two it took for the message to open. His frustration exploded as he realized he was not able to read what Erin had sent — the enormous sun directly overhead in the unclouded sky washed out his screen, rendering it impossible to decipher. He squinted, tried using his hand to block out the light, searched desperately for shade, but it was hopeless. He left the puzzled attendant standing open-mouthed by the Nissan, keys in hand, driver's side door ajar. An exasperated howl burst forth from the depths of Josh's gut as he frantically scampered across the street, dodging cars, ignoring the indignant honks directed toward him. He stopped under an arched white stucco overhang, in front of a gift shop, the outsides of its windows draped with cartoon emblazoned T-shirts. Back pressed against one of those shirts, sweat rolling freely from his temples and down his cheeks, breath coming in short, shallow gulps, he read:

Hey there,

You're in LA??? No way!!! I'm in Denver. Funny how that works, right? So, this is going to sound kind of unbelievable, but guess what? Remember that culinary school in France? I'd pretty much given up on them, but then they got in touch, and I can't believe it, but I'm in! They told me I can start in June. How nuts is that?? It's all happening so quickly. I'm super excited but I've also been kinda sitting here thinking about how to break it to you. I guess you could tell I've been avoiding you for the last few days. And now it turns out you're in L.A. Weird.

So I gave notice at LAKreativ (note the different email address!), gave up my apartment, and put my stuff in storage. I drove to Colorado and got here a couple of days ago. I'm going to live with my parents for a few months to save some money. I'm doing a little consulting for a couple of app start-ups. I'm also doing some bartending.

Listen, Josh, I know this is all pretty unexpected. I just want you to know how much I treasure you. You're a great friend. But I have to jump on this opportunity. You of all people understand how I feel about not sleepwalking through life. If I pass this up, I'll never forgive myself. I know you know where I'm coming from. That's one of the things I so appreciate about you.

When you get back to N.Y.C., hit me up and we'll get on the phone and talk through everything. It's kinda hard to do it on email. But please don't think this has anything negative to do with you. On the contrary, you are one of the reasons I hesitated before accepting. But I gotta do this. It's now or never.

With warmth and affection,

E

TWENTY-SIX

He became aware of his dress shoes sliding along the concrete promenade, slipping on patches of sand drifting across the pavement. He had no memory of leaving the T-shirt shop or even a sense of how much time had passed. The blue water, waves breaking gently, shimmered in the distance off to his left, across that broad expanse of beach he'd checked out earlier. On his other side were souvenir stands and fast-food shacks. A pot-bellied Mexican man in a straw hat and embroidered white shirt was selling ceramic skulls of varying sizes — lurid, haunted faces painted in bright, garish colors.

"Day of the Dead," the portly man said through a heavy accent as Josh neared, slowing to look. "Check it out." The man spread his hands out over the display before him, eyeing Josh impassively.

Josh nodded weakly and kept going.

The sun reflecting off the sand was strong; he could feel his neck and forehead burning. He had removed his jacket but was still moist with perspiration. In the distance, up ahead, he spotted the outline of a Ferris wheel and roller coaster emerging through the last remaining wisps of haze along the shore. After what felt like a long time, he reached a set of wide steps and followed them past a row of palm trees up onto the Santa Monica Pier.

Directly in front of him was a merry-go-round, the spinning carousel dotted with colorful stage lights. He stepped inside, beneath a vaulted circus tent, relieved to be under shade. Excited children straddling painted horses gripped long thin poles with their small hands, waving to their parents, who, calling out over a tinny music track, busily snapped pictures and beamed back at them. A spasm of remorse washed over Josh as he thought of his own kids. These kinds of parent-child moments may have been prosaic, repeated millions of times every day across the planet. But it was the prosaic moments that made up a life.

He recalled the time he and Claudia had brought Amy to a merry-go-round much like this, when she was young enough for them to still believe this sort of outing with her was possible. As Josh had lifted her up to place her atop one of the ponies, she had screamed, her little body twisting, desperately trying to wiggle free, struggling with all her might, as if Josh were forcing her head under water and breaking free was her only chance for survival. Amy's inherent inability to balance, the noise, the spinning, the lights had all been too much, sensory overload she'd been unable to process. Josh remembered how everyone, kids and adults alike, had stared. Or had pretended not to.

He moved away, shuffling farther along, across the pier's slatted wooden surface. It had begun to feel completely ridiculous that he was even in Los Angeles. How did he arrive here and what was he doing, standing on the Santa Monica Pier, watching other people's children flash by on a merry-go-round? He was disoriented by an unsettling sensation that he wasn't on the other side of the country at all but instead had somehow mistakenly landed in some strange, vaguely malevolent exotic locale on the other side of the world — Sudan or Bhutan, say — where he neither spoke the language nor understood the customs.

He was now over water, out beyond the shoreline. He felt surrounded, hemmed in by beefy, white-skinned tourists, some with European accents, others speaking in the flat tones of the Midwest, taking pictures, looking about, strolling along as soft ice cream cones melted onto their hands, their kids trailing behind, chomping into puffy swirls of pink cotton candy.

Josh approached the amusement park rides, the Ferris wheel nearly directly over him, screams coming from the direction of the roller coaster. He kept going, past the arcade games, the bike rentals, the caricaturist perched on his stool with his easel and Sharpies. The crowd thinned as he reached the Harbor Office, a gray two-story wooden building, bisected by a row of vertical windows. To its right was a restaurant with the same window design, offering diners a commanding view of the sea and sand. Josh came upon a row of fisherman, their backs to him, crowded shoulder to shoulder, facing west toward the expanse of open water that extended to the horizon and beyond. This was where the pier ended. He heard the fishermen chatting in Spanish as they kept a close eye on their poles and lines that floated in the grimy, brackish water.

He turned around and contemplated the building he had just passed. Suddenly aware of being intensely hungry, he went up some steps to the restaurant, but it was dark inside and the door was locked. Nearby was a bench along the side of the Harbor Office, a quiet spot where the tourists didn't venture. From here, he had an elevated view back to where he'd just come from. An achy exhaustion settled over him. He had been upright for too long; his sweaty, swollen feet throbbed in his black loafers. He let his body go slack, relieved to sit.

He had been determined to get out to L.A. to pursue his destiny, to reinvent himself. Now, here he was, he'd made it, even if things weren't exactly unfolding as he'd scripted them. Not that he was all that surprised by this. On some level he'd always known it. Whatever it was — destiny, fate, providence? — was never going to allow him to have this moment. The universe just didn't work that way. But still, he'd gotten here, he'd gone as far west as he could go. Technically at this moment, to be precise, he'd gone even farther, past the water's edge, beyond the end of the continent. He thought he could feel the pier rocking, the waves lapping against the pilings. Though that might have just been his imagination.

Stretching out from the other side of the beach, past the souvenir stands, past the rides, past the parking lots, past the coastal highway, the vast city, seemingly borderless, streamed in every direction. Somewhere in the midst of it all was Erin's apartment and Don's office — what he had imagined to be the touchstones of his new life. Until a few minutes ago, that was.

He pictures himself flying, soaring over Los Angeles until he is finally far enough east that he can break free of the city's pull. Now he is over desert, a wide, stark emptiness. He approaches the bright lights of Las Vegas, glittering below. Josh zooms in on the bar where he and Don had had their alcohol-infused evening. At this very moment someone else is sitting at that very table they had shared. That someone else is ordering drinks from that same aging waitress in the low-cut top, and she is flirting in that same trying-a-little-too-hard sort of way. Perhaps the people sitting there are having a similar conversation to the one Josh had with Don, hoping to make a deal, trying to land the next big opportunity. Striving, always striving.

Josh keeps going, leaving the desert, continuing up into the high snow-covered mountains. On the far side of the majestic Rockies, he hovers over Denver. Somewhere in that city, a place Josh has never seen, Erin is making lists, figuring out details, in her usual organized way, planning for her big adventure, dreaming of possibilities, what might happen, who she might meet. She stops what she's doing and takes a moment to think about Josh. Or maybe she doesn't.

A short jog south and east, and he reaches Oklahoma. There are Don's kids from his first marriage, the ones Don never sees. Long since grown up, of course, they get up every morning and go to work, like everyone else, so they can cover the mortgage and make their car payments. Like everyone else. Then they come home and take care of their own kids, Don's grandchildren, whom he has never even met. Josh wonders what those grandkids have been told of the grandfather, the man who flew the coop for the bright lights of Hollywood all those years ago.

Josh resumes his cross-country flight, slowing when he gets to Nashville, picking up the route Claudia and her college roommate had taken on that ill-fated spring break trip. Josh follows their car as it weaves its way too quickly through the Appalachians to meet its destiny farther on. If only he were able to warn them. Claudia always said that trip both defined and changed her, but Josh was never entirely sure what that meant. He had needed specifics, and Claudia had been reluctant, or unable, to provide them. She seemed to think Josh should just get it.

Josh leaves the accident site in West Virginia, makes a left turn, and before long he is over New Jersey. There's the house in Plainfield where his mother still lives, and there she is at the kitchen table, doing the crossword puzzle in her solitary way as she has every day for more years than Josh can remember, seated in the same chair, pencil poised by her ear. Down his street and a couple of more turns and there is his high school and the woods behind the football field where Josh got stoned with the other asocial teenaged weirdos. He often feels, even now, that those dreary, chilly autumn afternoons, faint echoes of football practice carrying through the trees, were where he felt his greatest sense of belonging, of acceptance. He is momentarily enveloped by a sense of nostalgia, but he shakes it off. There is more ground to cover.

And then there it is, spread out before him, the Big Apple, the Center of the Universe, the City That Never Sleeps. It's the place where Josh finally became Josh, finally figured out who he was, or at least as much he could, as anyone can. His personal landmarks are dotted throughout the city, the apartments he'd lived in, the apartments he'd gotten laid in. Every corner of Manhattan seems to hold memories and meaning. There is the James Gang office, and there, by Washington Square, is Russell's apartment.

A quick shot north, and he's in Westchester County. Turn left to Yonkers or right to Larchmont? It's an easy choice; Yonkers means nothing to him, while he spent ten years in that house in Larchmont. He can see Claudia just getting home on this cold, blustery January day. She rushes from her reliable Honda Pilot and into the house. Ethan runs toward her before she can even take her coat off with a million things to tell her and a million requests and needs. Amy, spinning in the corner, receives Claudia's kiss with a brief, shy smile and then retreats back into her private world and resumes spinning. And where is Marcus? Josh isn't sure. He hopes he's not there, but he probably is, lurking, looming, smirking somewhere. Josh watches Claudia struggle with the always abrupt shift from work to mommy mode; another prosaic, universal scene. As he watches her hurry about during the pre-bedtime scramble, he feels a tenderness toward her, an ache, something he has not experienced, at least not to this degree, not like this, for a very long time.

* * *

Josh's extended reverie was interrupted by a ping from his phone heralding yet another email. *What the fuck?* he thought. *First, no one will get back to me, and now everyone has something they want to say. And none of it good.* He reoriented from his daydream, eying, without seeing, the tourists below him, the wide beach dotted with sunbathers.

Skimming quickly, terrified that one more piece of bad news might push him over the edge, Josh relaxed slightly when he saw this email was from James. Josh slowed himself and read through at a deliberate pace.

James reported that he had just signed a new client, "*in dire need of a full slate of marketing support.*"

It's a handbag company, James wrote, *that's moving into a whole new area. They are starting a new line of sexy underthings — they call it 'everyday lingerie for the everyday woman.' First on the to-do list: change that fucking tagline. Jesus, where do they get copy like that, off a fucking cereal box? But the best part? They have (wait for it) MONEY!!! And a lot of it, apparently. It's backed by Russian oligarchs and run by a couple of Israelis, ex-Mossad agents turned entrepreneurs. So either we're going to make a lot of $$ or they're going to have us whacked and chopped up into next Passover's gefilte fish. Personally, I'm willing to take my chances. I'm that confident. So, needless to say, I could use your exceptional skills. But I need to know if you are available. I'm meeting with Sergey (the lead Russian) and Rony (the lead Israeli) next week, so if you want to be a part of this, I would need you in New York for that kickoff meeting. As an added incentive, if you behave yourself, I'll let you cover the photo shoot with the scantily clad models.*

Seriously, though, Josh, if you are truly set on relocating out to La La Land, I don't want to stand in your way. I'll wish you the best, and I'm always here to help. But just in case you are having second thoughts about your Plan B, I want you to know that you would be my first choice to run this new account. So I just need to know what you've got in mind, because if I can't have you, I'll need to hire some other equally unqualified asshole pronto. So get back to me ASAP, okay, and just tell me: Are you in or are you out?

Josh laughed softly as he set his phone down on the bench next to him. No one phrased things quite like James. He looked again at the ocean, at the sunbathers, at the city stretched before him. The sun had shifted into the western sky, over the water, the sky growing paler, a more washed-out shade of blue. He watched a shirtless guy in khaki shorts guide a metal detector across the sand. Every once in a while, he would stop, inspect something, pocket it, and move on. Down the pier a ways, a white-haired man with a sunburned, weather-beaten face had attracted a crowd by turning his body into a roosting spot for the imperious seagulls that circled above and strutted cockily along the pier's railings and low rooftops. One bird was perched on the guy's head, a couple were on his shoulders, a few others rested on his forearms. The tourists were eating it up, snapping pictures with their phones. The birds were half as large as your average New York City pigeon, and to Josh's eye, considerably tougher and more assertive. Watching them squat on top of the old guy, Josh was slightly freaked out. The birds seemed to be calling the shots; they were the alphas, glaring with their small, dark eyes at anyone who they might perceive as a threat to their dominance. At least New York's pigeons knew their place in the pecking order. So to speak.

His thoughts returned to Claudia; he struggled to locate what he was feeling now. Josh began to think the unthinkable. Maybe his true destiny actually did lie in returning to what he knew best — in returning to Claudia and their children. Maybe this was what his universe, in its annoyingly indirect way, had been trying to tell him, not just now but over all these past months.

He knew, even as the thought entered his mind, how ridiculous this sounded. It was absurd, wholly unworkable. That ship had sailed. Their paths had diverged permanently. Claudia was with Marcus now. But what if this were only a temporary divergence, one that was still amenable to an intervention, a course correction? When he'd first decided to move out of the house, he'd told Claudia he just needed some time, a year, to reevaluate. It seemed more than coincidence that now, almost exactly a year later, his universe was sending these signals to him.

He had a vision of themselves, years from now, looking back on their life together. This year would be only a dimly remembered glitch, a sabbatical in what would otherwise be thought of as a generally good marriage — not without its problems, certainly, but one that had been strong enough to survive those rough patches. He saw himself, white-haired, shriveled and wrinkled, sitting on a porch, Claudia's hand in his. *Remember that year apart?* he would say to her. *You were with that other guy — what was his name?* And she would laugh and shrug dismissively and then gently rest her head on his shoulder.

He knew any rapprochement would be overwhelmingly difficult. The hurt from all sides was deep and profound. Claudia had more than once declared herself done with him. And even if there were a small part of her open to reconciliation, even in the best of circumstances, she would be extremely skeptical. But it was her nature to be skeptical anyway. He mused over what it would take to win her back. He'd start by taking responsibility, by owning up, by admitting that he'd lost the thread of the marriage, become overwhelmed by details, by negativity, by their many issues, their core connection subsumed by Amy's many needs. But, he would argue, he was in a different place now. And, at its heart, he would make her believe, the marriage was still viable. The love could be salvaged, resuscitated. They could invigorate the chemistry that had brought them together so many years ago. He needed to make her understand that he recognized the gravity of what he had done, but that he had grown, changed, and now felt ready to take on more of what was expected and required from a special needs parent, a special needs spouse. His epiphany was genuine. He missed his family.

And — no small part of this equation — he didn't, couldn't, believe that Marcus was the man Claudia was meant to spend the rest of her life with. Marcus was so smarmy, such a dweeb. Josh knew Claudia better than anyone; he just didn't see *their* chemistry. He didn't see the appeal, not deep down. She was with Marcus because Josh was no longer a possibility. But he could make it a possibility. At least he could try. It all began to click now, to make a certain lopsided, crazy sense.

He suddenly remembered, in the midst of everything else going on, that he'd gotten a text from Claudia a few days earlier telling him she wanted to make a plan to see him when he returned to New York, that she needed to talk to him as soon as possible. He had brushed it off at the time, figuring it had something to do with him not sending back the papers. But now it began to dawn on him that she may have been having some of the same thoughts as him. All during their relationship, they had had this weird habit of thinking the same thing at the same time. It could be downright eerie, and they used to laugh about it. Was it not possible that she was now having parallel feelings of regret, of yearning?

It was true that he also yearned for Erin. There was no denying that, and those feelings were not going to resolve themselves any time soon. But he also recognized that this whole elaborate exercise — moving out, Don, Erin, California — might just have been his universe's way of getting him to understand where he truly belonged, to open his eyes to what had been hiding in plain sight all along.

He read James's email again. *Are you in or are you out?* Josh hesitated another minute before responding, though he now knew what he was going to do, what he had to do, what he was meant to do. He tapped out his reply then held the phone in his hand and stared at it. He had written a single word. There was no reason to elaborate further. James would appreciate the directness.

As soon as he pressed *Send*, he could sense the pressure easing. He closed his eyes, felt the fading California sun, the sticky breeze, on his skin. There was a certain security, tangible, almost physical, in knowing that a response would soon be coming, in knowing he could count on it, in knowing what it would say. Reliability was not something to be taken lightly. He looked again at the message he had just sent. He waited.
In.

END